A VISIT FROM THE DEAD

Sean suddenly stiffened, his chest a cavern of ice, his heart burning with bitter cold. The smell of damp earth dripped down into his lungs, gagging him. His thoughts exploded, as if they had been frozen and shattered and scattered into the wind.

"Forget her," he heard a woman say in a throaty whisper, the voice a distant echo from his past.

Fight or flight charged his body with a million volts of energy. He spun around, only to stumble backward at what he saw. Standing before him in a puddle of crumpled clothing was a woman. Naked, her skin was dirty and pallid and mottled with bruises. Her hair was a tangle of gritty knots, her lips gray, her face gaunt, lifeless. Except for her eyes, which he couldn't resist, her gaze reached deep down inside him and took hold of his very soul.

"Who the hell—"

He was silenced against his will when she raised her hand. Unable to move, he could only watch in horror as she stepped forward, stopping only when her body grazed his, his skin burning wherever her flesh touched him. "Don't you know?" she asked, her words fading. Her breath, the smell of decay, turned his stomach.

Dead Love

DONALD BEMAN

LEISURE BOOKS NEW YORK CITY

A LEISURE BOOK®

December 2001

Published by

Dorchester Publishing Co., Inc.
276 Fifth Avenue
New York, NY 10001

ISBN 0-8439-4951-1

Printed in the United States of America.

Visit us on the web at www.dorchesterpub.com.

ACKNOWLEDGMENTS

Dr. Mike Merrill, physician, journalist and soon-to-be-novelist. Linda Lavid, for her help with Spanish. Elaine Harrigan, a reader with an amazing eye for character and story. And Sean MacDonald, for letting me play with him.

Dead Love

Chapter One

Nothing shouted, *Welcome home!* as Sean Mac-Donald ran along the once familiar country roads, now lined with concrete curbs and silly city sidewalks. Even the lazy intersections had been citified with traffic lights and prisoner's stripes, and were jammed full of minivans. While all of the old apple orchards and corn fields had been cut down and plowed under and replanted with wannabe Hollywood houses, complete with perfectly pruned shrubs, weedless lawns sprayed Technicolor green and surrounded by armies of politically correct ceramic sculptures—bug-eyed gnomes, dancing dwarves and ugly little trolls—all blind, deaf and dumb.

The moment he turned off Lake Road and started down Western Highway, Sean spotted the old fieldstone church he passed half an hour before. Though only a distant memory, the small country cemetery behind the church was the solitary exception to the silence that greeted him upon his return to Blue Fields, its call as seductive as any siren's song. Sensing that same odd feeling in his chest again, he glanced down at the receiver on his wrist the size of a watch, the transmitter a narrow band strapped around his chest beneath his sweatshirt. His pulse was a steady 145, right about where it should be for the relaxed pace—146 strides every tenth of a mile, every fifty-four seconds, a nine-minute mile—he slowed to after turning back, as if he were suddenly unsure of himself. A tap of the tiny button on the side of the small digital display called up the elapsed time; there were less than two minutes remaining on the one-hour limit he'd set for himself.

Another tap of the button recalled his pulse.

At six foot, and more stocky than trim, Sean MacDonald didn't have what the running gurus preached was the ideal build for a distance runner—two pounds per inch of height—which meant he was thirty pounds too heavy, according to the self-proclaimed prophets. But he ran anyway, his running as important to him as his writing. Just trying to stay a few steps ahead of the Devil was his stock reply whenever anyone asked him why, at his age, he ran five miles a day. He also claimed running helped him keep his sanity, yet one critic questioned even that when he reviewed Sean's last book.

"Fuck 'em all," he snarled and broke into an all-out sprint. His pulse was unchanged for the first dozen strides, then jumped to 150 . . . 156 . . . 163 . . . and hit 166 just as the alarm sounded, reminding him to back off. "And fuck you too," he grumbled and pushed himself to 176 before he grudgingly slowed to a brisk walk, cooling down. As he glanced at the houses lining the road, he shook his head, wondering, *What in the hell were you thinking when you agreed to come back? You don't belong here anymore.*

Having just completed a month-long book tour, Sean had had his fill of stale cookies, warm punch and little old ladies asking him if there was lots of sex in his book, only to frown and walk away when he told them Some, but not *that* much.

His change of heart was the result of a phone call he received from a complete stranger, Elaine Anders. After he politely but firmly declined her request for a book signing at the local library, she asked, "Please, Sean, for your hometown readers?" In that fleeting moment, no more than a heartbeat, he was certain he'd heard Judith's voice—something that had been happening more and more lately—and found himself unable to refuse the request to come home after thirty years.

With this last book, Sean had put an end to the love-hate relationship with the character he'd created from a childhood nightmare, in spite of what they meant to each other. "It's time for me to move on," he told his editor, even though he knew all too well this mirrored image would continue to haunt him—drifting in and out of his life—an uninvited spirit with a mind of its own.

He laughed, " 'Til death do us part!" as he cut across the threadbare lawn toward the cemetery imprisoned inside a falling-down wrought-iron fence infected with rust and crawling with ivy.

Hesitating, his hand hovering inches above the gate, Sean asked himself one more time if he really wanted to go inside and risk unearthing the memories he'd buried here a lifetime ago. Fictional characters were easy—he could give them life with a few dozen keystrokes, or take it away just as quickly, and never give it a second thought—but Judith was a different story altogether, one whose end had never been written. At least not for Sean.

"She's dead, for chrissake," he grumbled as he swung open the gate and immediately shuddered at the unnerving sound of metal grating against metal, scrapping away the peace and quiet of the warm October afternoon. He gingerly lifted the gate—an old trick suddenly remembered—and eased it shut. But it didn't work; the rusted iron hinges complained just as loudly the second time.

Once inside the cemetery he felt lost and stopped to get his bearings. Not only were the trees thirty years taller and wider, their branches casting unfamiliar shadows everywhere, but dozens of headstones had been devoured by hungry weeds, or knocked over by frightened vandals. There had also been more than a few additions since he was last here, which only added to his confusion until his gaze fell upon a familiar shape—another—then a third.

With a confident nod, he plotted a course and began to navigate his way through the maze of weathered sandstone markers, miniature marble mausoleums and angels frozen in flight. When he lazily kicked his feet through the dusting of autumn leaves, he uncovered a small American flag lying on the ground and stopped to pick it up. The fabric was tattered and threadbare, the colors faded to elusive tints of red and blue and white-turned-gray. The skinny wicker stick was bent and splintered. He carefully fit the small flag back into the corroded bronze plaque it had fallen from.

Without cheating and looking at the headstone, Sean put his memory to the test. But as hard as he tried, he simply couldn't remember who the flag honored, even though there was a time when he could name everyone here. He'd also known all of the dates, birth and death, and could reel off the names of husbands and wives, children who had died too soon, spinster aunts and bachelor uncles, and even those distant relatives who had left and returned, one by one, to sleep here. *You were one strange kid,* he thought, repeating what the other kids said whenever they saw him taking a rubbing off the face of a headstone, the crinkly sheet of parchment destined to hang in his room with the others.

Drawing a blank, he placed the tips of his fingers on the face of the headstone and slowly traced the barely visible letters that read JONAS BLAUVELT, 1741–1778, SON, BROTHER, FATHER AND LOVING HUSBAND—HE GAVE HIS LIFE TO BRING US TO THIS NEW WORLD.

Whatever apprehension Sean had felt about returning to Blue Fields seemed to fade as he drifted from headstone to headstone, reacquainting himself with one old friend after another, such as ADELAIDE WEST CONKLIN, 1783–1810, DEVOTED WIFE AND LOVING MOTHER, WHO DIED IN CHILDBIRTH WHILE GIVING LIFE TO PRECIOUS LITTLE ADELE. And BEATRICE ANN HOUSTON, 1805–1807, GOD'S LITTLE GIFT, WHO WENT TO SLEEP ONE NIGHT AND AWOKE IN HEAVEN. Or EZIKIAL JAMES HILL, 1846–1864, OUR ONLY SON, WHO BRAVELY GAVE HIS LIFE TO PROTECT AND PRESERVE THE UNION. MAY HE ENTER THE KING-

DOM OF HEAVEN AND STAND GUARD AT THE FOOT OF THE LORD'S THRONE.

That relaxed feeling changed the moment Sean found himself in the back of the cemetery, not far from where he set a modest stone marker into the ground three decades earlier—secretly—and with his own hands. He chose this spot because it was where he and Judith had made love that summer and long into the fall, safely hidden behind the rows of silent stone sentinels no one dared challenge in the dark. Without a name or a date—marking a grave that was never dug, for a body never found—the small block of polished granite bore the simple inscription I WILL ALWAYS LOVE YOU.

As he cautiously stepped into the clearing, Sean spotted a corner of the marker peeking out from underneath the blanket of new-fallen leaves painted every possible shade of red and orange. He waited. Nothing, not even the slightest twinge. He took a shallow breath and shut his eyes, trying to force them to show themselves. Yet not a single hidden memory answered his call.

This is crazy, he told himself and knelt down, intent upon clearing away the leaves and confronting his fears, only to be startled by the unsettling sound of the iron gate creaking open.

Jumping up, he spun around and quickly laughed at himself when he heard a familiar voice call out, "I thought I'd find you here."

As tall as Sean, Pamela Eagleston's smoldering red hair was cut boyishly short, and the only makeup to be found on her smooth yet angular face was a quick brush of iridescent red over her lips.

With a friendly wave and relaxed smile, she started toward him, lazily weaving her way in and around the headstones, slowing to read one, then another, but not stopping. As she drew closer, a stiff wind rose up out of nowhere, trapping her inside a furious swirl of leaves. Appearing momentarily blinded, she stopped and shut her eyes, as if waiting for the wind to blow itself out. But it seemed to grow even stronger, pulling at her hair and clothes.

Shivering, as if she was suddenly cold, Pamela zippered up her leather jacket, lowered her head and made a beeline for Sean.

The wind abruptly gave up on her and slithered toward Sean, coiling itself around him, but gently. In that instant, fragments of the neverending nightmare he'd imprisoned in his soul were set free. An elusive shadow moving about with feline grace. Another, faceless, mirroring his every move. Whispers. Guarded secrets. Anger. The air turning cool, damp, then bitterly cold. A leadened silence that seemed to last an eternity, followed by a suffocated cry that still echoed in the recesses of his mind.

Grabbing Sean's hand, Pamela snuggled up against him and gave him an affectionate peck on the cheek. "Okay," she asked with a mischievous smile and a gentle nudge at his shoulder, "where is it?"

About to kick the leaves away and show her the headstone, Sean was distracted by a voice in the back of his mind, shouting *Run!* while another, distant and faint and not his own, pleaded with him to stay. Before he could answer, the wind whipped the leaves into a frenzy, exposing the small block of stone lying at his feet.

"What the hell—"

Dropping to his knees, Sean started rubbing the face of the headstone as if he were trying to erase the words that had been added—a lover's reply lazily scratched into the sand with the tip of a finger and forever frozen in time—changing his youthful vow of eternal love to read . . . AND I WILL ALWAYS LOVE YOU, SEAN.

Chapter Two

Sean fielded the pair of rolled-up towels Pamela had tossed over the chain-link fence—a ribbon of galvanized steel lace circling the serpentine reservoir in the soft light of the moon.

"Be careful," he cautioned as he dropped the towels onto the ground and moved closer to the fence, his arms outstretched.

"Just stand back," Pamela replied as she scaled the eight-foot-high barrier with the strength and stealth of a large cat, jumping to the ground beside him with equal feline grace.

Stifling a laugh, Sean asked, "Where the hell did you—"

"Don't ask," she whispered, "you don't want to know."

Scooping up the towels, he chortled, "I'll remember that," as he started down the gently sloping hillside crisscrossed with jagged rows of knee-high evergreens and dotted with scraggly brush.

Pamela fell into step beside him, the two of them slowed to a labored walk by the loose, sandy soil. "Okay . . . where's this *secret* swimming hole you've been carrying on about ever since that woman called and talked you into coming home for a book signing?"

Never one to wait for an answer, or to hold one back for that matter, she took his hand and squeezed it affectionately. "Well?"

Sean gestured off in the distance toward a small stone bridge spanning the mouth of the manmade lake and slowly drew an imaginary s-shaped curve over the moonlit surface of the water. "When I was a kid, the old Hackensack Creek snaked its way from that bridge and the pond we called the forty-foot . . . which was strictly for fishing . . . through the woods that no longer exist to the seven-foot, which was at the base of the field we're now standing in. *That's* where all of the younger kids went swimming, except when the Jackson-Whites showed up, and everyone cleared out. And fast!"

Sean gave a distasteful shiver upon recalling what those girls—inbred and most of them mothers before they were fifteen—had looked like. Dirty and dark-skinned, with misshapen features, they used the stream to bath in, soap and all, while trying to lure one of the local boys into staying behind and scrubbing their backs.

"Farther down the creek, hidden in the woods, was the ten-foot. That was the private, and I mean *private* domain of the older guys, and their girlfriends. The younger kids weren't allowed."

He added with a throaty growl, "And no bathing suits, either."

Darting up ahead, Pamela spun around and spread her arms, blocking his path. "And did you take this *mystery* girlfriend of yours there?"

Though he didn't show it, Sean was surprised by Pamela's question. In their two years together she hadn't once shown even a flicker of interest in any of the women in his past. Passing it off as no more than an attempt to get a rise out of him, he said, tongue in cheek, "Don't ask . . . you *really* don't want to know."

Laughing, he broke through Pamela's blockade and started running toward the far end of the reservoir, his gaze fixed upon the cloud of mist clinging to the surface of the water. Before he had gotten too far, he heard her behind him, gaining on him, which only served to spur him on, determined not to let her catch him.

Sean had never known a woman as competitive as Pamela, or as physical. At first, when everything was new—when they were still telling harmless white lies and holding back the truth until they were sure it was safe to go there—he had found her exhilarating, and quickly rose to the challenges he thought she posed. After the hunger in their bellies had been satisfied, and the lies replaced with bits and pieces of the truth, he had come to the realization that he was the spark, not her, unconsciously egging her on, just like now. He had also discovered that for some reason he needed to prove to himself that she would give chase, which was when the doubt had set in: the fear that one day he would run, unable not to—not knowing why he did it—and she wouldn't follow him.

But then a ten-year spread in their ages and a million-dollar difference in their bank accounts, her's being the larger, might also have had something to do with his newly discovered insecurity; at least that's what he had told himself.

"I'm too old for this shit," Sean said as he slowed to a lazy walk, only to have Pamela run into him. The impact sent them both tumbling in the sand toward the water's edge.

Lying sprawled on the ground, a tangle of arms and legs and towels and moonlit shadows—trying to catch their breath—Pamela asked quietly, almost apprehensively, "I know it was a long time ago, but do you think there's a chance you could *still* love her?"

Sean hadn't expected Pamela to ask something like that and wasn't sure what to say, if anything.

Gathering his thoughts, he chose his words carefully. "How can you possibly love someone you only knew for a short time . . . and thirty years ago at that?"

The moment he'd said it, Sean knew it didn't ring true and wanted to take it back, to somehow make it right. Before he could, Pamela said in a solemn, womanly tone of voice, her words laced with a hint of disapproval, "Love isn't something you simply turn on and off like a faucet . . . either it's there or it's not."

Rolling over onto her stomach, she propped herself up on her elbows and leaned into him. "So, my romantic young man . . . who puts headstones over empty graves, professing his eternal love for girls he only knew for a short time . . . do you still love her?"

Sean knew that if he didn't answer her, and quickly, Pamela would hound him until he did, which was something he didn't want, not here and especially not now. "I have the *memory* of loving her, which . . . now that I think about it . . . is probably due—"

Don't even go there. "No," he said emphatically. "I do not still love her."

What he hadn't said, what he refused to admit even to himself, was that he was afraid the feelings were still there, buried somewhere inside him, and if he wasn't careful they might slip out, along with all the unwanted memories. "Am I

22

making sense?" he asked, hoping that he had, and that Pamela would drop the subject.

After a moment, Pamela sighed and gave him a tender but unquestionably cool peck on the cheek, before climbing to her feet. This was her signature way of ending a discussion that upset her.

Gathering up the towels, she shook them out and gave him a less than gentle nudge with her foot as she said with a crystal-clear note of impatience in her voice, "C'mon . . . get up . . . let's go find the rest of those demons of yours and flesh them out."

As Sean stood up and brushed the sand off his clothes, he muttered under his breath, "One man's devil is another man's god."

Without turning to face him, Pamela said with an exasperated sigh, "It was just a prank, sweetheart. Cruel and thoughtless, but nonetheless a childish prank. Forget it and move on . . . *okay?*"

Sean shook his head and picked up where their argument had left off at dinner. "I told you, no one could have known—"

He hesitated, still unwilling to tread on that ground. With a shake of his head, he started around the reservoir in silence, moving steadily closer to the isolated patch of fog hovering above the surface of the water a stone's throw from the shore.

"Where you two made love?" Pamela finally asked, completing Sean's unfinished sentence. The tone of her voice—sounding more like an accusation than a question—belied the need for an answer.

With a towel in each hand, the ends dragging over the ground, she joined Sean, walking side by side, her fist bumping into his open hand as if she was asking him to hold her. He didn't.

After a moment, she said with a definite sense of certainty, "Why do I get the feeling there's something you're not telling me?"

Sean was about to disagree—to mount a knee-jerk, typically guy type of defense of himself—when he realized that she was right: There was something he couldn't tell her, but not because he wouldn't . . . he couldn't. Everything was off in the distance, beyond his reach, shadowy silhouettes lurking about, as if they were waiting for something, or someone. *But what? And why?*

Growing more frustrated by the moment as he tried but couldn't remember, he said in a quiet voice, "I'm sorry, I shouldn't—"

"Don't!" Pamela snapped. "You don't owe me any apologies. We both have demons in our past we haven't come to terms with."

She paused, as if trying to find the right words. "I just don't wear mine on my sleeve the way you do, which . . . in a strange way . . . I envy you for."

Sean was surprised to hear her admit to what he'd suspected from their very first meeting two years ago at the New York Academy of Fine Art. At thirty-six, she had been hiding from who and what she was—heir to a vast charitable trust—blithely teaching painting and drawing for a pittance. Her disguise had been complete with shocking shoulder-length orange hair, diamond studs lining both ears and a small emerald stud piercing her nose.

"Right here," Sean announced as he stopped and kicked off his shoes. Taking a towel from Pamela, he spread it out on the ground and gestured toward the patch of fog. "*That's* the old ten-foot."

She started laughing. "How the hell do you know that?"

"Simple," he said with a shrug. "The ten-foot always steamed in late spring and early fall. And on cool summer nights too."

Slipping off his sweater, he nonchalantly tossed it onto the towel. His shirt was next. Unbuckling his belt, he stepped out of his pants, then his briefs, to stand naked in the moonlight.

"According to the experts, there's an active fault running through the county which, they claim, explains the fog. Something about one of the wells feeding the reservoir passing over a release point and surfacing here. But we all thought

25

it was the Devil's work," he laughed as he sauntered into the water up to his knees.

"Too cold for you?" he teased. "Just going to watch?"

Pamela promptly peeled off her clothes. Taut and trim, yet every bit a woman, she cut a sensuous silhouette in the dark.

"I suppose I'm just as crazy as you are," she said, laughing, as she ran into the water and dove headfirst beneath the surface, only to jump back up just as quickly, her arms wrapped around herself in a futile attempt to get warm. Shivering, she took one look at Sean, who was still dry, and started kicking water at him.

Laughing, he dove backwards toward the mist with Pamela in pursuit. He felt her hand graze his calf, grab his ankle and pull herself to him just as he surfaced. She bobbed up beside him in the neck-deep water, the two of them shrouded by the mist, which turned the waxing moon overhead into a fuzzy blur. "My God," she whispered. "You're right, the water is *unbelievably* warm here."

Sean slipped his hand around Pamela's waist and pulled her to him. "Warm enough to make love?" he asked as he gently drew her closer, revealing that he was already on his way to being aroused.

Pamela snarled, "Like you did with *her?*"

Kicking off his hip, she started swimming for

26

the shore. Halfway there, she stood up and began walking, her head down, her stride purposeful. Vaporous tendrils rose up from her naked body in the cool night air, creating the illusion that she was on fire.

Sean was at her side before she could reach the shore. Taking her wrist, he turned her around. "What has gotten into—"

He stopped, his wide-eyed gaze fixed on a figure moving out of the shadows and slowly walking toward them. "We're not alone," he whispered under his breath, and pulled Pamela to him.

"Nice try," she snarled as she pulled herself free of his grasp and turned away, only to stop dead. "What the—"

Naked, her liquid black hair cascading down over her ivory-white shoulders—the moon's heavenly gaze toying with her breasts as it wrapped its arms around her hips and buried its face in the shadowy hollow of her loins—the stranger glided past Pamela as if she didn't even exist and walked up to Sean.

Speaking in a rasping voice, she said, barely above a whisper, "Hello, Sean," and reached out, brushing the tips of her fingers over his chest, her nails skating over his skin and sparking a fire inside him that he couldn't quench.

His heart racing, his muscles straining, he tried to pull away but couldn't—his thoughts, his actions no longer his to control. Her gaze, empty and expressionless until now, suddenly came to life as her eyes began to glow like embers in the dark. But they were cold, not hot, and strangely inviting. He tried to look away but couldn't as he felt himself being drawn into the flameless fire, a bottomless void, as if he were free-falling straight to hell.

After a moment, she nodded and slowly slipped past, grazing his arm with her breast, searing his skin and sending a shiver he couldn't stop throughout his body. Smiling, she gave a subtle tick of her head—as if she was inviting him to join her—before diving into the lake and disappearing beneath the blanket of fog.

Chapter Three

Propped up by a mountain of lace-fringed pillows pushed against the shiny brass headboard, his only accommodation to modesty a corner of the bedsheet—a Victorian floral print crawling with English ivy and morning glories in full bloom—Sean was sitting with his arms folded over his chest, watching Pamela.

Although she was wearing nothing more than a pair of black bikini panties and matching lace bra, she looked anything but sexy to him with a cell phone pressed to her ear and an angry scowl on her face as she paced back and forth over the huge Oriental rug. Her eyes, which turned from honey brown to burnt sugar whenever she talked business, appeared to be tracking every silent word spoken by the caller, the fifth trustee from the museum in less than two hours. The first one had weighed in shortly after six, rudely ending Sean's attempt at patching things up from last night.

Sean suddenly realized just how pissed he was for having fallen for the conditions Pamela had laid down for their four-day weekend together: a much-needed break from work for the both of us, was the way she'd put it. For his part he had agreed to leave behind his laptop and any talk of his new book in exchange for Pamela not bringing her cell phone and a briefcase full of work. The one thing he'd refused to agree to, however, was her request that he leave his running shoes and shorts at home. After all, he could write in his head and save it, but he couldn't run there.

As if having sensed his growing irritation, Pamela covered the mouthpiece with her hand and smiled sweetly. "Sorry . . . trouble in paradise. I'll only be another minute or two . . . I promise."

Sean batted the air with his hands and grumbled, "More like paradise lost." He had all he could do to keep from jumping out of bed and snatching the phone out of Pamela's hand and tossing it out one of the windows of the third-floor suite in the bed-and-breakfast they'd found on the outskirts of Blue Fields.

Sensing that he was getting close to the edge, he decided it was best to put as much distance as he could between them, at least until he calmed down. Hopping out of bed, he snatched his running shorts off the chair. In the process of slipping them on, standing storklike on one leg, he heard Pamela say, "C'mon, relax!" and felt her poke him in the back. Knocked off balance, he stumbled out of his shorts and fell face-first onto the bed into a harmless patch of silk-screened ivy and lavender flowers.

"Son of a bitch," he growled as he rolled over and sat up, bridling his desire to tackle Pamela to the floor and fuck her, simply to piss her off. That thought was quickly followed by the comic image of Pamela holding the cell phone to her ear—still talking and frowning and looking around—while he screwed her.

Sean replayed that scene over again in his head, letting it defuse every ounce of his aggression. Taking a deep breath, he said in a resigned tone of voice, "This simply isn't working. Why don't you head back into the city and take care of the problems at the museum? I'll find a ride home after the signing this evening."

Pamela abruptly clapped the cell phone shut. "I bet you'd like that too. And no doubt from *that* woman, I suppose. Right?"

Sean knew he shouldn't say it—knew all too well that it would only fuel the fire from last night that Pamela had refused to let die out—but he couldn't help himself. "Are we jealous?"

31

Pamela snarled, "You egotistical bastard," and threw the phone at him, her aim right on target, sending it straight for his head.

Fielding it with a one-handed catch, smiling, Sean hesitated only for as long as it took him to decide which open window was closest, before tossing it outside. He cocked his head, listening, and nodded at the sound of the phone hitting the ground. He then said somewhat self-righteously, "You and I had a deal, Pamela Jean. No laptop for me this weekend and no cell phone for you."

He wagged his finger. "*You* didn't keep your word."

Pamela suddenly charged him, looking anything but ladylike.

Stepping aside with the grace of a toreador, he slapped her silky bottom as she lunged past him and fell onto the bed. Rolling over, her eyes burning with indignation, she looked as if she wanted to tear him apart. Before she could sit up— knowing all too well what her blows felt like— he straddled her hips and grabbed hold of her flailing fists. Pinning her down, but not without a struggle, he asked, "What's gotten into you?"

He lowered his voice to a tender pitch. "I love *you* . . . not some thirty-year-old memory. When are you going to believe that?"

Though he had tried, Sean had been unable to come up with an explanation for Pamela's sudden jealousy. Desperate, he gave it another pass, picking and poking at the events of yesterday and last night in the hope of coming up with something, anything, that he could put his finger on and say with certainty—That's it!

Still fighting to break free of his hold, Pamela snarled, "Okay . . . then tell me who the hell that woman was last night."

Sean sighed. "I've already told you a dozen times . . . I can't remember ever having seen her before last night."

Pamela asked in rapid-fire succession, "Then how did she know your name? And how did she know that we were going to be there? And where the hell were her clothes? Do the women in this hick town all walk around outside in the middle of the night, stark naked? And where the hell did she go to . . . she just vanished!"

Sean had already asked himself those very same questions and a few others, ones that he knew he couldn't tell Pamela, such as why had her touch started his heart racing and sent a chill through his body? And what was it that he saw in her eyes that he couldn't resist, yet at the same time wanted to run away from?

Pamela abruptly softened all over. "I hate this. Can we try and pick up where we left off this morning, before the first call came in?" She shut her eyes. "Which I am *truly* sorry for."

Sean was touched by her sudden change of

heart, but only for as long as it took him to realize it was a test. Everything was a test for Pamela, especially when it came to men, even him. She didn't do anything on instinct, or judge anyone on her intuition: She had to have proof that what they said and who they were were true.

"Want a pad and a pencil to keep score?" he asked as he let go of her hands, shook his head and rolled off her. "Or have you given the test so often that you can score it from memory now?"

He stood up and began dressing. "Tell me, Dr. Eagleston, have *any* of the men in your life *ever* passed your little tests?"

Sean was standing on the top step of the front porch, framed by the gingerbread decorating the century-old Victorian dripping with 1890s' candy colors. With a bewildered shake of his head, he returned the polite but stone-faced nod from Pamela's chauffeur, John Sutherland, as he expertly maneuvered the Rolls-Royce Silver Wraith II around the small circular drive.

Sitting in the backseat, another cell phone stuck to the side of her head, Pamela waved as the car passed in front of him, though her gaze was focused on something other than him.

The moment the Rolls was out of sight, Sean tossed a ring of keys into the air—snatched them back—and started around the house to where Pamela had parked her car last night. "It's really

not me . . . never has been," she had said without
any outward sign of emotion when she handed
Sean the keys not ten minutes earlier.

Before he could say anything, she had crossed
his palm with the title, which her chauffeur just
happened to have had with him. "You've always
liked it," she had said, refusing to look at him.

What Pamela had done hadn't made any sense
at all to Sean, and still didn't. While money had
always been her way of covering up her feelings,
or using it to buy someone off just to avoid
having to deal with them, he had never once seen
her do anything on the spur of the moment. She
always approached everything, even their relationship, in a logical and methodical way.
Doesn't make sense.

Sean drew to a stop in front of the garage,
which was unquestionably the architectural off-
spring of the house that his boyhood friend,
Michael Gordon—a fugitive from the world of
A T & T—had saved from the wrecker's ball and
masterfully turned into an elegant bed-and-
breakfast. He smiled, wondering who had been
more surprised, Michael or him, when he and
Pamela had appeared on the doorstep looking for
lodging. *Me*, he decided as he slid open the barn-
style garage door and stood admiring the Maserati Ghibli.

With spoked wire wheels, wood-rimmed steer-
ing wheel, polished walnut paneling on the dash

and doors and not a hairline crack in the dove-gray leather, the 1965 pearl-white roadster was a classic.

A wave of doubt suddenly swept over him, followed by ripples of self-recrimination from what he had said to Pamela. And not just this morning, but last night too. The part of him that loved her, though apparently not the way she wanted or needed him to love her, regretted having said what he did, even though he had meant it. He had wanted to take it all back the moment the words had been given their freedom, but something had stopped him—exactly what, he didn't know—twisting his thoughts and tying his tongue.

That wasn't like him, which only added to the irritating conflict he felt growing inside him, yet he couldn't put his finger on what it was, or stop it. He found himself second-guessing his decision to tell Pamela anything about Judith, and especially about the headstone. *And taking her for that swim last night hadn't been a good idea, either. What were you thinking? And that woman . . . whoever the hell she was . . . had been the final straw.*

The more he struggled to resolve his feelings, to sort out what had happened, what he had said, what they both had said, the more his thoughts seemed to slip through his fingers. Unable to concentrate, he gave up and stood staring at the car, wondering what he should do with it, if anything. He could leave it right where it was and tell her to come get it, or he could keep it, if only to teach her a lesson. He just as quickly brushed that thought aside, reminding himself once again that she wouldn't have just handed over her car to him like that. *What the hell is happening?*

Frustrated at not having an answer, he gave up and glanced at his watch, but more out of habit than anything else. Seeing that he still had a good three hours to kill before having to shave, shower and get to the library by seven for the reception, he began toying with his options of what to do with his free time, stuck in a town he no longer knew and facing a sky that was threatening to open up any minute. That exercise lasted for as long as it took the image of the epitaph on Judith's grave marker to crowd his thoughts, the words—no longer just his own—echoing loudly inside his head.

"So do what the lady said," he muttered quietly to himself. "Go see if you can find those demons of yours and flesh them out."

Chapter Four

As chairman and CEO of the two-hundred-million-dollar John T. Eagleston Foundation, Pamela was in her element on the executive committee of the Museum of Modern Art: a world of facts and figures and powerful men and women, subjects she knew as well, if not better, than any of her counterparts seated at the long, narrow marble table in the wood-paneled conference room of the museum.

As far as she was concerned the issue was cut-and-dried: either the board agreed to dedicate one of the galleries to exhibit the Gerard bronzes, or she would withdraw her offer to donate the collection of fifteen larger-than-life-sized sculptures valued at over forty-million dollars. Hailed as modern masterpieces—"the beauty of Michelangelo and the power of Rodin," one critic had written of Monique Gerard's sculpture—the collection was to be a memorial gift in her father's name, a bequest that included an endowment to assure proper care of the sculptures while also providing for periodic refurbishing and rotation of the works on display.

With each bitter exchange between the committee members, Pamela's thoughts drifted further and further away from the meeting, until all she could think of was what had happened earlier that morning. She had lost control, which was unlike her, and upset her no end. But not nearly as much as what she had said and done to Sean. In hindsight, she realized he had been right, that she hadn't kept her part of the bargain. She was an addict when it came to the foundation, though in a way it wasn't that much different than Sean's addiction to his writing. Only she hadn't been able to face up to her habit as he had, when he had up and walked away from his tenured position at Hart College to write fulltime, going from Dr. Somebody to Mr. Nobody overnight. As for his running, though she knew he would never admit it if she asked him, it too was an obsession he couldn't live without.

What bothered her the most, however, was that she didn't know what had made her feel the way she had and prompted her to say and do the things she did. She sorely regretted what she had done with the car—not the fact that she'd given it to him, but the way she had given it to him. And leaving, as if she was running away from something, was even more confusing. That simply wasn't her style.

Outspoken? Guilty as charged. Passionate? Without a doubt, and she wouldn't have it any other way. But jealous? No. After all, this wasn't her first turn around the block. *Far from it!*

Now—fifty miles from Blue Fields and ensconced in the boardroom of the museum—she couldn't for the life of her taste a single bitter drop of the venom that had poisoned her, though she could remember with unerring clarity every acrimonious word she had spoken while under its toxic influence. This impasse served to bring out Pamela's analytical side, the part of her that Sean had once referred to as "your dominant-male half." The thought of what he had gone on to say, as if he was admitting to a carefully guarded secret—"My therapist says that it goes perfectly with my dominant-female side"— brought a smile to her face, which she quickly reined in lest it be misconstrued by anyone at the table.

Pamela quickly refocused her thoughts on what had happened, intent upon putting her finger on that exact moment in time when her feelings had changed, when she had begun to feel threatened and started to attack. She replayed in her mind what had gone down between her and Sean yesterday and last night, and earlier this morning. She worked backwards, scene by scene, looking for the spark that had ignited the fire in her, forcing them apart.

While Sean was well on his way to an enviable royalty income from his books, he was no match for Pamela, financially speaking. She lived off the income from her assets, and quite well at that. Even then, more than half of that income was left untouched and reinvested, expanding her personal worth day by day. And Sean outright refused to ride on her coattails, which had impressed her from the very beginning of their relationship; albeit a stormy one at first. All of this only made what Pamela had done with her car that much more painful for her to think about, but not because it wasn't hers anymore: She feared that by treating him like a gigolo, something she had always been concerned about, she might have burned her bridges.

You can be a real bitch sometimes, do you know that?

"Dr. Eagleston . . . are you with us here?" David Ross asked impatiently, rudely rapping his knuckles on the table. A pompous little troll of a man, Ross had made his fortune in telemarketing.

Pamela sat up. "Forgive me," she said apologetically, though she felt anything but sorry. "My thoughts must have wandered for a moment, but I assure you that it wasn't for lack of interest."

No sooner had she said this than she realized it was a lie: She cared more about what had happened between herself and Sean than what had transpired in the meeting over the last three hours.

This isn't supposed to be happening . . . not to me!

In an effort to buy time, to collect her thoughts, she asked, "What exactly have you come up with?"

Ross, his voice scarred by decades of three packs of Camels a day, said brusquely, "We have agreed to submit our unanimous recommendation to the full board that the funds for the project be appropriated from the capital improvement reserve, rather than waiting for the development people to raise the money."

He paused and smiled and said with a certain self-satisfied twist to his words, "The only hitch is that I—"

He caught himself. "*We* want to use an outside design firm for the gallery . . . not that we don't think highly of your—"

Without thinking, Pamela stood up, causing everyone else seated at the table to rise in unison, except for David Ross, who sat stuffed in his chair. "David . . . I really don't—"

"Sit down, my dear," he said with a flick of his hand.

You little shit. "I'm fed up with your childish games and your adolescent need to control everything, David. The foundation's offer for the Gerard bronzes is hereby withdrawn."

Silence blanketed the boardroom as Pamela picked up her journal and started for the door, her thoughts already halfway up the East River Drive on her intended exodus from Manhattan.

About to slip out into the hall, she turned and said with a mixed sense of apprehension and relief, "I'm also submitting my resignation from the board effective the end of this month. There are some things that I must . . . no, that I *want* to take care of."

"United Nations Plaza," Pamela told the cabby as she pulled the door shut behind her and slid back in the seat.

"No . . . wait!" Laughing, she erased with a hasty wave of her hand what she had just said. "Make that Thirty-four Sutton Place."

Although she had moved over two months earlier after having waited a year and a half for the renovations to be completed, she still, for some unexplained reason, hadn't succeeded in programming her brain with her new address. *So much for your dominant-male-side theory, sweetheart,* she thought, and returned to un-

winding the reel from this morning and yesterday, searching for that single frame when she had
been bitten, and had begun biting Sean. Replaying those scenes over again, she was struck by
the thought of the wind that had kicked up in the
cemetery, chilling her to the core. In that fleeting
moment, she had gone from feeling happy to see
Sean and be with him, sharing his memories, to
feeling threatened by what had happened between him and another woman. *That's it!*

Handing the driver a twenty, she hopped out
of the cab without waiting for change and stood
curbside, lost in thought.

"But it's been thirty years, for heaven's sake."

Reaching back still further, Pamela recalled
the evening that Sean had told her about the call
he'd gotten from Elaine Anders, and about the
book signing at the Blue Fields library. Though
he hadn't come right out and said it in so many
words, she had sensed that he really didn't want
to go. It was as if he felt he had to, as if he had
to settle an old debt. *But to whom?* Later that
evening he had sat down and told her about Judith for the first time, recounting their brief but
passionate love affair. He had made it sound like
a confession yet never once mentioned what had
happened between them to end what read like a
storybook romance.

Pamela was now convinced that something

must have happened that Sean didn't want to talk about. "Or maybe he can't—"

"Good evening, Ms. Eagleston," the stocky little doorman said smartly as he opened the polished brass door, the thick glass panel etched with a three-dimensional art nouveau swan in flight. "Will you be needing a cab for dinner tonight, or will you be dining in?"

"Neither," Pamela snapped as she darted past into the lobby.

Stopping on a dime, she turned back. "Oh, and Tony?" She pointed at him. "Have the garage bring my Mercedes around."

She turned and made a beeline for the stairs, passing up the old elevator, which she didn't have any patience for just now.

"Which one?" Tony called out, hurrying after her.

"The SL," Pamela shouted over her shoulder as she bounded up the stairs two steps at a time. "And make sure the tank's full."

With her hands on her hips, wearing only panties and a bra, Pamela stood in the center of her walk-in closet, trying to decide what to bring with her. She glanced at her watch. If she was lucky—even though it was a Friday and traffic heading out of the city would be bumper-to-bumper—she just might be able to get to the library before Sean left for home.

"But only if you drive like a bat out of hell," she muttered as she began grabbing anything that wouldn't wrinkle and tossing it into the square-cut canvas flight bag sitting on the floor.

Jeans, a long-sleeved cashmere sweater—on the light side of navy blue—and a pair of old penny loafers fit the bill for what to wear now. Reaching beneath a sea of silk and satin in her lingerie drawer, she retrieved a packet of crisp one-hundred-dollar bills, still wrapped with a paper strip from the bank.

Folding them over, she stuffed the cash into her jeans and pocketed the collection of credit cards lying on the dresser.

About to shut the drawer, she paused when she saw her pistol, a 9mm Luger, safely strapped into the custom-made calfskin shoulder holster, along with a spare clip. A special issue to the SS, her father had brought the gun back with him from the war, including the horror story on how he'd gotten it. She thought seriously about taking it with her, which instantly begged the question, *Why?*

One reason after another not to take the gun popped into her head, offering the usual sound and sensible advice. With a sharp wave of her hand, she dispensed with them all, tossing the pistol into her bag and sliding the drawer shut with a swing of her hip.

Chapter Five

As the police officer climbed out of his cruiser, not appearing to be in any real hurry, Sean gestured excitedly toward the cemetery. "It's over there . . . I didn't want to—"

He was silenced when the officer raised his hand and began to circle the Maserati, his expression equal parts skepticism and envy. Hooking his thumbs over his belt, he sauntered to a stop a few feet from Sean, who was holding a cell phone and standing near the driver's-side door. "This yours?" he asked with a sideways glance.

The young man's dirty blond hair, slate blue eyes and square jaw sparked a distant memory. Distracted, Sean glanced at the engraved brass nameplate pinned to the flap of the officer's shirt pocket. *"Murphy?* You aren't by any chance—"

"I asked if this was yours," the officer repeated firmly.

"No," Sean replied without thinking.

With a smile and a shake of his head, he quickly countered, "I mean yes." He couldn't help laughing at himself for what he'd said and tried to set the record straight. "Yes . . . the car is mine."

Murphy frowned.

You look just like your father, Sean thought, and was about to tell him that, to try and smooth things over. He also wanted to ask about his boyhood friend, but judging from the expression on Murphy's face, he decided that no matter what he said, or how he said it, he would only be digging the hole he was standing in that much deeper.

He finally said somewhat tentatively, "It was a gift," and slipped the title out of his pocket. As he handed it over, he was filled with apprehension and tried to remember whether or not Pamela had signed over the title. In an effort to reassure himself that she had, he decided she was too organized not to have done it. But it didn't help; he was still nervous and was sure it showed.

"Call it a thanks-it's-been-fun-but-it's-over present."

Murphy grinned. "She have a sister?"

"Not that I know of. But I'll ask . . . that's if

I ever see her again," he said, and flashed a cocky smile in the hope that Murphy couldn't see through his thinly veiled bravado as the thought of what had happened this morning finally sank in.

Murphy leaned up against the side of the car as he unfolded the title and read it. "So . . . where do you live, Mr. MacDonald?"

Thankful for Pamela's thoroughness—knowing that Murphy wouldn't be asking that question if she hadn't written in his address and signed over the title—Sean replied with a sense of relief, "Red Hook. It's a small town on the Hudson, just—"

"North of Rhinebeck," Murphy interrupted. "Yes, I know."

He handed the title back to Sean. "What brings you downstate, Mr. MacDonald?"

Suddenly reminded of why he had called 911, Sean asked bluntly, "Do you want to see what I found . . . or do you want to stand here and bullshit?" Ignoring Murphy's surprised look, Sean turned and started toward the cemetery. "Well, are you coming?"

"You sleep with that?" Murphy asked.

When Sean turned back, an inquisitive frown on his face, Murphy pointed to the cell phone.

Realizing how relieved he had been when he found the phone in the car and eagerly used it, Sean suddenly regretted what he had said to

Pamela earlier that morning. His discomfort was made that much worse by the recollection of the puddle of useless bits of circuitry and plastic oozing out from underneath the huge front tire of the Rolls-Royce. He made a mental note to apologize to her for what he'd said and done. *That's if you get the chance,* he thought, as he gingerly tossed the phone onto the driver's seat.

"Shall we?" he asked, gesturing toward the cemetery and following his own point. "At first I thought it was just some prank, but I decided it was best not to take any chances, and—"

"You grew up with my father, didn't you?"

That question brought Sean to an abrupt halt, allowing Murphy to catch up and walk ahead of him. Leaning up against the fence and partially blocking the open gate, Murphy smiled, changing from the uniformed policeman he was into the spitting image of the young boy Sean had once known. "I recognized your name on the title."

A sense of having been toyed with flared up inside Sean, instantly pissing him off. "Then why the hell did you—"

"Habit," Murphy was quick to say. "Technically speaking, we're not supposed to *assume* anything." He stepped aside, inviting Sean to slip past into the cemetery. When Sean hesitated, still angry and showing it, Murphy said softly, "Just doing my job."

Somewhat placated, Sean sidestepped through the gate and pointed off to the right. "Over there," he said and snaked his way through the headstones, pulling up to a wavering stop.

Murphy stepped beside him and immediately motioned with a sweep of his arm for Sean to step back, which he obeyed without question. "Did you touch anything?" he asked, his fierce gaze raking the ground.

"I know the drill," Sean replied drolly as he drew his hands behind his back and stood staring down, re-examining the pieces of clothing strewn about on the ground: a plaid wool skirt, a hunter-green sweater, a bra that appeared to have been violently ripped off a woman's body and a pair of white cotton panties—torn to shreds and spotted with blood—and a solitary brown penny loafer.

Draped over a nearby headstone were the remnants of a lavender silk blouse. A few steps away was a purse, the other shoe and a small notepad, the pages ripped out and scattered all about.

Without comment, Murphy withdrew a plastic bag from one back pocket and extracted a pair of surgical gloves from the other, which he struggled to pull on as he slipped past Sean and squatted down. Taking care not to disturb the lie of the brown leather pocketbook, he lifted the flap, reached inside and fished around and came up with a wallet. Standing up, he fingered it open and fanned the plastic sleeves until he found what he was looking for.

"Shit," he growled through his teeth and slowly shook his head. "It's times like this that I hate this *fucking* job."

Leaving the wallet folded open, he gently tucked it into the plastic bag, zipped it shut and handed it to Sean as if he didn't want any part of it. "Know her?" he asked quietly as he turned toward the entrance and motioned with a disgusted wave of his hand for Sean to follow. "Try and stay in your footsteps . . . okay?"

Immediately upon seeing the photo on the driver's license, Sean took a step back, as if he had been pushed. "Shit," he sighed, echoing Murphy's reaction. Though it had been dark last night, and the photo anything but flattering, the long black hair, high cheekbones and wide-set eyes were a dead match. In that instant of recognition, Sean regretted having come back to Blue Fields as he turned to follow Peter Murphy, unaware of the leaves tumbling after him, a sudden gust of wind blowing itself out the moment he darted through the gate and pulled it shut behind him.

"You need me for anything," he asked, "or can I go?"

He handed the bagged wallet back to Murphy. "I've got a book signing to get to at the library, and I have to—"

"All I need is your statement, Mr. MacDonald. It won't take long. But first I have to call and get the forensics unit here."

He turned toward his car. "Gimme a minute or two, okay?"

Sean replied affably, "No problem." Stuffing his hands into his pockets, he stepped back, only to be caught up in a sudden swirl of wind that whipped around him and pulled him to the fence, taking his breath away. Adrenaline suddenly coursed through his body, but the urge to flee drained away just as quickly at the sound of a whisper—a soft, soothing *shhhhhh*—as the air was filled with the faint but unmistakable fragrance of Shalimar.

Those elusive shadows suddenly reappeared in the back of his mind, but still too dark and too far away to make out. He shook his head and told himself it was nothing more than his overactive imagination, repeating what Pamela had said to him before giving him a reassuring kiss. The moment that thought filled his head, setting him at ease, the air turned cold and damp and stale with decay, sending an uncontrollable shiver through his body.

"You okay?" Murphy asked as he walked up and stood in front of Sean, no more than an arm's length away. "You look like—"

He stopped, his head cocked to one side, as if he was testing the wind. "What's that smell?" he

Donald Beman

asked, glancing past Sean and peering into the cemetery. "You don't think that she's—"

"I seriously doubt it," Sean said with a shake of his head.

Murphy stiffened, his body wired. "How can you be sure?"

Sean was about to explain but stopped, knowing that he couldn't. "So . . . what is it you want to know?" he asked as he slowly but deliberately walked away from the gate, doing his best to ignore the gentle howl of the wind, as if it were calling him back, while at the same time fighting the urge to run like hell.

54

Chapter Six

Once a tavern along the north-south highway during colonial times, and laying fair claim to hosting General Washington, the heart and soul of the Blue Fields library—a two-story sandstone block building—had served as a general store, a private residence and even the local post office during its former life.

The addition, a pristine frame and glass structure designed by architects unquestionably well intentioned and no doubt eager to please, yet hampered by a limited budget—blinding them to the past—was wrapped in aluminum clapboard siding and topped with a faux cedar-shake roof. To Sean, however, wanting nothing to have changed, it failed to capture the true colonial character of its much older twin. Not even the rain, a solid curtain of water falling straight down, could hide the jarring break with the past.

Though it was already ten to seven, there were only two cars in the parking lot, which reawakened in him the ever-present fear that no one would show up. Over the last five years he had experienced everything from having fifty people queued up at a little mall bookstore in the Hudson Valley—the line snaking its way out into the food court—to being confronted by a group of feminists angrily protesting his portrayal of the Devil as a woman. They had become downright ugly after he had commented that it seemed only fitting to him, since the female of the species was the natural-born predator. Without a doubt, however, the most memorable book signings— what he had dubbed the book signings from hell—were the ones where no one showed up, and he was left sitting alone at a table in a trendy suburban bookstore on Little League night.

The crackle of lightning and clap of thunder helped to turn that sickening feeling into panic. Real or imagined, Sean found himself struggling with the primitive urge of fight or flight, with retreat gaining favor. "Grow up," he told himself as he made a sharp U-turn and pulled into the newly paved parking lot.

He circled it once and again—the fan belt slipping and squealing as he splashed through the puddles—before choosing an unlit spot in the farthest corner, as if he was trying to hide.

The air inside the addition smelled of sawdust and fresh paint and still wet varnish. Sean was immediately struck by how large the main room was, until he realized that many of the shelves had yet to be filled with books. After sending out a spray of water with a shake of his head, he marched up to the young woman standing behind the checkout desk and asked with a cheerful smile, "Ms. Anders, please. I'm Sean MacDonald, I'm here for—"

He stopped in midsentence when he saw the girl's twilight-gray eyes grow wide and her face turn pale, a ghoulish complement to her straight, shoulder-length black hair.

She began fidgeting with the book she was holding, then cleared her throat and asked in a whisper, "You don't know?"

Sean laughed nervously. "Let me guess. The signing's tomorrow night . . . and I'm a day early . . . right?"

He was as much chagrined as he was hopeful, given the turnout.

Glancing down, he brushed off the water that had beaded on the sleeves of his Harris Tweed sports coat. When he looked up, the young woman still appeared to be at a loss for words. *Shit.*

"It wasn't yesterday . . . was it?"

"Patty?" an older woman asked as she appeared in the doorway of the office behind the desk. "Would you be a dear and get—"

She came to an abrupt halt, a startled look on her face, which was quickly replaced with a warm smile. "Welcome home, stranger."

Without waiting for Sean to respond, she stepped around the desk and gave him a gentle kiss on the check. Though her long red hair was now tarnished with silver, her green eyes not quite as bright, Annie Parker hadn't changed. Just seeing her made Sean smile, the same way it had whenever she walked into class, fresh and clean and covered with freckles, which were now nowhere to be found. "I can't believe it, you look as lovely as you did—"

Blushing, Annie pressed her finger to Sean's lips, silencing him as she said with a sigh, "I apologize for the turnout. I'm afraid half the town . . . the half that reads! . . . is at the wake."

"Must be someone really important," Sean noted, hiding his relief and disappointment behind a mask of respectful solemnity.

Her face darkened. "You don't know?"

Sean replied with a wide-eyed grin and shrug of his shoulders.

She said with a quiet reverence, "It's Elaine Anders."

"What!" Sean responded in disbelief. "When? How?"

Annie took Sean's hand and led him toward a table stacked with copies of his book. Pushed up against the wall behind it was a pair of aluminum folding tables covered with paper tablecloths and set with a punch bowl, plastic cups, paper plates and napkins, and plastic trays filled with an assortment of bite-sized pastries.

Sitting him down at the table of books, she pulled up a chair beside him, took a breath and sighed. "Elaine had been missing for over a week. As a matter of fact, she disappeared shortly after she had successfully talked you into coming here."

Annie blinked and turned away, as if she was trying to avoid his inquisitive gaze. It was her signature pose, forever etched into Sean's memory after the first time they had made love.

"They found her body—"

She paused. When she finally spoke, she sounded weary. "I was going to call you, but I guess I didn't want to—"

"Do they know what the cause of death was?" Sean asked, and immediately wished he hadn't when he saw Annie stiffen all over.

"I'm sorry," he said softly. "I wasn't thinking."

Annie turned back. "So, how's the book doing?" She sounded and looked upbeat and cheerful. "Make the best-seller list yet?"

She picked up a copy of *Death Mask* and fanned the pages. "It's strange reading a book written by someone you once—"

She smiled. "I've read every one of your books. Even the first one which, just between two old friends, was a real—"

She appeared unsure of herself.

Sean smiled. "A real struggle to read?"

Annie nodded, her gentle laugh instantly infecting Sean.

He reached out and took her hand. A sudden roll of thunder overhead startled them both into laughing like a couple of giddy teenagers instead of the fortysomething adults they were. When they sighed and leaned into each other, the warmth of Annie's body seeped into his, the smell of her hair and her sweet breath calling up memories he thought he had neatly wrapped up and put safely away. In that instant, he wanted everything to be just as he remembered it, even though those memories had been tampered with; rewritten by time. He wanted to bury his face in her long red hair and wrap his arms around her, losing himself once again in the soft curves of her body.

Before he could reach that point of no return, turning fantasy into reality as he often did, he sat up and asked, "How's John?"

Annie began to absentmindedly pick at the lint on her black wool skirt. After a moment, she said without the slightest hint of emotion, "He divorced me ten years ago and took a trophy wife. That's when I went back to school and got my MLS. So here I am, Annette Parker, the town librarian, fat, forty and single again."

She gave Sean a quick peck on the cheek and stood up, still holding his hand. "Sign a book for an old girlfriend?" she asked with a bright-eyed smile, her mood having turned on a dime again.

It was over as fast as it had begun: that tenuous bridge to the past had been crossed, contact made, followed by a hasty and reluctant retreat. Sean wasn't sure whether he felt sad or relieved, which only added to his growing sense of melancholy as he released his hold of Annie's hand and picked up the pen lying on the table. He didn't need time to think about what to say, or how to say it; he simply and easily penned, *You are as beautiful as I remember you . . . and you still make me laugh.*

About to sign his name, he hesitated, smiled and wrote with ease, *All my love, Sean.*

Turning to the title page, he signed his full name with a flourish, which immediately drew a soft chuckle from Annie and the wry comment, "That signature of yours certainly has changed."

She took the book from him and wrapped her arms around it the same way she had always carried her books home in high school.

"I'm sure folks will straggle in after the wake,"

she said reassuringly and glanced outside. "Even in this hellish rain."

No sooner had she said that, than the front door creaked open and a woman quietly slipped inside, her head bowed, her gaze cast aside. Soaking wet head to toe, she looked as if she had been walking in the rain for hours, not dashing from her car to the front door. Though she was a complete stranger, she moved in a vaguely familiar way, calling up the distant memory of someone once known but forgotten. Now and then she glanced about the room, her gaze falling upon Sean for an instant, darting away, then flitting back, unblinking, as if she was trying to decide if she knew him.

"See," Annie said as she started toward her office, leaving Sean alone with his thoughts, a place he didn't want to be.

To his relief, more and more people began arriving—women with men in tow, looking like reluctant little boys being dragged into the library by their surrogate mothers. Before long there was a small crowd, but not nearly enough people to make the books on the table disappear. One by one the women marched up and welcomed him to Blue Fields. Their varied smiles told as many different stories of a dead friend as did the worry on their faces, the wrinkles silently sketching the fear they felt for their own safety but didn't dare speak of. Sean had all he could do to

keep from asking how Elaine Anders had died,
and if they had caught whoever did it? He hoped
that someone would ask him if he had known
her so that he could say no, then ask what had
happened to her before they could slip away. But
no one did, though he was certain he could hear
them talking about it, their voices hushed, their
backs turned, carving him out their lives. He
soon felt like a stranger, a drifter, in the town
that he had known before any of them, his memories now little more than the dirt beneath their
feet.

As he smiled politely and asked each of them
for their first name—writing cryptic notes as if
he knew every one of them personally—Sean
couldn't help thinking of his conversation with
Elaine Anders, and the startling turn in the sound
of her voice: One moment he had been talking
with a stranger, the next minute he was listening
to Judith. Though her voice was different, older,
it was her, *her* words, *her* turn of a phrase, *her*
expectant silence.

Is that what you're running from? he wondered. But that wasn't a question, it was an in-
dictment—one long held but never served—a
charge for which Sean had no defense, and he
knew it.

"Hello, Sean," a woman said in a low, rasping
voice.

Those two words, faint and frail, had been

spoken with a familiar ring to them—lyrical, in perfect harmony—scattering his thoughts. When he glanced up, he found himself staring into the hollow gaze of the woman who had been the first to enter the library. Her dress was wet and wrinkled, her silky-brown hair plastered to her head and neck. She smelled of soil, but sweet, not sour. "Why did you leave me?" she asked, and started coughing.

Confused, his thoughts not his own, Sean broke free of her mesmerizing gaze and glanced down, intent upon writing a brief note and being done with her. "What would you like me to—"

"Hello, sweetheart," was followed by the reassuring touch of a hand on his shoulder and a gentle kiss on the top of his head.

He spun around to find Pamela standing behind him, smiling, her finger pressed to her lips. Reaching out, she caressed his cheek with the back of her hand as she mouthed *I love you*. She then gestured with a subtle nod of her head for him to turn around.

About to comply, he felt something slip inside him and wrap itself around his heart, its touch as warm as a summer's night.

Breathless, he turned around, fully expecting to find that woman waiting for him. But she was gone, her place in line taken by another woman. Nattily dressed, with a ruddy Irish face and thin-lipped smile, her small eyes were framed by a delicate pair of gold wire-rimmed glasses. Handing Sean one of his books, she said with a perplexed frown on her face, "That woman who was ahead of me wrote something in here and just walked away." She turned and gestured toward the door, which was just easing shut.

With the click of the heavy brass latch, the comforting touch inside Sean's chest turned airy and cool as he looked down to see the phrase *You promised you would always love me* smudged onto the page, as if it had been written with a muddy finger.

"Shit," he whispered under his breath.

"What is it, sweetheart?" Pamela asked as she leaned over his shoulder to see what he was staring at. "This is more than just a prank," she said with an angry note in her voice as she reached down, lifting the book out of his hand and cautiously brushing her fingers through the words, smearing the cryptic note.

Closing the book, she said with unquestioned authority, "I think that we should head back into the city tonight and get as far away from whoever it is who's playing this sick game."

"No," Sean said with a subtle but firm shake of his head.

"But—"

"I'm tired of running."

"*Running?*" Pamela asked. "What are you talking about?"

Chapter Seven

The drenching downpour had given way to a brilliant October sunrise—crystal-clear skies washed with blue—leaving behind a crisp, refreshing chill in the air. The relentless rain had also stripped many of the leaves off the trees on the hills surrounding the reservoir, cooling but not quenching autumn's fiery flames.

When Peter Murphy waved his hand over his head, Sean hurled a stone the size of a golf ball into the lake. It splashed some fifty feet beyond and an equal distance to the right of the scuba diver standing in knee-deep water. Clad in an orange wet suit, the barrel-chested man was tethered to a nylon line that sank beneath the surface and reappeared on the shore wrapped around the waist of his equally burley partner. Parked a few steps behind him was a truck, the rear door rolled up, its sides lettered with the words NEW YORK STATE POLICE—UNDERWATER RECOVERY UNIT. Nearby, their arms folded and talking quietly among themselves, was a trio of uniformed state troopers. At the water's edge, sitting atop an aluminum suitcase turned on end, was a bespectacled man in his fifties, chunky and bald, fighting to stay awake. He was wearing waders, a shirt and tie and a black nylon windbreaker with the words MEDICAL EXAMINER stenciled in iridescent white on his back.

Pamela cradled a Styrofoam container of hot coffee in both hands as she snuggled up against Sean and asked, "Are you *positive* the woman we saw here was the same one in the licence photo?"

Sean simply nodded.

Pamela shook her head. "I can understand why you decided to tell them what we saw here, but did you have to tell them that we were swimming, and naked yet! They must think we're crazy."

Sean replied with a patient sigh. "I don't care what they *think*, I'm tired of running away from everything. I've been doing it all my life. You even told me that . . . or have you forgotten?"

Judging from the turn of her head and her skeptical frown, it was apparent that Pamela didn't agree with Sean's position on this.

"They asked why you didn't go in after her, didn't they?"

Sean leaned back on his heels and said with a drawl, "Yup."

"And what did you tell them?"

"I threw the question back in their laps. I asked them if they were with their wife or fiancée . . . or girlfriend . . . would they chase after some naked woman who had suddenly appeared out of nowhere . . . made a pass at them . . . and dove into the water."

Sean shook his head. "It's a no-brainer. They would have done exactly what we did, which was get the hell out of here."

Pamela stood nursing her coffee, her gaze drifting off into the distance. "Is there *anyone* you can think of who could have possibly known about—"

She hesitated and began to chew on her lip. "Did anyone besides you know about the grave marker, and that it was you who put it there? An old friend, someone who might have seen you putting it there, such as the pastor of the church? *Anyone?*"

Sean had asked himself those same questions at least a hundred times, ninety-nine of them having been last night as he lay awake beside Pamela, playing everything back in his mind, over and over again. He gave a casual shrug. "There's only one person who knew about Judith and me, who's still in Blue Fields, and that's—"

He shook his head. "Annie and I were best friends, still are, she would never have—"

"You and the librarian!" Pamela laughed. "You're kidding?"

"Sweetheart, she's just a—"

"She's *just* beautiful, *that's* what she is. And she couldn't take her green eyes off you all night. Are you blind? You're single, successful and in great shape. Any woman worth her—" Pamela held up her hand. "Whoa, girl, hold it right there." She turned to Sean. "Why am I only like this here, in this town?"

Sean took a deep breath and exhaled slowly. "I don't have a clue . . . but if it's any consolation, you're not alone."

He gave her a reassuring hug and a kiss on her cheek. "But whatever it is, I intend to stay and find out what's going on." Grinning, he stole Pamela's coffee from her, took a long sip and said through a thinly veiled laugh, "Who knows, maybe there's a story in it?"

"Stay?" Pamela asked quizzically. "As in not go home?"

Sean replied with a wide-eyed smile.

"You're serious, aren't you?"

"Yup," he said with a sharp nod as he turned and focused his attention on the line of bubbles breaking the surface of the water in a steadily tightening circle in the area where he'd tossed the stone. "Wanna take a little vacation and stay here with me?"

Pamela leaned up against him and whispered, "I'd love to."

"Really? You're kidding, right? Don't you have all sorts of problems at the museum that you—"

"Nope," Pamela quipped. "I cleared the decks and packed my bags. If I need more clothes, I'll have John drive them up to me. You're stuck with me, mister."

Before Sean could say anything, Pamela asked in a more serious vein, the hint of a frown wrinkling her forehead, "That woman who came into the library last night . . . the one who wrote that bizarre note in the book and vanished . . . did you tell the police—"

"Dr. MacDonald!" Peter Murphy shouted. "We found her!"

Walking a few steps behind the waitress, who was garbed in colonial dress except for her shoes, Sean and Pamela ducked beneath another rough-hewn beam in the dimly lit dining room of the '76 House and came to a stop beside a small wooden table set to the left of a massive field-stone hearth ablaze with a crackling fire.

After setting the menus on the table, the woman stuck her hands into the pockets of her apron and shook her head. "Oops, forgot my pad," she muttered under her breath and scurried away.

Sean pulled out one of the spartan ladder-back chairs and gestured for Pamela to have a seat.

Glancing up at the low-slung ceiling and down at the wavy, wood-planked floor, Pamela jiggled the rickety-looking table and asked with a playful smile, "Is this place safe?"

Sean laughed. "Not if you're a traitor."

"Traitor?" she asked, sitting down. "What are you saying?"

Sean sat across from her and began humming to himself, as if he was playing a dirge, while drumming his fingers on the table.

"This is where Major André was tried for treason during the Revolutionary War. And he was hung not far from here, on what's now known as Andre's Hill. I presume that Dr. Eagleston knows who Major André was?"

Pamela replied with a gracious nod. "She does, thank you. She also knows of his accomplice, the infamous Benedict Arnold, who got away scot-free and never paid for his crime. Unless you call living in London on a pension from the Crown, an outcast even there since London society never trusted him because of what he'd done, scot-free. Sort of ironical, don't you think?"

Sean simply shrugged, as if to say that he couldn't care less.

Donald Beman

The waitress breezed up, a pad in one hand, a pen in the other.

"You folks having dinner," she asked, "or just drinks?" She squinted at her watch. "If you're gonna eat, you better decide what you want now . . . the kitchen closes in fifteen minutes."

Pamela raised her hand. "I want a drink first. I'll have a double scotch . . . Chivas . . . on the rocks."

Pamela's passion for scotch equaled her love of fine wine, both of which she could hold better than any man Sean had known; and he was no exception to that rule. By his own admission, he was a cheap date, since two martinis were his limit. After that, he progressively lost all inhibitions with each successive sip.

"And you, sir?" the waitress asked as she began to work at retying her linen apron around her ankle-length skirt.

Pamela answered for him. "The gentlemen will have a double Tangeray martini on the rocks, please . . . with extra olives."

Sean reached out, placing his hand on Pamela's. "Hold the drinks. Instead, bring us a bottle of wine. A red burgundy, but nothing young. And set aside a second bottle of the same vintage."

Pamela propped her elbows on the table and rested her chin in her open hands. "Care to tell me who's going to drive?"

Sean glanced up at the ceiling, then back into her expectant gaze. "We don't have to drive anywhere if we don't want to; we just have to be able make it up the stairs and stumble into one of the rooms they rent to dinner guests."

A sly smile spread across Pamela's face. "Why not skip dinner? When did you say your friend Murphy was going to be here?"

"Friend?" Sean asked reticently. *"Officer* Murphy said he would be here right after he gets off duty. Hopefully, he'll know more about the autopsy on that woman than he did this after—"

"Hi!" Peter Murphy said on a cheery note as he marched up and ceremoniously dropped a manila envelope onto the table as if he were serving them a summons. "Want some company? I'm *starving.*"

Chapter Eight

It only took Pamela one bump of her head on the pitched ceiling in the tiny bathroom to remind her that at a tad over six feet, she stood head and shoulders above the average colonial woman, and easily half-a-foot taller than most men of that time.

With an appreciative smile, she dropped her towel over the wicker stool beside the huge claw-footed tub. Reminded of how playful Sean had been before he had hopped out of bed and gone running—which had surprised her, given the amount of wine he'd had last night—she wasn't about to take any chances: She carefully buried the palm-sized cell phone inside the plush folds of terry cloth. She then topped it with the manila envelope containing the autopsy report she'd talked Peter Murphy into leaving with her, and gingerly eased herself down into the steaming hot bubble bath.

A good soak was Pamela's tried-and-true remedy for a hangover, in spite of the fact that her headache always got worse before it got better. Nevertheless, she was convinced that her prescription for a hangover was far more civilized than running five miles the morning after, which Sean claimed sweated everything out of him.

"Must be a guy thing," she sighed and sank still deeper, until only her head and knees were above the mountain of bubbles.

A bubble bath, and the hotter the better, was one of Pamela's few truly stereotypical female traits. As for Sean, there were few things he disliked more than taking a bath, which he likened to soaking in his own dirt and grime. Where she was methodical and analytical, he relied upon his intuition. She was assertive, to the point of being aggressive, even confrontational, while he tended to be circumspect, but not by any means passive. And she had a head for numbers, which he didn't, and didn't even seem to care that he didn't.

Pamela smiled when she realized that simply looking at their relationship this way was by its very nature more male than female.

All of this said, however, she had nonetheless come to accept the fact that they were a perfect match for each other, and that Sean truly loved her. But perhaps even more important than his love was the fact that he accepted her for what she was without trying to change her, unlike the other men in her life, who had tried telling her what to think and what to say and what to do.

There was, however, one trait they both shared: their passion for each other, a raw sexual desire they had only recently learned to exercise some control over. And then only because Sean was an early bird, up at four to write and in bed by nine that night. While she was a night owl, staying up until after midnight, more often than not reading, then dragging herself out of bed the next morning. Making love was the last thing on her mind at six A.M.

"Maybe you're getting old," Pamela said as she plucked up the manila envelope with a pinch of her soapy-wet fingers.

Although she had listened attentively to everything Peter Murphy had to say, the wine had taken its toll on her memory, and she wanted to make certain she hadn't missed something. Besides, regardless of Sean's trust, Peter was the enemy until he proved otherwise, which was another dichotomy in their personalities.

She began reading the report, weighing every word, every phrase. She was looking for any contradiction to what Peter Murphy had told them about Jean Gleason—the great-granddaughter of

Jonas Blauvelt, the man whose grave her clothes had been scattered atop—that the ME thought she had been dead for some as yet undetermined period of time, but definitely died before witnesses claimed to have seen her alive.

Wait a second. Pamela placed a soapy finger on one entry and raced through it in silence: *Found evidence of damage to the cardiac tissue and the lungs similar to that caused by direct contact with something such as dry ice. There was, however, no evidence of frostbite or freeze burning of the lips, mouth or esophagus. Biopsies are being sent to the lab for analysis, along with blood and lymphatic tissue for a complete tox screen. Because of the bruising of the lower abdomen and legs, and the severe trauma to the genitalia, smears were taken to test for semen.*

Tossing the autopsy report onto the floor, Pamela fished the cell phone out of its hiding place and tapped a few keys, calling up a number from the programmed memory. After no more than two nods of her head, she said in a firm, businesslike voice, "This is Pamela Eagleston . . . I want to speak with Charles Andrews."

Pamela sighed, "Is he with a client?"

She shook her head. "I see . . . then interrupt him."

"Charles? Pamela here. Sorry to break in on your partners' meeting, but I need you to take care of a few things for me."

She paused, listening with her eyes; however, her frown said that she really didn't care a wit what her attorney had to say.

"I want you to get hold of that friend of yours in Albany . . . that big-name forensic pathologist you were telling me about."

Reaching out, she blindly patted the floor and came up with the autopsy report. "I want him to perform a second autopsy on one Jean Gleason. The case number is RC, nine, nine, four, seven, two, zero. It's—"

She stopped to listen. "Yes . . . yesterday . . . and there's a good possibility it'll be ruled a homicide by the supervising ME."

Pamela sat up, then slid back down out of a false sense of modesty, which brought a smile to her face. "And Charles? I also want your criminal law guru to familiarize himself with every detail of this case he can dig up . . . and right away. Sean and I could be suspects here, and I want to be prepared should—"

She shook her head. "Please . . . just do what I ask."

She nodded. "Thank you. Now, when you—"

"Pamela Jean Eagleston!" Sean called out and could be heard scratching at the bathroom door. "Is that a cell phone you have?"

Damn. Pamela replied innocently, "Cell phone . . . me?"

At the sound of the doorknob turning, Pamela

slipped the phone beneath the surface of the water and flashed a broad smile at Sean as he peeked into the bathroom. "Just talking to myself."

She grinned. "Comes from being around you."

She tried to shoo him out of the bathroom by tossing a handful of soapsuds at him. "Go . . . get out . . . I'll be out in a minute."

With a mischievous smirk on his face, Sean stepped onto the bath mat and squirmed out of his sweat-soaked T-shirt. He then bent down to untie his running shoes. "I think I'll join you."

"Like hell you will . . . you're all sweaty and yucky."

Seeing he was serious, Pamela stood up and stepped out of the tub, dripping with bubbles.

Sean's smirk grew into a lecherous smile.

"You can be a real prick sometimes, do you know that?"

When she scooped up the towel, the suds-covered cell phone slipped out of her hand and slid across the floor.

Sean frowned and folded his arms over his chest.

More upset with herself for getting caught than she was angry with Sean, Pamela spit out, "Don't get upset; I only called—"

"I know . . . your attorney . . . I heard."

When Pamela reached for him, Sean pulled back and said with obvious resentment, "I know you think that I'm naive when it comes to people and their motives. But I prefer to think that I'm simply curious . . . and perhaps a bit more tolerant than you are . . . rather than dense. Or dull-witted. Which is exactly how I sometimes feel you think of me. One thing I am not, however, is stupid."

Surprised, Pamela said in a contrite voice, "No, sweetheart, you are *definitely* not stupid. I suppose curious is really what you are. Though at times I can't help thinking this curiosity thing gets out of hand. Just remember, curiosity killed the cat."

"I'm going out," he said and walked out into the bedroom, heading for the door. "I don't know when I'll be back."

"Sean . . . wait . . . you'll catch your death of a cold if you go out like that."

"We cats have nine lives . . . remember?"

Pamela shot back, "And which one are you on now . . . have you kept count?"

As he closed the door behind him, Sean said with a sarcastic twist, "You're the big CEO . . . you're good with numbers . . . *you* count."

Chapter Nine

The small courtyard behind the '76 House was cloaked in a curtain of privacy by a stockade fence, giving new meaning to the expression pied-à-terre. The early morning sun, still struggling to burn away the leftover fog, cast half the courtyard in warm, hazy sunlight, the other half in a cool shade. Overgrown flower beds planted with wilting blue and white petunias and clusters of yellow marigolds were surrounded by a kaleidoscope of hardy asters and chrysanthemums standing at attention up against the fence, immune to autumn's early frost. Snaking through the grass sorely in need of cutting was a black rubber garden hose.

Sean turned full circle, inspecting the old fence for breaks. He checked the gate to make certain he had latched it shut behind him. With a reassured nod, he bent down and untied his running shoes and kicked them off. After a second look around, though he was anything but shy, he peeled off his sweat-soaked shorts and tossed them onto a white wrought-iron bench pitted with rust.

Turning on the hose, he waited for the water to run clean and cold. "You're wired backwards," Pamela had told him the first time they had taken a shower together; instead of him shrinking from the cold as most men did, he had become aroused. And now was no exception to that rule as he stood in the cool, sunny October air, the cold water cascading down over his body, enjoying the illicit sensation of being outdoors and naked, and in broad daylight.

Although he was lost in his own pleasure, Sean was not deaf to the sound of the wooden gate slowly creaking open behind him, and closing. The soft scuff of metal told him the latch was being secured. Happy that Pamela had followed him, he listened for her footsteps. They were muffled but not silenced by the ankle-deep grass. He held his breath when he heard her hesitate, the faint rustle of clothing rising above the gentle whisper of the wind.

He was barely able to contain himself as thoughts of her undressing—the two of them together, naked in the open air, the fear of getting caught—added to his tumescent state.

Though he anticipated her touch, he still jumped.

"You're hands are cold, why don't you put—"

"Shhhh," was all she said, silencing him.

In one breath he wanted to be in her, now—in the next he wanted the anticipation, the excitement, to last forever. He began to turn around. She held his head in her hands, as if to tell him not to look. He gave in to her fantasy as she leaned against him, her breasts, as cool as her hands, pressing into him, her body becoming one with his as she wrapped her arms around him and held him tight, taking his breath away. He felt her cold hand slowly move down and take hold of him, the tips of her fingers, her nails toying with him as she bit the base of his neck, his shoulder, hungrily nipping and nibbling and licking each bloodless wound.

He tried again to turn and face her, but she held firm. "I want you," he groaned, his heart pounding harder and harder.

"Shhhh," was all she said as her hands, her mouth, her tongue, her teeth, revealed a hunger he had never known her to have.

He shut his eyes, imagining her over him, sliding down, her warm, moist flesh devouring him inch by inch. In his mind, he reached out, drawing Pamela down to him, telling her he loved—

He suddenly stiffened and arched his back, his chest a cavern of ice, his heart burning with bitter cold. The smell of damp earth dripped down into his lungs, gagging him. His thoughts exploded, as if they had been frozen and shattered and scattered into the wind. Every point of contact where fingers, lips, tongue and teeth had touched his skin now burned, as if acid had been poured into open wounds.

"Forget her," he heard a woman say in a throaty whisper, the voice not Pamela's but instead a distant echo from the past.

Fight-or-flight charged his body with a million volts of energy. He spun around, only to stumble backward at what he saw.

Standing before him in a puddle of crumpled clothing was the woman who had slipped in and out of the library. Naked, her skin was dirty and pallid and mottled with bruises. Her hair was a tangle of gritty knots, her lips gray, her face gaunt, lifeless. Except for her eyes, which he couldn't resist, her gaze reaching deep, down inside him and taking hold of his heart, his very soul.

"Who the hell are—"

He was silenced against his will when she raised her hand.

Unable to move, he could only watch in horror as she stepped forward, stopping only when her body grazed his, his skin burning wherever her flesh touched him. "Don't you know?" she asked, her words fading. Her breath, the smell of decay, turned his stomach.

Gagging, he asked, "What do you want?" and just as quickly realized that he didn't want to know.

Reaching out, she slowly brushed her hand over his chest, the tips of her gnarled fingers, though ice cold, igniting a familiar fire inside him. Only now the flames were strangely cool, almost refreshing. Before he could tell her that she was wrong—that she couldn't possibly be who he thought she was, who he feared she might be—she was struck by beams of sunlight punching holes through the wall of fog, snuffing out the light in her eyes.

With a faint cry, more sorrow than pain, she turned away and stumbled toward the gate. Pulling it open, she disappeared into the retreating fog, a dark, vaporous wake trailing behind her.

Chapter Ten

Much to her dismay, Pamela was wide awake, while Sean was lying sound asleep beside her. Half sitting up, not a stitch of clothing on, she had one hand behind her head, the other resting lightly on his chest. Although they had been together for two years, she still found the unusually slow beat of his heart unnerving, in spite of his assurance, said with a definite bravado, that it was simply the resting heartbeat of a conditioned athlete.

Once, in the beginning, after they had exhausted each other making love and were drifting off to sleep in a tangle of arms and legs, she had become alarmed when she felt the beat of his heart growing slower and slower. Frightened, shouting his name and shaking him, she had startled him out of a deep sleep. Even now the thought of the confused look on his face made her smile.

That fond memory, however, lasted only for as long as it took Pamela to remember why she couldn't fall asleep now. She brought her hand to her face. While the odor was gone, washed away, the memory of the rancid smell from the blouse she had picked up off the ground in the courtyard—defying Sean's warning not to touch it—still lingered in her mind. From that moment on she had listened to him attentively, not interrupting even once to ask a question, as he proceeded, without prompting, to restore what he had cut and clipped and edited from everything he had told her. With each passage rewritten, pasting a withheld memory here, an untold sensation there—adding back closely guarded thoughts—she had finally come to understand why he had been acting the way he was. And the comment he had made at the library, "I'm tired of running," said as if he was talking to himself, finally made sense.

But no matter how much she understood, she hadn't been able to buy in to his belief, his fear, that Judith was somehow alive. And as much as she loved him, she couldn't help wondering if he had lost touch with reality, unable to separate fact from fiction.

The one thing he hadn't told her, even though

she had asked, and more than once, was what had happened to end his relationship with Judith. And it wasn't that he wouldn't tell her; he had said that he couldn't remember. His vague response had only added to her growing doubts, while heating up the unwanted jealousy she could feel simmering inside her.

Given her nature, Pamela had to have a rational explanation, not only for what Sean claimed had happened this morning, or the last two days, but for everything. And especially for Judith's yet-to-be-explained disappearance thirty years earlier. Until she had those answers—until she could literally place her fingers in the wound—Sean's explanation for what was happening would have to remain nothing more than a product of his imagination. "In *real* life, my dear," she whispered, "when you're dead . . . you're dead."

Tipping the scale in Sean's favor, however, was the fact that she couldn't write off what she had seen when they had been swimming: There had been a woman there; she had heard her speak to Sean; and she had seen with her own eyes his reaction when she had touched him, though she hadn't told him that. The discovery of the body had confirmed that what they'd seen wasn't a hallucination, even though the findings in the autopsy report had made it sound as if she and Sean had fabricated their story, as if they were trying to cover something up. What bothered her most, however, were her own feelings, particularly the venomous bite of jealousy.

But even though she knew that she'd been bitten, and when, she couldn't do anything to stop it from poisoning her thoughts.

Angered by what had come between them, Pamela decided to retrace the steps she and Sean had taken from day one in hope of finding something, a thread of hope, however tenuous, that would offer a rational explanation for what Sean thought was happening.

Stealing out of bed, she quietly collected her clothes and dressed in the soft afternoon light filling the small bathroom.

After turning off the engine, Pamela sat quietly for a moment in her Mercedes, gathering her thoughts. Always the organizer, she wanted to be certain she hadn't forgotten anything in the note to Sean that she'd pinned to her pillow. She had told him that she was taking the car, offered her apologies if it left him stranded, and told him where she was going. She had listed her intended stops in order: a walk around the reservoir to see if she could find some sign of that woman—something a man might have missed; a stop at the cemetery where it had all begun, not knowing what she was looking for; and finally a talk with Annie Parker to see if she'd known the woman who had written that cryptic note to Sean.

She had even tried guessing when she might be back, allowing an extra half hour in case she got lost, which she had noted with a long row of exclamation marks. While she had told Sean where she was going, she hadn't told him what she was doing, or why, simply because no matter how she had tried phrasing it, it still came out sounding like she didn't believe what he'd told her.

"Well . . . let's get on with it," Pamela told herself as she climbed out of the small roadster and stood facing the cemetery, which was already fading to gray in the advancing twilight.

It was just that waning light that had forced her to cut short her walk around the reservoir, fearful that she wouldn't have enough light to read the headstones in her effort to uncover a connection to the two women who were now dead, Anders and Gleason, and with Annie Parker's help see if there might be a link to that woman in the library. Although she had told herself that Sean must have overlooked it, or had simply forgotten to mention it to her, Pamela couldn't help wondering if there wasn't something about these women he didn't want her to know.

She just as quickly shook off that thought, not wanting any part of that divisive and equally destructive feeling. "It must be this place. Or *her!*"

She laughed and started toward the gate as a brisk autumn breeze began swirling around the cemetery.

Although she had rejected the thought that Sean might have deliberately held something back, that nagging doubt had sunk its teeth into her, refusing to let go. With each step closer to the rusted wrought-iron gate, Pamela felt herself growing more and more angry with Sean for not having told her what he had thought from the very start. What upset her the most, however, was that he hadn't told her what he felt, and not about what was happening, but his fear about his feelings for Judith. She couldn't help wondering if he really did love her, and quickly asked herself if there were other things that he wasn't telling her, thoughts and feelings that he didn't want her to know, or didn't trust her with.

"Stop this!" she snapped angrily and drew to an abrupt halt, her hand held out, about to push open the gate. She drew back, unsure of herself, wondering if she really wanted to go inside.

Indecision was not Pamela's style, which only made her irritation with Sean that much sharper. When she tried to sort out her thoughts, she was confronted with one unwanted feeling after another, leaving each question unanswered. The sound of laughter echoed in the back of her mind as images of Sean—standing naked in the water, unaware that he had responded to the touch of that woman—filled her head. The more she fought those thoughts, the sharper they became, their razored edges like barbed wire, cutting her with each attempt she made to pull herself free of them.

Pamela shut her eyes and covered her ears, refusing to give in as she blocked open the rusted gate. Once inside the cemetery, she was suddenly blind to those images and deaf to the ridicule raging inside her. She cautiously opened her eyes and slowly slid her hands off her ears. Silence filled the air, which was damp and heavy, and dead calm. She could feel it, every vaporous molecule, pressing against her, weighing her down. Not a whisper was to be heard inside the rusted iron fence. Nor was anything moving: not a blade of grass, not a tattered flag, or even a single dried leaf.

Yet outside, all around her, the trees were bending and yielding and snapping back—but in slow motion—their branches flailing in futile protest. Slowly, breath by breath, day gave way to night, trapping her in the perpetual gray of twilight, as if she were caught in the eye of a storm, one of time and tempest.

Pamela struggled to get hold of herself as she began reading the headstones and repeating the names aloud. She did it as much to imprint them in her mind as to hear the sound of her own voice. But no sooner had she spoken than her words were swallowed up by the eerie silence. Even her footsteps were devoured by the hungry void as she moved from grave to grave, weaving her way back and forth through the cemetery. The more she tried, the less able she was to remember anything she read, her thoughts eluding her like the silent ebb of a midnight tide slipping out to sea, cloaked by the dark of a new moon.

Upon exiting the final row of headstones, the air turned wintery cold and her breath began to condense into a cloud of white in the rising dark of night. She stopped when she saw that the ground had been raked clean. A chalky rectangle had been dusted onto the wilted grass. Nearby, a shiny new headstone, lying flat on its back, proclaimed the interment of JEAN BLAUVELT GLEASON, 1952–2001. In the center of the soon-to-be grave site was Judith's marker. Stuck into the ground beside it was a long-handled shovel, yet not a single turn of fresh earth was to be found anywhere.

Without warning, the bed of grass, the marker—the promise of eternal love forever etched in stone—sparked lurid images inside Pamela's mind of what Sean had done here thirty years ago with another woman, engulfing her in flames of jealousy.

Before she could quench that fire, she saw Judith, a faceless figure. Sean was lying beside her, aroused, erect, dripping with desire. He was kissing her and fondling her breasts, repeating scene for scene what she and Sean had done not two hours earlier.

"No," she muttered and shook her head. "This isn't happening." But it was, and she couldn't do anything about it, let alone explain why it was happening. "Get out of here," she growled and started to leave, but stopped when she felt something drip on the back of her neck. She glanced up. "Dear God!"

Directly above her, silhouetted against the face of the moon, was a man, naked, impaled on the barren branches of the huge oak tree, the limbs twisted and snapped and stripped of their leaves. His eyes were wide open, his face etched with terror, his scream muffled by a branch piercing his throat. The splintered ends of his broken bones protruded like spiny quills. The flesh on his chest, his belly, his loins, had been clawed to shreds, stripping him of his humanity.

The spell was broken by the spatter of blood on her face.

Turning away, she wiped her cheek with the sleeve of her white cotton sweater, smearing the blood across her mouth. The warm, salty taste made her gag and spit as *Get out of here!* echoed through her mind, turning her deaf to any other thought but flight.

About to run, she was struck between the shoulders by an unseen blow, sending her sprawling onto the ground, the wind knocked out of her. Before she could move, she was pinned down by one frozen hand as another reached deep into her chest, grabbing hold of her heart. The icy grip instantly released memories of what she'd read in the autopsy report as she fought for every breath. Unable to bear it any longer, she gasped, "Please . . . I can't—"

A blast of cold air stuffed her feeble plea down her throat, choking her. She fought to be free, but her captor only became stronger, its chilling howl rising to a shrill, shattering the newly chiseled headstone. Though it was unclear, muffled by the angry storm raging around her, Pamela was certain she could hear a voice, belonging to a woman, young—but at the same time old—her cries of sorrow echoing far into the night. About to lose consciousness—every thought but survival ripped from her brain—she was given her freedom. She curled up into a fetal ball, shivering uncontrollably as the air grew calm, its touch warm and soothing. Seconds became minutes as time wound down, as if to stop and watch and wait.

Warmed back to life, Pamela struggled to her feet. Every muscle in her body ached. Her joints were stiff, as if rusted in place. Her bones felt brittle, about to break. With each welcome breath, she uncurled her body and stood erect. When thoughts of where she was and what was happening crept back into her mind, she shuddered and wrapped her arms around herself, but she received no solace from her own embrace. Alone, frightened, she thought of Sean, of his strong arms around her, his warm body pressing—

A crushing blow struck her on the chest, knocking her backward onto the ground. Fear exploded into rage as she leapt to her feet.

"Who are you?" she demanded, peering into the shifting shadows cast by the moon. "And what the hell do you—"

A violent wind swept her up and held her suspended in the air as that invisible hand slipped beneath her ribs and up into her chest, its icy fingers grasping her heart and squeezing the life out of her as the shrill voice grew louder and louder. This time she could hear the hint of perverse pleasure in the rising wind.

Desperate, her life slipping from her grasp, Pamela cried out without thinking, "He loves me, not you."

A vortex, a conical swirl of ice and water, wrapped itself around her, ripping and tearing her clothing from her body.

Naked, her arms outstretched, she was whipped by the relentless wind again and again, leaving her red and raw and bleeding. She could feel her heart beating slower and slower, which brought to mind Sean's heart—strong and stead-fast—and his love for her.

Tipping her head back, she looked up into the face of the moon and whispered, "I love you . . . I will always—"

She was silenced by the angry wind filling her lungs, drowning her beneath wave upon wave of liquid air. About to pass out, she was given a reprieve as everything grew calm again, the tamed wind caressing her numbed body. With a breathless sigh, she gave in to its healing touch, only to be brutally violated by a cold vaporous shaft, hard as ice, ramming deep inside her—thrusting again and again and again—tearing her flesh as blood dripped down her legs.

Tears fell from her eyes and froze to her cheeks as Pamela unshackled herself from the bonds of reality, separating mind from body—trading heart for soul—death no longer feared but wel-come.

"Pamela!" Sean screamed as he raced toward the back of the cemetery, frantically slapping at the dense fog blocking his path.

"Leave her alone!" he bellowed as he threw his arms around her legs, his face smeared with blood as he tried to pull her free.

Peter Murphy was a step behind him, a gun in his hand. "Jesus Christ!" he gasped as he stum-bled to a stop, staring up at Pamela.

Holstering his gun, he stepped forward to

help, only to be thrown to the ground.

Sean tightened his grip as he looked up into the whirlwind and said in a frightened voice, "If you truly love me, let her go."

A moment passed. Another. The raging wind roared, then sighed to a whisper, leaving the air crystal clear and bone dry. Not even the crackle of a leaf could be heard.

Without warning, Pamela fell into his arms, her battered body limp and lifeless, sending them both tumbling to the ground.

Chapter Eleven

Dr. Robert Jeffrey paused to consider Sean's question. A child prodigy who had breezed through college and Harvard Medical School to graduate at the age of twenty-one, he was not one to shoot from the hip. After a moment, he said on a somber note, "Quite honestly, we have no way of knowing when, or even *if* she will come out of the coma. Based upon all the tests we ran, it appears that she's in the grip of an exceptionally virulent virus, which means we can only wait it out since by the time we're able to type it and treat it . . . that's *if* we have a treatment, which I doubt . . . she will either have fought it off or succumbed to it."

While he had peppered Bob Jeffrey, an old friend, with dozens of questions about Pamela's condition, and what the prognosis was for her recovery—every one of them in great detail, though offering little hope—Sean had been unable to answer the two simple questions that Bob Jeffrey had asked of him: What in God's name happened to this woman? Who could possibly have done something like this . . . something so cruel and inhuman?

The easy part was who, though he didn't dare say it. How could he? The strange part was that he thought he knew what had happened, though he didn't know how he knew. It was just there, hundreds of black-and-white fragments floating in his mind. He tried but couldn't piece them together. Angered, he imagined himself reaching into his brain and ripping them out, synapse by synapse, only to pull back with a start as if he'd gotten a shock.

"I don't want to make it sound like there's no hope, Sean, but the profile of the cardiac enzymes in the blood indicates she may also have suffered a heart attack, which means that her heart may be compromised, further lowering her chances of recovery. The abnormal EKG confirms that *something* happened to her heart; we just don't know exactly what it was. The good news is that these symptoms can also be the result of severe external physical trauma to the chest . . . even from CPR . . . both of which we know occurred."

Bob Jeffrey grew calm as he cast his gaze about the darkened hallway outside Pamela's room on the seventh floor of the Harkness Pavilion, one of two dozen buildings in the Columbia Presbyterian Medical Center complex in upper Manhattan overlooking the Hudson River. When he finally turned to face Sean, he said with a perplexed frown, "It's strange, but I can't help thinking that we're dealing with some sort of rejection response by the body, much like we see with organ transplant patients. In this case . . . whatever it is . . . it's targeted the heart."

He shook his head. "I'm afraid all we can do at this time is to keep her hydrated, pump her full of antibiotics as a precaution, monitor her closely and—"

"Pray for her," Peter Murphy said in a subdued and clearly compassionate tone of voice as he walked up and stood beside Sean.

Sean looked as if he had been found washed up on the beach somewhere after a storm, but Murphy was clean-shaven, bright-eyed and neatly dressed—and out of uniform—which prompted Sean to wonder, *What the hell are you doing here?*

Bob Jeffrey glanced at his watch but didn't appear to actually look at it. "If there's any change in her condition, Sean, no matter how slight, they have instructions to page me." He placed his hand on Sean's arm. "I know what you went through when you lost your wife . . . what we both went through, since she and I were good friends . . . I'll do everything I can, I promise."

On that note, he smiled, though it appeared to be more of a reflex response—learned from years of insulating himself from disease and death—and disappeared down the dimly lit corridor.

Tuning out the noisy clatter of dishes and conversation all around him, Sean wrapped both hands around the white ceramic mug—his fourth cup of coffee in less than an hour—and melted into the booth of the old railcar diner on Broadway and 158th Street.

"Well?" he asked and took another hit of black coffee. "What's it going to be, Peter . . . truth or dare?"

Using his last triangle of buttered toast, Murphy sopped up the leftover yolk from the four sunny-side up eggs he'd dusted off and said matter-of-factly, "I told you . . . I'm on my own time."

The wedge of toast, dripping with yolk, disappeared behind his closemouthed smile, followed by a crispy piece of bacon pilfered from Sean's plate in exchange for a mischievous grin.

Sean's thoughts were divided right down the middle: half of them were locked up tight in the left side of his brain, seeing an off-duty cop and telling him not to trust the man; the other half were sequestered in the right hemisphere and saw the spitting image of the young man he had once considered his best, if not his only friend when he was growing up. These same thoughts also told him to believe Murphy's story, that he had taken a personal day and driven into the city out of concern for Pamela, and for him too.

Murphy raised his mug and asked solicitously, "More coffee? Or have you already pumped enough caffeine into your body to keep you going for a week?" He smiled again, this time an ingenuous, boyish smile, and waved the waitress over. "My limit is two cups. Any more than that and I'm wired for hours."

He held out his mug for the waitress to fill. "It's a good thing I never did drugs; I would have been a natural-born addict."

Sean felt himself giving in to the right side of his brain.

"If I know your father, and I think I do . . . at least I did thirty years ago . . . he would have kicked your ass if he had even caught you smoking."

Murphy laughed. "I did, and he did." He poked at the uneaten home fries with his fork. "You really liked my dad, didn't you?"

Caught up in a sudden swell of boyhood memories, Sean nodded and let his guard down as he recalled countless Saturday afternoons in the fall and the hundreds of Johnny Unitas passes he'd thrown to Raymond Berry in the end zone. He also remembered Mike telling him that he was going to play wide receiver for the Baltimore Colts when he grew up. But that he, Sean, would never make it as a quarterback. "You're smart and you can really throw," he had said with the cocky confidence of a seasoned NFL scout. "But you're too short, Mac, gotta be at *least* six-three to cut it."

Sean was about to regale Peter with what he was certain were never-before-heard stories about his father when he noticed what he thought was Peter's gaze narrowing and drawing a bead on him. It brought to mind a surveillance camera about to record everything he said and did. In a heartbeat, right or wrong, he decided that Peter Murphy had unconsciously clocked in and was now on duty.

Maybe you were never off duty in the first place. Sean began to retreat, donning that familiar armor and preparing to defend himself, when he thought of his promise to stop running. Sounds more like a threat, Pamela had told him. He leaned forward, his weary gaze fixed on Murphy, and asked without the slightest concern for the consequences, "Why don't I believe you?" Though he was surprised at himself for having said what he did, it had felt good, so he decided to go with his feelings. "Why don't you stop fucking around and just ask me outright what you want to know . . . okay?"

Murphy sat up, shoulders back, jaw square. "How did you know she was at the cemetery?" he asked and took a hasty sip of coffee.

The rapid-fire query had confirmed his hunch. Sean shot back, "I already told you . . . she left me a note." He slipped his hand into his pocket, retrieving a crumpled-up wad of paper. "See for yourself," he said and sat back, watching with a sense of amusement as Murphy unraveled Pamela's note and meticulously smoothed out the wrinkles with the back of his nails, as if he didn't want to get his fingerprints on it.

He asked without looking up, "So why did you call me?"

Sean quipped sarcastically, "This is a trick question, right? You probably want to see if I give you the same answer twice. I told you when I called, *I didn't have a car*. But the answer's right in front of you anyway . . . she apologized for leaving me stranded . . . or isn't reading comp a requirement for your job?"

When Murphy appeared to stiffen, Sean realized he'd gone over the line and raised his hands in mock surrender. Murphy rapped the table with his knuckles. "That still doesn't explain how you knew to go *directly* to the cemetery, instead of the reservoir."

"Call it intuition." Sean grinned. "It's my female side."

Though Murphy had shrugged off Sean's comment, he appeared to guard his words more closely when he asked, "When we were waiting for the ambulance, what did you mean when you said 'it couldn't have been her'? Who were you talking about?"

Before Sean could respond to the question, not that he could tell him the truth or anything even close, Murphy leaned forward and asked in a secretive voice, "And when we found her hanging from that tree . . . I still can't figure out what the fuck was holding her up . . . who were you talking to? Did you see somebody?" he asked in obvious bewilderment. "Because I sure as hell didn't."

He glanced away, as if he were chasing after another question. When he turned back, there was a look of disbelief on his face, clouded by confusion. "And when I got knocked on my ass by—"

He shook his head. "By *whatever* the hell it was. You shouted *leave her alone*. What the hell did you mean by that?"

Sean knew there was no way he could possibly explain what he had meant, let alone who he was talking to. As it was, he still didn't believe it himself, or didn't want to. "Don't ask," he muttered without thinking. "You *really* don't want to know."

It was as if he'd waved a red flag in front of a bull; Murphy's face tightened into a knot as he slid out of the booth and stood up and threw a twenty onto the table.

"If you want a ride back, let's go,'cause I'm leaving."

Spinning around, he was out the door of the diner before Sean could drain his mug.

Sean quietly slid the uninviting wooden armchair over to Pamela's bedside and collapsed into it with a weary sigh of relief. His arms and legs felt more like limbs of an old tree—bark and pith and just as heavy—instead of flesh and bone. He tenderly covered Pamela's hand with his as he leaned back and shut his eyes, desperate for sleep but afraid to give in to it. He wanted to be the first person Pamela saw when she opened her eyes, in spite of Bob Jeffrey's renewed caution only moments earlier that it could be days, weeks or even longer before she regained consciousness.

"That's *if* she regains consciousness," Sean whispered, admitting to what he had until now refused to let himself consider.

The guilt wasn't far behind. Facing it squarely, he let it wash over him, unafraid of a feeling he'd never suffered from. He never wallowed in what he believed was a pool of self-indulgent pity, crying for everyone to forgive him. Now, with someone he dearly loved lying close to death because of what he had done—in this case what he had not said—he found his conviction sorely tested, along with his lifelong immunity. He sat blindly staring at the amber-green monitor mounted to the wall over Pamela's bed, his gaze tracking the beat of her heart as it rose and fell on its short journey across the small screen. He couldn't help thinking there had to be a reason she had gone to the cemetery. *You never did anything without a reason.* He began wondering what she could possibly have been looking for. Before he could take his inquiry too far, he stopped, certain that he'd heard her say something.

He sat still, his head turned, holding his breath and listening with his whole body. He gently squeezed her hand.

"Pamela . . . it's me, Sean . . . can you hear me?"

Leaning forward, he whispered, "I love you."

Her eyelids fluttered but remained closed. Her lips began to quiver, as if she was trying to speak. He watched, wide-eyed, as she moved her head from side to side ever so slightly. Standing up, he bent over and whispered into her ear "What is it, sweetheart?"

In a gurgling voice, Pamela said, "Don't touch me."

Sean flinched, as if he'd been punched in the gut. When he pulled back, he was certain he saw tears at the corners of her eyes. "Why?" he asked, the guilt he thought he was immune to infecting his every feeling.

Pamela suddenly began coughing and gagging and an alarm began toning. Startled, he looked up at the monitor to see the thin green line tracking her heartbeat stumbling across the screen, the numbers falling rapidly. About to yell for a nurse, he was silenced when Pamela grabbed his wrist. He tried to break free but couldn't. Frantic, not knowing what else to do, he placed his free hand on her shoulder to hold her down and try again. It was as if he'd fallen through the ice: bitter cold engulfed his hand and shot up his arm. "Dear God!" he cried and grabbed his chest.

"Get away from me!" Pamela cried out as she knocked his hand away and began gasping for air. With each labored breath she shook her head, repeating, "Get away," over and over again, her feeble words wrapped in a vaporous cloud of white that settled over her like a shroud, chilling the air all around her.

"What the hell is going on?" Bob Jeffrey demanded as he stormed into the room with a pair of nurses in tow, pushing a cart.

The monitor suddenly flat-lined—a piercing electronic shrill.

"Hand me the paddles!" he ordered.

There was no need to think, no choice but one for Sean.

"Wait!" he shouted and bent down. Taking care not to touch her, he whispered in Pamela's ear, "I don't love her."

Pamela's eyes burst open as a beam of excited electrons reappeared on the monitor and the nerve-shattering alarm went silent. Her wide-eyed gaze was empty, colorless, the only sign of life the faint flicker of a tiny shadow in the back of her mind.

Sean would only shrug his shoulders in muted response to the pained expression on Pamela's face that appeared to be asking him *why?* just before she shut her eyes, her breathing once again calm.

Chapter Twelve

Sean broke stride midspan on the upper level of the George Washington Bridge, stopping squarely in front of a small green sign announcing the NEW YORK–NEW JERSEY border in reflective white letters. He tried to imagine a line drawn in thin air five hundred feet above the Hudson River but could only think of the small-minded men who had put up what he decided was a stupid sign.

This was Sean's first stop in a twenty-five-block jog uptown from the hospital. He hadn't even stopped for a single red light. Having taken his cue from a drunk, he had brazenly stared down the cars into stopping and zigzagged his way through the intersections.

In hindsight, however, his jaunt through a part

of the city most people wouldn't have risked driving through had not been a smart thing to do. But having rushed out of the '76 House without a penny in his pocket—and damned if he was going to call Peter Murphy and suck up for a ride home—he had been left with two choices if he wanted to get back to Blue Fields: walk or run.

He guessed he had another fourteen miles to go. Having hitchhiked to and from the city more times than he cared to remember during his high school years, he had committed every tenth of a mile to memory—176 steps every eighty seconds—including every twist and turn and bend in the back roads from Blue Fields down to Fort Lee, where the massive steel span leapt over the river to Manhattan. His destination? Where else but the promised land of his youth, Greenwich Village, in search of the prophets: Kerouac and Ginsberg to feed his mind and naive spirit of adventure; the Modern Jazz Quartet, Brubeck and the black ghost Miles Davis to soothe his soul.

"So much for religion," he said as he struggled with his lifelong fear of heights and inched closer to the railing. It was one of the few secrets he had kept from Pamela. As much as he tried, however, he couldn't bring himself to look down. The best he could do was look straight ahead, his gaze fixed on the twin towers of the World Trade Center in the distance, poking up through the haze and smog choking the city as if snorkeling for clean air.

After a moment, he smiled mischievously and spit as hard as he could and started laughing at what he'd done when the wind blew the spray back into his face. It was one of the things he did that really bothered Pamela—a disgusting guy thing—along with his peeing in the bushes, which, she said, no girl would ever do.

"You're just jealous because girls can't pee standing up."

It had been like this for the last hour: Sean arguing with himself out loud like some homeless vagrant as he jogged up Fort Washington Avenue, what he had seen and heard and felt wrestling with what Bob Jeffrey had said to him with a condescending shake of his head, leaving no room for discussion: It was *definitely* the air-conditioning unit . . . it was the *only* plausible explanation for the vapor. As for her reaction, it was an autonomic response by her severely compromised immune system to the sudden drop in temperature, and nothing more than that.

With a handful of pompous and self-serving conclusions, Bob Jeffrey had discredited everything Sean thought he had seen.

As certain as he was of what he'd witnessed, Sean couldn't help siding with Bob Jeffrey in thinking that there had to be a rational explanation for what had happened. And not just in

Pamela's hospital room—or last night in the cemetery—but over the last three days. He knew it didn't take a rocket scientist to explain what someone had written on the headstone, the swirl of wind in the cemetery, the sudden changes in temperature, the voicelike howl of the wind, the patch of fog on the reservoir, even the woman who had appeared out of nowhere in the courtyard.

The easiest thing to discount was what he had felt. "What you imagined," Bob Jeffrey had said in a patronizing tone of voice. "The mind does strange things, Sean, when we're under severe stress."

The part of him that was suddenly so willing to accept scientific explanations for everything, however, was the same part he had long ago come to distrust; his deliberative and supposedly rational side. This realization, and the unforgettable sight of Pamela suspended in midair— naked and battered and bleeding—served to fan his internal fire, an anger he hadn't felt in years, as he flipped through the mental snapshots of what he'd seen and played back what he'd heard, and most memorable of all what he had felt. To his irritation, he found himself doubting his own feelings, something he never did. "Fuck it," he growled. "And fuck you and you're *'self-induced psychotropic phenomenon.'* "

Lacking the energy for another round—a tag-team match between what he knew he had seen and Bob Jeffrey's logical, scientific explanations— Sean thought of Pamela in an effort to distance himself from the growing doubt and self-incrimination. He recalled Bob Jeffrey's reassurance that she had taken a turn for the better and was, as he'd put it, out of the woods. When pressed on exactly what about her was better, he had said with a casual shrug of his shoulders, "Call it a hunch, but she just seems better to me."

You hypocritical son of a bitch! You preach science, then you turn around and tell me you've got a fucking hunch?

As much as he wanted to hold on to that edge—if for no other reason than that it felt good—he couldn't as what he'd whispered into Pamela's ear echoed loudly in his mind, drowning out every other thought. He had actually spoken to her. But he had chosen his words carefully—*I don't love her*—intending them to offer hope to both of them. Nonetheless, it meant that he must have believed what he had told himself all these years couldn't possibly be true, and what no amount of science could explain away: She was alive.

Once Peter Murphy was up to speed with the rest of the cars, he eased off the gas and held his partially restored WWII Jeep at a steady fifty-five miles per hour. Even at that speed, however, it rattled so much that it sounded like it might shake apart any minute.

"Do you have any idea how long it would have taken you?" Murphy asked. "It's at least twenty miles back to Blue Fields."

Sean glanced outside, lazily scanning the trees and rough-hewn, wood-planked guardrails bordering the Palisades Parkway.

"Ten miles," he replied as they sped past a familiar pair of tree-trunk-thick posts that appeared to have once held up a sign.

An amused smile began working its way onto Peter Murphy's face. "My father was right about you . . . you really are strange."

"Eccentric," Sean countered with a sense of pride. "Writers are eccentric. Normal people, people like you, are strange."

Sean began laughing to himself. "I'm too tired for this shit." He sighed and slumped up against the flimsy passenger-side door. "Let's call a truce, okay? I'll tell you the truth . . . the whole truth and nothing but the truth, so help me God . . . if you'll level with me. Can do, Officer Murphy?" Sean asked, rolling down the window and pushing his face into the wind. "Only I go first."

Murphy nodded.

Sean cut to the chase and said with a wry smile, "It's a three-part question. Were you on or off duty last night . . . are you here in an official capacity now . . . and how the hell did you know I was walking back to Blue Fields, and on *this* road?"

Settling back, Murphy appeared to relax, if such a thing was possible in the spartan seats of the battle-worn relic.

Reading into the pitch of his body, the subtle turn of his head—his boyish smile—Sean's trust in Peter was turned up a notch as he waited to hear what he had to say for himself.

"Yes . . . *technically* speaking . . . I was on duty. But that was *your* doing, since you called the station looking for me, not my home. As for now . . . no, I'm just Joe Six Pack. And although I didn't know for certain, I figured that you might be walking back since Dr. Jeffrey said you mumbled something to that effect after you and he had what he called a 'philosophical disagreement.' "

Murphy tapped the microphone of the two-way radio mounted to his console. "And with this, finding you was pretty much a piece of cake." He started grinning. "Why do think the parkway police didn't pick you up . . . because you're a writer?"

"*Eccentric* writer." Sean laughed as every contentious bone in his body seemed to creak at the same time. Patting the radio, he asked hopefully, "Can this help me find out how Pamela's doing?"

Murphy beamed. "I'm one step ahead of you.

Dr. Jeffrey said to tell you that she's stable and getting stronger, but that she's still unconscious. I gave him a few numbers . . . the Seventy-six House, Mike Gordon's place, my house and the station . . . just in case he needs to get hold of you with the news as soon as she wakes up."

If she wakes up, Sean thought, and leaned out the window again to keep from dozing off. "Okay, it's your turn, Murph," he said, using the nickname he'd called Peter's father. "Fire away."

Without hesitation, his relaxed smile no doubt acknowledging what Sean had called him, Murphy asked, "Were you the one who put that little grave marker in the back of the cemetery . . . the one with the inscription that appeared to have been vandalized?"

The quickness of his response told Sean he had a shopping list of things he wanted to know. *Fuck it.* "Yes; thirty years ago this month as a matter of fact. It was—"

"I know, some old girl friend who left town.

"Did you know Elaine Anders . . . *personally,* that is?"

Relieved that he didn't want to know anything more about the marker, Sean sighed. "No."

"Ever meet her?"

"Strike two. I only spoke with her on the phone, and then only once."

"Know what her maiden name was?"

"I haven't the slightest—"

"Martin."

Sean sat up rigid as a post and wide awake. *"Ellie Martin?"*

"Yeah . . . and what about Jean Gleason?"

Drawing a blank, Sean just shook his head.

"Try Jeannette Blauvelt," he said in an accusatory tone of voice. "You must have known her . . . and the Anders woman too . . . you grew up with them, for chrissake!"

Unaffected by Murphy's pique, Sean said quietly, "Yes, you're right, I did. I even dated them. But that was after she—"

Don't, he told himself and shook his head.

"Who's this *she* you keep talking about?" Murphy asked, his impatience growing.

"It was nothing," Sean muttered. "Forget it."

Sounding annoyed, Murphy asked, "And the others?"

Sean snarled, "What *others?*"

Murphy stuck his fingers into his shirt pocket and pulled out a neatly folded sheet of paper. "Here," he said solemnly.

Snatching it out of Murphy's hand, Sean tore it open and scanned the long list of names neatly typed in alphabetical order.

"Shit."

Chapter Thirteen

Conscious, but trapped just beneath the surface—
a prisoner of her own mind and body—Pamela's
thoughts were suddenly filled with carefully
guarded secrets, precious memories, each one
called up against her will. She watched as Sean
knelt between her legs, naked and aroused.
Bending down, he kissed her shuttered eyes, one
and the other, then her lips, her neck, his tongue
slowly circling her nipples and gliding down over
the womanly yet firm swell of her tummy as he
steadily moved lower. Parting her warm, moist
flesh, he hungrily drank her in as wave upon
wave—

Stop it! she cried out in muted silence and
called upon every ounce of strength, every sinewy fiber in her body, to end what was happen-

ing. But she couldn't move, let alone open her eyes, as the images continued to play. And in black and white, a tawdry twist to their love-making, the most intimate thoughts only she knew laid bare as she was poked and prodded, inside and out.

The second time the unwanted touch was soft, and not Sean's but a woman's. Sickened, Pamela was aroused against her will and pleased again and again, until every nerve was frayed. Her breasts and nipples were tender, her loins raw and dry. Every inch of skin was smoldering, while inside she was bitterly cold, her heart and mind locked in an icy embrace.

Dr. Faraahd turned to Bob Jeffrey. "This is the sixth time in the last two hours that her heart rate has risen and stayed elevated like this." Galeal Faraahd's gentle voice and diminutive size was in stark contrast to her penetrating gaze, which was made even more strident by the swirl of long black hair pulled back into a severe bun. "It lasts for three to five minutes. Each time it's occurred she's broken out into a mild sweat, but no shivering."

The young resident's mysterious Mediterranean eyes grew darker as her brow wrinkled like furrows in the sand. "I think she's cognitive and aware of what's happening around her. It's just that her motor functions are somehow impaired. When I noticed—"

She glanced away from Bob Jeffrey's attentive gaze, her smooth olive-toned cheeks bronzed with a subtle blush. After a moment, she turned back and said confidently, "When I noticed a faint vaginal odor . . . which recurred with the onset of each cardiac event . . . I examined the patient more closely and found physiological evidence of sexual arousal, which leads me to—"

"You did *what?*" Bob Jeffrey asked, his response laced with both surprise and disapproval as he scanned the event log he'd asked Dr. Faraahd to keep during her nightlong vigil. "You have no right to examine a patient when she's unconscious like this."

Bristling, the young woman said in a firm, clinical tone of voice, "As a woman, and based upon the tests, I think that I—"

Bob Jeffrey waved his hand, dismissing her attempted rebuttal.

"You were out of line, young lady. In light of what the patient appears to have been through, I find it inconceivable that you . . . a woman! . . . would have done anything of the kind."

Pamela wanted to shout "Shut up and listen to her, you stupid man!" But she could only think it, and even that was difficult as her thoughts continued to thicken from the arctic cold.

Goddamn you! suddenly rang inside her head when she felt Judith unlock the door to those special memories she thought she'd safely hidden away. She could feel her exploring Sean's first touch, replaying the stolen moments over and over again, as if she was trying to memorize them. The more she struggled to hide her thoughts and mask her uninhibited responses to Sean's tender lovemaking, the colder she became. Yet on the surface she was burning with passion, her body a fire without flames, as Judith put to the test everything she'd found, reliving every erotic moment for her own vile pleasure.

With a patronizing smile, Bob Jeffrey motioned for Galeal Fahaard to have a seat in the chair beside the bed, which was where she'd been when he walked in a few moments ago, her stethoscope over Pamela's heart, listening intently, her gaze fixed on the amber green monitor over the bed.

Turning, about to leave, he said casually, "Oh, I almost forgot. Ms. Eagleston has visitors. I left instructions for the desk to hold them until after eight o'clock, then send them up."

He shrugged his shoulders. "Why don't you take a break while they're here, but stay within earshot just to be on the safe side?

"Okay?" he asked—appearing not to care in the least if it was all right with her or not—as he walked out of the room.

Dr. Faraahd promptly slipped her stethoscope beneath Pamela's hospital gown and sat gazing at the monitor, comparing sight with sound.

Donald Beman

Speaking in a whisper, she said, "Pamela?" She took hold of her hand, squeezing it, but gently. "Can you hear me?"

Yes! Yes, I can! Pamela tried to shout, only to wince in pain, but inside not out, when Judith tightened her frigid grip.

"Very interesting," Dr. Faraahd muttered when she saw Pamela's heartbeat trip and stumble. She raised her hand, ready to hit the CODE button on the monitor as she continued to watch and wait.

In an effort to fight Judith's hold on her, Pamela flooded her mind with thoughts of Sean—his crooked smile, his guarded laughter, the strength of his embrace, even his simple presence.

"I love you, Sean," she sighed, her soft-spoken words fragile and brittle, like the unnerving sound of thin ice cracking.

The beam of electrons shooting across the face of the screen jumped, her pulse growing stronger with every beat of her heart.

With a sigh of relief, Dr. Faraahd lowered her head and began whispering to herself, mixing Arabic with English as she shut her eyes and placed both hands over Pamela's heart.

"Last rites?" a nurse asked playfully as she breezed into the room carrying a red plastic tote tray filled with sterile packages.

Walking up to the bedside opposite Galeal Faraahd, she said in a made-up secretive voice, "Better not let Jeffrey see you doing that; he'll think you're into some sort of faith healing or something."

She set the tray on the nightstand and went about her preparations to draw blood from Pamela. When the doctor didn't move, she asked softly, sounding apprehensive, "Dr. Faraahd, are you all right?" She reached out and touched Galeal's hand. *"Dr. Faraahd?"*

Dr. Faraahd jumped back, as if she'd been woken from a trance. Wide-eyed, the two women began laughing, sounding more relieved than anything else. She nodded. "She's stable now, thank God."

She brushed the hair off Pamela's face and placed her hand on her forehead. "Before you draw blood, Mary, would you please take her temperature for me?" Grabbing the clipboard off the bed, she flopped into the chair and began jotting down her observations.

"Ninety-six-point-two," Mary announced as she traded in the small, handheld electronic thermometer for a sterile syringe.

"Isn't that awfully low?" she asked.

Galeal simply nodded and kept on writing.

When the trap in Pamela's vein wouldn't flow, even after a second saline rinse, Mary tied Pamela's arm above the elbow and began tapping her forearm. "Gotcha," she muttered and quickly

slipped in the needle. "Well . . . I'll be!" she said.
"Her arm twitched . . . she must have felt it . . .
good for you, girl."

Galeal jumped up—the clipboard in one hand,
a pen in the other—and stood hovering about the
bed like a bird of prey.

"Take it out and do it again," she said excitedly.

"But I already have a vein."

"Just do it . . . now."

With a perplexed frown, Mary swabbed another patch of skin over Pamela's barely visible
vein and deftly slid in the needle.

Pamela flinched.

"See!"

We can feel pain, can we? Pamela's thoughts
raced ahead of her, driven as much by vengeance
as her will to survive. She tried calling out, *Stick
it into my heart, maybe it'll kill her!* but her
thoughts were frozen into silence before they
could find her lips.

Watching the monitor, seeing that Pamela's
heartbeat was growing steadily stronger, Galeal
told Mary, "Do it again."

Yes!

"But—"

Galeal growled, "Don't argue with me," as she
tossed the clipboard onto the chair behind her
and slipped on her stethoscope. Motionless, head
cocked, she listened to Pamela's chest while her

sphinxlike gaze was riveted to the monitor over the bed. "Now," she ordered, and placed her finger to her lips, asking for quiet.

Do it! Do it! Do it!

Pamela felt her arm twist and jerk, telling her that she'd been pricked, though she hadn't felt any pain.

Again, stick the bitch again!

Galeal nodded reassuringly and said solemnly, "Once more."

Pamela's arm twitched again, but this time her fingers curled up into a tight ball. Galeal's gaze was nervously flitting back and forth between the monitor and Pamela's clenched fist.

"Do it again," she instructed. "Only step back a little."

The instant Mary pricked the skin, Pamela's arm folded up like a steel trap snapping shut, her fingernails barely grazing Mary's cheek and leaving behind a row of reddening welts.

You bitch!

Mary's Irish-green eyes lit up her face. "How did you—"

"Woman's intuition," Galeal said with a guarded smile. "Now, draw the blood and send it to the lab with a critical tag. Then go find Dr. Jeffrey . . . stat." Her gaze narrowed as she said softly, but firmly, "Even if you have to drag him out of a class."

Nodding obediently, Mary carried out her orders with speed and precision. About to slip out into the hall, she stopped, sidestepped—nodded and smiled graciously—and continued on her way.

"Excuse me . . . is this Pamela Eagleston's room?"

Dr. Faraahd looked up and stiffened ever so slightly. "Yes."

She was unable to hide her disappointment at having to leave Pamela's bedside as she made a point of busily pulling up the sheets and snugging them tightly around her. "I'm Dr. Faraahd."

She glanced down at Pamela, then back up. "I'm afraid she's still in a coma."

Galeal snatched the clipboard off the chair and started for the door. "I'll be at the nurses' station just down the hall if you need anything." She smiled and gestured toward Pamela. "I think she can hear, so please feel free to talk to her, even though she probably won't respond. The sound of a loved one's voice can sometimes help."

Pamela's senses were wired for a signal that would tell her it was Sean, but the moment she heard the fall of unfamiliar footsteps—slow, almost apprehensive, as if the visitor was uncertain—she knew it wasn't him. Before she could try to open her eyes, she was distracted by a stirring in her chest: the sensation of a wind rising up inside her, cold at first, then cool, and growing steadily warmer as the visitor drew near.

She felt the gentle touch of a hand on hers. She tried to tell the person to go away but could only cough, her throat parched and burned from the cold. She felt the soft pat of a hand on her shoulder, as if the visitor was trying to comfort her.

Everything inside her grew still.

After a dozen futile tries, she managed to say in a weak, rasping whisper, "Get away from me," as she made a feeble attempt at brushing away the hand, only to start retching and gagging and coughing up a thick white fluid that was instantly churned into a bright red froth as rivulets of crimson streamed from her nose.

Go to hell, you fucking bitch! echoed in her mind as towering walls of ice rose up around her, encasing her in a glacial tomb.

Chapter Fourteen

Sean suddenly began running faster and faster, trying unsuccessfully to distance himself from the shadow he'd seen in Pamela's eyes, followed closely by what she had said to him, her words—get away from me—refusing to be silenced. Her plea was sharpened by Peter Murphy's unexpected question: and the others?

As Peter told it, each of the women who had disappeared had gone through the same bizarre metamorphosis, changing from the devoted wife and loving mother everyone in Blue Fields had known to a virtual stranger. They all suffered from the same affliction, an insatiable appetite no man could satisfy. At first, they were discreet about it, but as the disease progressed—a cancer without a cure, infecting body and mind—they had become steadily bolder in gratifying their visceral needs. Then, without warning, they simply disappeared. At first everyone believed they'd run off with their latest conquest, some unsuspecting out-of-town stranger, until the body of one of the women was found in the cemetery: naked, her clothes in shreds and spotted with blood, her body brutally ravaged and half-frozen, though it was only late October.

That discovery had cast a pall over Blue Fields that had taken years to lift, only to fall once again, resurrecting old fears, when Elaine Anders's body had been found. The veil had darkened when Jeannette Gleason's body was recovered from the reservoir.

Murphy had gone on to say on a somber note, "There are some people in Blue Fields who believe you have something to do with this. I know you grew up here, but if I were you, I'd be damn careful when I was out running. The town you once knew isn't the same . . . lots of people from the city . . . if you know what I mean."

Sean had wanted to say, and almost did, "It's not me they have to worry about, it's her." In that moment, he'd crossed the line a second time, accepting as fact what he had convinced himself couldn't possibly be true. "She can go fuck herself for all I care" had slipped out of his mouth, prompting Murphy to ask, "Who the hell is this *she* you keep talking about?" only to be stone-walled by Sean.

In spite of what he'd said, however, there was a part of Sean that still refused to believe what had happened. It was that part he chose to listen to now as he shook himself free of his fears and shifted his thoughts to the note Pamela had left for him before going to the cemetery. He assigned a time slot to each of his intended stops, allowing himself what he guessed was ample time to revisit each of the places Pamela had been to. The idea of asking Annie to join him for dinner entered and exited his mind with equal speed, but not before it succeeded in piquing his curiosity.

The only thing he now needed was a starting time. After a few taps of the button on the wrist-band monitor—seeing that it was almost 10 o'clock he settled on 11. That would give him what he guessed was enough time to circle back to Mike Gordon's, shave, take a quick shower—grab a bite to eat—and be on his way.

Though it wasn't his nature, Sean began to make a mental list of what to look for and what to ask Annie. Halfway through the exercise, he realized that without his laptop and the ability to write, his obsessive side had taken over and was busily organizing every minute of his day. Slowing to a lazy jog, he smiled at the thought that a schedule was really no more than a plot, save for one difference: He could revise a plot as many times as it suited him without anyone the wiser, while in real life his first draft was his last, his words and actions frozen by the hands of time.

About to start running again, he was startled by the nerve-jangling sound of tires screeching. "Get in!" Murphy yelled as his Jeep jerked and clunked to a stop beside Sean. "It's Pamela."

Sean darted past the security guards at the entrance to to the Harkness Pavilion. Upon seeing a crowd of visitors queued up in front of the row of elevators, he made a beeline for the stairway, scaling the first few flights two steps at time, but cutting back to one when the muscles in his legs cramped up. Upon reaching the seventh-floor landing, he paused to catch his breath, which is when he noticed that the side of his T-shirt was soaked with blood and realized that what he'd felt when he bailed out of Murphy's Jeep must have been the corner of the flimsy door tearing his shirt and ripping the skin off his ribs.

"Fuck it," he growled as he jerked open the door and stepped into the hall, frantically looking to his left and right, trying to get his bearings. With a nod of his head, he turned right, drawing upon every ounce of self-control he could muster to keep from running when he heard hurried footsteps behind him and anxious voices calling for him to stop. Just as he felt a hand on his arm, then another on his other arm—trying to pull him back—he turned and calmly walked into Pamela's room. "Jesus Christ!" he gasped when he saw the bloodstained sheets on the bed, startling the orderly into dropping the crimson pillowcase he was holding.

Spinning around, he confronted the two nurses standing behind him. "Is she dead?" he asked and held his breath.

At that moment, Galeal Faraahd walked into the room.

Sean reined in his urge to shout "Where the fuck is she?" and instead took a much-needed breath. Steadying himself, he asked apprehensively, "What happened to her? Where is she?"

Galeal nodded reassuringly. "Ms. Eagleston's in the ICU, but she's stable. You can—"

"The hell with this *stable* shit!" Sean yelled, startling Dr. Faraahd into stepping back. "Just tell me the truth for chrissake . . . and in plain English! . . . and tell me where I can find her."

She reached out and put her hand on Sean's shoulder.

"Ms. Eagleston had to be rushed into surgery earlier this morning. It was a ruptured pulmonary artery, which, thank God, we were able to repair in time. We have no idea what caused the rupture. According to the surgeon, it was a crude break in the arterial wall, as if . . . and these are her words . . . something had been scratching at it. The other good news is that she came out of the coma, but only briefly."

Galeal beamed, the tone of her voice suddenly more womanly than medical when she said, "And presuming there isn't another Sean in her life, she said that she loved you."

She raised Sean's arm and said with unquestioned authority, her demeanor belying her size, "Looks like you're going to need a passel of stitches." She laughed. "And I need the practice."

Sean pulled away. "What about her heart?"

Galeal's gaze narrowed. "How did you know about her heart?"

He ignored her question and stood glowering at her, making it perfectly clear that he wanted an answer. "Her heart!"

With a compliant nod, Galeal said quietly, "I had asked the surgeon to examine her heart while her chest was open—" She paused for a moment, as if to gather her thoughts. "There was evidence of damage to the cardiac muscle, however—"

"What kind of damage?" Sean demanded. "And how bad is it?"

Galeal's reply was filled with compassion. "I realize this may not make any sense to you . . . and if it's any consolation, it doesn't make much sense to any of us here either . . . but the tissue showed signs of what appeared to be frostbite. As to whether there will be any long-term affect, I'm afraid only time will tell."

Chapter Fifteen

Carved in relief on the sides of the huge marble sarcophagus Sean was sitting on—lazily flipping through an old leather-bound journal lying open in his lap—were six mythological griffins, feral lions, their feathered wings spread wide and dripping with rust-colored stains. Bridled to an empty stone chariot, their gaze was cast toward heaven, as if they were watching for a sign that would tell them Judgment Day was here and flight was now theirs.

Why the hell did you come back here? was the one question that had repeatedly slipped in and out of his thoughts as he slowly worked his way through the cemetery, front to back, methodically recording the names from every single headstone. Spanning three centuries and filling dozens of pages in his journal, he had hoped they might offer a clue that would tell him what Pamela had been looking for, certain that she must have known something he didn't. After all, she was the logical one, not him, always weighing the facts and carefully thinking everything through— something that he rarely, if ever, did—then planning out her every step before taking any action. It was one of the things that had always impressed him about her, since he tended to act on his instincts, a trait—especially when it came to judging people—that Pamela had once warned, "will someday be the death of you, Sean Mac-Donald."

After collecting the names, a tedious two-hour task, Sean had climbed atop the massive stone coffin and settled down to rearrange them into alphabetical order, then chronologically by date of birth. He had also grouped them into families, sketching crude family trees from memory. While combing through the hundreds of entries, he had noticed that there were a half-dozen names without death dates. One or two he could have passed off as his having failed to jot down the dates. But not that many, not even with what he had come to realize was his steadily growing inability to concentrate, to remember things, leaving him with the feeling that his thoughts weren't his own, as if someone else was in his head.

Telling himself that Pamela would go back and double-check, he had relocated each of the gravestones, only to discover to his surprise that the dates of death had, in fact, been left off. The questions that had popped into his head had ranged from could it be a coincidence? which he instantly discounted, to maybe their families had purchased the headstones years ago, like they do plots. But what if they got married? had finally driven home the obvious, that the headstones all marked the graves of women, and all but one of the names—Isabelle Evangelista—fit neatly into the family surnames populating the abandoned country cemetery.

Confused, he had made another round, which was when he was struck by the realization that each of the headstones were identical in size and shape to the one he'd placed in the ground for Judith. But even more unsettling was the fact that the inscriptions—a graceful freehand—matched the style of the two words that had been added to the epitaph on Judith's headstone.

As he flipped through the journal, impatiently slapping at the pages in search of any other names he might have missed, Sean muttered to himself, "Looks like your list is incomplete, Peter."

Surprised by what he'd said—wondering if he'd meant that their bodies were yet to be found, or if they were yet to be taken—he growled, "This is crazy," and slammed the journal closed. "Or maybe *you're* crazy!"

"Sí! Estas loco hombre," a woman laughed.

Startled, Sean jumped up, sending the journal tumbling onto the ground. Before he could hop down and chase after it, the stranger stepped around in front of him and went for it. Wiry and thin, with dark auburn hair and skin that was almost but not quite black, there was a stiffness in the way she moved that belied her youthful appearance as she hurried over and bent down to pick up the journal. When she turned back, she said with a mischievous twinkle in her bright amethyst-blue eyes—a striking contrast to her dark, earthy complexion—"Sorry, didn't mean to frighten you."

On the surface she appeared relaxed, yet at the same time there was a subtle, springlike tension about her body. Sean's immediate reaction was to back away, to distance himself from her. But there was something about her that he found irresistible, a curious combination of cultures, as if she were a hundred women, not one.

He watched her intently as she smoothed out the wrinkled pages—paused to read the list of yet-to-be-found women he'd compiled on the last page—before handing the journal back to him.

"You aren't the Grim Reaper, are you?"

Sean laughed, yet at the same time shuddered

inside at the bitter irony of her comment as he stepped down off the sarcophagus and stood eyeing this woman who had just walked into his life.

She returned his inquisitive gaze, but only for an instant, before blinking away and glancing about the cemetery. Although she had turned full circle, her back now to him, her gaze had passed over him, leaving him with the bizarre sensation that she'd sliced through him, cutting him in two. Sensing that she was watching him, Sean caught a glimpse of her out of the corner of his eye. To his surprise, her gaze was blank, her eyes cold and empty, her lips thin and drawn—looking more like a smirk than a smile. It was as if her earlier expression had been painted onto her face and wiped clean. *It's your imagination,* he told himself, opting for a logical explanation for what he saw—*what you think you saw*—and especially how he felt, turning a deaf ear to his instincts.

"Believe it or not, I think my grandmother is buried here." Her mouth grew taut, her words sharp-edged. "No doubt alongside the man who gave me these blue eyes and turned this Moorish skin of mine a shade lighter," she said, as if tainted by lesser genes.

She abruptly turned and held out her hand, her face suddenly soft, her eyes alive, as if she had traded her kiln-dried clay mask for one of flesh and bone. "My name's Carmen . . . and you are?"

"Sean . . . Sean MacDonald," he said as he took her hand and immediately felt a familiar sense of reassurance in her firm but gentle grip.

As if rehearsed, they asked in unison, "Do you live here?" and immediately began laughing.

Sean was first to speak. "I grew up here. But I left thirty years ago, when I went off to find my fame and fortune. And you?"

Carmen fired off, "Manhattan . . . Riverside Drive . . . a few blocks from Columbia Presbyterian Medical Center. Know the area?"

Without waiting for an answer, she asked, "So, tell me, what in the world brings Sean MacDonald back here after thirty years?"

"Business of sorts. I'm a—"

"Wait, let me guess." She reached out. "Give me your hands."

Leaning back, Sean asked cautiously, "Why?"

Carmen propped her fists on her hips. "Don't you trust me?"

He did and he didn't, yet he complied nonetheless. But he only offered her one hand, the other drawn behind his back. He watched as she began to trace with the tip of her fingernail the creases in his palm. Her touch, part curious, part sensuous, sent a chill through his body. With her head bowed, her attention fixed on divining whatever secrets his ancestors might have hidden in his genes, Sean was surprised to find a spider's web of silver and gray spun beneath the surface of her dark auburn hair. This discovery, coupled with her stilted movements and the fact that she appeared untouched by time one moment, yet centuries old the next, started him searching for other clues that might tell him how old she was.

"I worry a lot," Carmen said softly without looking up.

Sean started laughing. "Do you read minds too?"

She glanced up, her gaze narrowed and focused. "And if I can?" she asked solemnly. "Are you afraid of what I might find?"

Caught off guard by her question, left with the feeling that she really had read his thoughts and was just toying with him, waiting to see what his answer would be, Sean said with an anxious twist to his words, "I suppose we all have secrets we don't—"

"*There* you are!" Annie Parker called out as she threaded her way through the cemetery and came to a stop beside them.

Carmen frowned and looked away, but not before Sean saw what he thought were tiny cracks around her eyes and mouth; that delicate crazing on fine old china found just beneath the painted glaze. Without warning, that all-too-familiar feeling of fight-or-flight surged through his body, his every instinct—echoed by Pamela's warning— telling him to leave. Yet once again he refused to listen to a voice he trusted, having decided that he wanted to know who this woman really was and why she was here—*and why now*.

Slipping her arm through Carmen's, Annie said with a gracious smile, "Come on. I'll help you look for that grandmother of yours."

As if he'd been given his freedom, Sean sighed and glanced at his watch. It was almost 4 o'clock. Visiting hours at the hospital would be over at 9 o'clock, which left him just enough time to go running—a need for him, especially now, that was as bad as any addict's craving—then take a shower and head into the city.

"Please don't let her die," he whispered to himself as he started for the gate but immediately stutter-stepped to a stop. He had done something he hadn't done in thirty years, which was to pray. *Sort of,* he told himself in an effort to explain away what he'd said, refusing to believe that he could have possibly regained a faith he had so willingly discarded. He shook his head and growled under his breath, "You had your chance with me."

"*Who* had *what* chance?" Annie asked with a lighthearted smile in her voice as she stepped in front of him. "And just where do you think you're going, anyway?"

"The hospital," Sean grumped as he gave her a friendly peck on the cheek and continued on his way.

Donald Beman

She slipped into step beside him. "Want some company?"

He shook his head.

"I'll drive," she offered. "You can catch a nap."

Be nice; she means well. "I'm really not that tired, in spite of what I probably look like. Besides, I'm going running first, then I'm going to head into the city. But thanks anyway."

Annie darted ahead and spun around, this time thwarting his attempt to slip past her by standing firm and spreading her arms.

Puzzled by her gesture, Sean hesitated, trying to figure out what it was about her stance he found familiar.

"Running?" she asked. "Something new? Midlife crisis?"

Sean was rapidly growing impatient, but he knew it was him—his impatience with everything that had happened—not with her.

"No." He forced a grin. "I've been at it for the last eight or nine years." His grin showed signs of spreading into a smile. "Just trying to stay a few steps ahead of the Devil, that's all."

Annie grew quiet, her green eyes suddenly hard and metallic, before glancing away and offering that unforgettable profile of hers, which instantly called up a treasure trove of memories for Sean. Brushing the hair off her forehead, he started around her, but her rigidly outstretched arms made it clear that she wasn't about to let

144

him pass. "How about some dinner when you get back?"

He reached out and gently lowered her arms. Though he wasn't sure of just how to say it, he knew what he wanted to say, which was thanks but no thanks. He also knew that he had to put an end to whatever was happening before he said or did something he might regret. "Annie . . . listen . . . I really—"

"You can't just curl up into a ball and hide from this," she snapped as she took hold of his hands, pressing them together between hers and striking a prayerful pose, which he quickly broke free of. She stood firm nonetheless. "You need someone; we *all* do now and then. And not just *anyone,* but someone who cares about you." As if to reassure him there was nothing more to her offer, she said with a wry smile, "You can relax; it's over between us."

Sean needlessly checked his watch again. "What if I—"

"I found her!" Carmen called out excitedly. "Come see!"

Annie hastily patted Sean's arm. "You do whatever you're comfortable with. I'll be up in any event should you decide that you want a bite to eat . . . or just want someone to talk to."

She turned to leave but stopped. "By the way, do you know where I live now?" Sean shook his head. "It's that colonial sandstone on Western

Highway, the one with the barns and a guest cottage set off to one side. The old Steiner place, remember?"

Sean nodded and waved Annie away and was about to leave but stopped, his gaze suddenly fixed on Carmen as he watched her walk toward Annie, her gestures animated as she excitedly slipped between English and Spanish. Freed by the vaguely familiar cadence to her words, one of the memories Sean had imprisoned in his mind three decades earlier suddenly managed to escape. Although the images were dark and faded, he could make out the shadowy figure of a woman, tall and straight, her skin dark as the midnight sky above them. As if blind to his presence, she had ambled up and down the wavy rows of headstones, all the while nervously fingering a band of ivory-white rosary beads and talking to herself. She had spoken with a certain edge, as if she was arguing with someone.

Sean found himself struggling to remember what she had said, and what she looked like. He quickly gave up out of frustration, those distant memories still beyond his reach—shifting shadows hidden behind a veil of time—except for her cold azure gaze.

Chapter Sixteen

Pamela drew upon every ounce of strength she possessed as she tried to fight off the images she hated the most—Judith's memories with Sean, colorful vignettes, complete with every womanly sensation, every lustful thought—left behind to drift through her mind. But her efforts were to no avail as what Judith had once heard now fell upon her ears, striking her heart. What Judith had once tasted was now on her lips, her tongue, burning the back of her throat when she tried to swallow it away. What Judith had wanted was now her insatiable desire. What she had felt inside her, Sean filling her with his youthful passion, brought Pamela to the edge, and over, until the thought of what she'd been forced to do sickened her.

You fucking bitch! rang out as she imagined herself violating Judith's body, ripping and tearing her flesh, savoring the perverse pleasure of every brutal thrust. About to choke her into silence, the tables were suddenly turned on her as scene after bloody scene was resurrected from the depths of her mind—her own never-ending nightmare—a kaleidoscope of red and black. Coughing, Pamela asked in a rasping whisper, "How could you have loved her?"

Sean jumped up out of the chair he was sitting in beside her bed and placed his shaking hand on her forehead. "Shhh," he said in a soft, soothing voice. "It's all right . . . you're safe now."

She felt him stroking and caressing her face as his manly scent filled her senses and instantly drowned at every agonizing thought, every unwanted memory. She tried to speak, to tell him that Judith was alive just as he feared, but couldn't. She felt him take her hand in his and squeeze it gently, once and twice more, their secret code for those three precious words.

When she finally managed to open her eyes, they filled with tears when he whispered, "I love you," then bent down and tenderly kissed her lips, his sturdy face, worried gaze and lopsided smile dissolving into a watery blur.

Every invisible nerve in her body suddenly began firing, spinning a web of pain that trapped her words inside her throat and started her arms and hands and legs twitching in a nervous frenzy.

She wanted to scream "Don't do it!" when she heard the telltale click of the IV drug feed, pumping another dose of morphine into her veins. She braced herself as the first wave washed over her, numbing the pain in her chest and slowing her breathing, the next stealing her thoughts. Desperate, knowing that she had only seconds left, she fought to say in a frail whisper, "She's in—"

Gasping, sounding as if she was drawing her last breath, Pamela sighed and closed her eyes, her face blank, a portrait of death.

Chapter Seventeen

After shuttering the windows on the first floor of the old colonial sandstone, a nightly ritual now that she lived alone, Annie had switched on every light, turning night into day. Then she scurried about the house, tidying up before taking a shower.

Now, standing barefoot in the center of the small living room with a lavender towel snugged around her—her long red hair wet and shiny and matted down—she slowly turned full circle: She wanted to be sure that everything was perfect, that not a single cobweb or dust mote could be seen.

Proud of herself, she smiled and whispered, "You're a neat freak." A frown suddenly appeared, stealing her mood, when she remembered that was one of the reasons John had left her.

For that little trophy wife of yours.

Even after ten years, Annie still referred to her ex-husband's wife that way, in spite of the fact that the woman was now three times the petite size six she had been when John had married her, much to Annie's spiteful delight. In truth, however, her ego had been more bruised than her heart broken when John had left her.

"At least one of us is happy now." She sighed as she dimmed the lights to a soft amber glow and slipped into the kitchen.

With the refrigerator and stove expertly hidden behind faux pantry doors, and not a single appliance in sight, the room was a two-hundred-year-old vision out of the past—an oasis in the modern age—complete with a wood-planked floor, huge fieldstone hearth, vaulted ceiling held up with rough-hewn posts and beams and a spindly brass chandelier with bulbs that flickered like flames.

Set out on the rickety old table was an assortment of china platters filled with a smorgasbord of cheeses and pâté and tiny tea sandwiches, along with a special prize for dessert: squares of half-defrosted cake from her daughter's wedding three years before.

A trickle of cold water down her back brought to mind her still-wet hair. "And you've got to do something with this face of yours!" She laughed as she darted back into the living room and raced upstairs, making the towel around her unravel and fall to the floor just as she stepped onto the second-floor landing.

With a sweep of her hand she scooped up the towel and slipped into the steamy warmth of the bathroom, closing the door behind her. She quickly cracked it back open after reminding herself that she wouldn't be able to hear Sean knock. She suddenly drew calm. *That's if he shows up. Face it, girl, he didn't seem any too keen to come here. You pushed him into it, and you know it,* she told herself as she grabbed the hair drier and brush off the shelf beside the sink and turned to face the floor-length mirror behind her, which was still covered with foggy patches from her shower.

Each pass of the noisy drier over the surface of the glass slowly evaporated the condensation, filling in the missing pieces of the jigsaw puzzle in front of her. She stood examining herself in the mirror. Turning around, she glanced back over her shoulder. With well-rounded hips and ample breasts, her snow-white skin soft but firm, Annie had a figure that most women half her age would kill for, in spite of what she thought. She raised her arms over her head, stretching herself into a shapely hourglass.

Wondering if she really wanted to do this, if

she could actually go through with it, she grabbed the hair drier and brush off the shelf beside the sink. Bending over, she began to brush out her hair and blow it dry. As she lazily turned her head from side to side, she caught a glimpse of her profile in the mirror.

"You're fat," she told herself with disgust and turned away from her reflection. "That's why he wanted *her* and not you. I hate you; I always will." Even after thirty years it could still be heard, that bitterness snarled in a tangle of hurt and jealousy.

No sooner said than she turned to confront her reflection.

"You're not a little girl anymore, you're a woman. Take it or leave it." With a sharp nod, Annie stuffed the hair brush and drier back onto the cluttered shelf, threw the bathroom door open and marched down the hall. But she wasn't quick enough, as the realization that she hadn't been alone with a man in ten years caught up with her, chilling her even more than the cold air in her bedroom. She sought reassurance from the waist-up mirror over her dresser, only to reject what it told her: Doubt and disgust had conspired to redraw her figure, age her face, turn her red hair to rust and blow out the coppery flames in her smoldering green eyes.

She stepped to her closet and stood absentmindedly staring at the clothes before her, as if they were someone else's, not hers.

Why would he even give you a second thought when he's got a woman like her? she wondered as she withdrew a hanger with a pair of black wool slacks. She slipped a bulky-knit black turtleneck sweater off the shelf. Shy to the point of not wearing sheer silk blouses, Annie gave new meaning to the word *modest.* About to get dressed, she paused and shook her head. "No," she said firmly and proceeded to exchange that outfit for something hanging inside a clear plastic garment bag; a dark blue, close-fitting, floor-length caftan that laced up the front from the waist.

Rejecting out of hand the thought of what to wear beneath it, she slipped the caftan over her head. Smiling, amused by her newly discovered boldness, she laced it up, then loosened the laces halfway down. Small emerald studs in her ears restored the sparkle in her eyes, while a few swipes of lipstick and a stoke or two of eyeliner gave just enough color to her ivory-white Celtic face. An old pair of espadrilles completed the look of casual confidence.

You need a drink! was the first thought that came to mind when she saw herself in the full-length mirror on the closet door.

This isn't you, she kept telling herself as she made her way down to the kitchen in search of her best friend. As she stood in the dark pouring herself a glass of wine, she wondered why she felt this way. After all, she'd already slept with Sean. *And you used to swim naked as a jaybird with the man . . . and in broad daylight!*

"No," she whispered affectionately. "*Boy* was more like it."

A relaxed smile found its way onto Annie's face as she walked over and stood in front of the huge bay window in the kitchen, staring out into the night, the bottle of wine in one hand, a glass in the other, striking an all-too-familiar pose. With each sip of wine, the memories she had buried long ago began to surface for the first time in years, though the shadows they cast had never left her side. Thoughts of that first awkward night with Sean, the two of them hiding in the hayloft of the old red barn behind his house, rekindled flames of passion in her that she thought had died long ago. She was even more startled by the surprisingly real sensation of forgotten touches: a hand on her face, nervous fingers combing through her hair, hungrily fondling her breasts, then eagerly—but always gently—exploring every curve and hollow of her body.

Not wanting any part of what was to come, afraid that it would only hurt, Annie drained her glass and turned to leave. Instead, not knowing why, she sat down on the corner of the window seat and refilled the glass, a familiar shadow among shadows. Leaning back, she closed her eyes and breathed a sigh of relief, inviting the carnal past to have its way with her. Seconds became minutes, turning back the hands of time as she sipped the wine, adding fuel to the fire now burning in her belly. Nothing was missed, not even those embarrassing moments that now seemed more precious than ever before. She watched herself awkwardly guiding Sean from boyhood to manhood, acting more out of instinct than experience. She slowed what he had hurried, savoring every delicious moment of his youthful passion. She relived what she had once thought had been pain, not woman enough then to know it would turn to pleasure.

"But I do now," she said with a throaty growl as she saw herself lying beside Sean on a pilfered blanket spread out on a bed of prickly hay, a cool midnight breeze blowing in through the wide-open loft door. Rewriting the scene with the heart of a woman, Annie imagined herself rolling over, straddling him, his hands on her breasts as she slowly eased herself down, feeling every—

No! suddenly shattered the picture into a thousand useless pieces.

Annie stood up and peered into the darkened kitchen, as if someone was there, watching her. Frightened, then angry, she hurled the empty wine bottle at a shadow. It struck the massive stone hearth and exploded, scattering a minefield of jagged shards over the hardwood floor, blocking her intended retreat.

She fell back onto the window seat, her anger rising—her thoughts dulled by the wine—as she fought to see what had frightened her. "Who's there . . . who are you?" she demanded.

As the image slowly drew into focus, she shut her eyes. But it grew sharper and brighter, color overlaying line and form as distant sounds broke the silence of the past.

She covered her ears and shook her head. *No!*

Chapter Eighteen

Sean had finally succeeded in tuning out the nerve-jangling noises in the hospital: the irritating squeak and clank of the carts being wheeled up and down the hall, nurses shuffling in and out of the room, the guarded whispers that cut through the quiet, the nervous laughter that tried but failed to hide the worry and the thunderous explosion of footsteps following the alarm of a heart flat-lining. He had left one channel open, however, finely tuned to the frequency of Pamela's voice, no matter how faint.

Was it really sleep? Who could say. Was it restful? Far from it, since Pamela's delirious outbursts had left him weary, as if he, too, was fighting death. But then, what was the difference between a deep sleep and death? When we are—

asleep or dead—do we know we are? Is our soul dead when our body's dead? And how do we know that when we do die, our spirit, our soul— that which makes us who we are—doesn't take refuge in another body and live on, forever expanding our collective subconscious? Maybe that was the real secret to mankind's evolution on earth. Perhaps our souls never die, and who we are is the composite of those who have lived before us, only we're deaf to the call of their voices because we haven't learned how to listen. And even when we hear them, we try to forget, afraid of what we've heard, afraid of what they're saying, afraid to tell anyone. And when someone does admit to having heard them, we laugh at them and analyze the shit out of what they say until it's nothing but meaningless babble. Except to those who have heard and listened, and know enough not to tell.

The sound of a woman calling his name drifted into Sean's subconscious, but it was the wrong frequency, so he tuned it out.

"Sean?" she asked again and jostled his arm, but gently, leaving her hand on his shoulder. "What are you doing here?"

Scrunching himself into a knotted ball on the uninviting wood and vinyl armchair, he swept her hand away and snuggled under the blanket someone had caringly placed over him during the night.

"Go away," he grumbled. "Sean's dead."

"*¡Estas loco hombre!*" She laughed.

Sean smiled. *Carmen?* Though he had only wanted to think it, he muttered, "Go find your own tomb to sit on."

Carmen replied in a throaty chortle, "This is *my* graveyard, mister, and *I* call the shots here." The question that followed lacked any hint of humor, though it wasn't asked harshly. "Now, I want to know what you're doing in my patient's room." With that said, she snatched up the blanket and tossed it into the corner.

As he sat up and winced from the sunlight leaking into the room around the edges of the misfit curtains on the window, Carmen stepped back and folded her arms. Although she wasn't wearing that trademark white coat, the stethoscope draped around her neck and a stern institutional scowl said that she was a doctor, and that thought instantly recast the image Sean had saved of her from their earlier meeting. "You look different." He gave in to a yawn. "All grown up. Older, too, but at the same time much younger."

He suddenly realized what was different about her: She was looking at him, not avoiding his gaze as she had yesterday, and her eyes were clear, on the sunny side of blue, not ice cold.

Looking miffed, Carmen preened herself and

said with a hint of dismay, "I didn't realize that I looked *that* bad yesterday."

She tightened the knot her arms had been thread into. "Now." This time she sounded a bit irritated. "What are you doing here?"

Sean didn't have the energy, or the inclination, to play the game he might have played, simply for the fun of it. What he needed was a good, strong cup of coffee. With that thought, he said, "I'm the guy who brought her in," and smiled. It was more of a smug any-more-questions-Doctor? smirk than a genuine smile.

Though she appeared to relax, Carmen did a good job of hiding it. "Want a cup of coffee?" she asked. A smile lit up her smooth ebony face. "You look like you could use one . . . maybe two."

She gestured toward the door with a subtle turn of her head and said in a whisper, "C'mon . . . my treat."

Sean stood up and stretched the kinks out of his back as he said through a yawn, "The lady doctor really does read minds."

Carmen laughed. "I read your face, and your eyes told me that you *desperately* needed a fix. We fellow addicts know that look."

She glanced at her watch. "I've got about two hours before my first bypass. That should give us more than enough time to go somewhere and shoot up, presuming I don't get beeped."

She slipped her arm through Sean's and started for the door.

"And in exchange for the hit, *Doctor* MacDonald, you're going to tell me the real truth about why you were sitting all alone in that cemetery yesterday and talking to yourself."

Digging in his heels, Sean asked, "What *real* truth?"

Carmen pursed her face into a doubtful but still playful frown. "After you left the cemetery, Annie told me—"

"No vuelvas, chiquita," Pamela called out in an old and frail voice.

Carmen stopped and stood motionless, breathless, as if she was afraid to turn around and look.

With his thoughts tumbling back in time, Sean spun around and stood staring at Pamela in disbelief, all the while struggling with the Spanish. "Sweetheart . . . did you say 'Don't go back?' "

He shook his head. "I don't understand."

Carmen slowly turned around, crossed herself as she asked, barely above a whisper, her eyes more black than blue, *"¿Eres tú?"*

Pamela appeared to smile. *"Sí . . . soy yo."*

Pushing Sean aside, Carmen rushed to Pamela's bedside.

Reaching out, her hand quivering like a tuning fork, she asked, *"¿Por qué me dejaste?"*

Sean edged closer and took hold of Pamela's

hand and held it possessively. "What did you mean by why did she leave you?"

"Stay out of this!" Carmen ordered and tried to shove Sean away with a surprisingly powerful, back-handed sweep of her arm.

"Who the hell do you think—"

"*No.*" Pamela sighed as she meekly raised her hand and gestured toward Carmen. "*Ven aquí y perdona a esta vieja.*"

She began to blindly pat the bed, as if she was looking for something. "*¿Donde estan mis gotas?*" she whimpered in a childlike voice. "*No puedo irme sin ellas . . . ¿qué diriá la Virgen?*"

"Your rosary beads?" Carmen muttered under her breath and shook her head, as if she'd said something she shouldn't have.

Pamela nodded. "*Sí.*"

Sean stood up straight as a rail and said in a hush, "My God! It's *her . . . that woman.*"

Carmen picked up an imaginary object off the bed and placed it into Pamela's open hand. She gently closed her fingers around it. "*Tomas,*" she said with loving tenderness. "*Vaya con Dios.*"

Pamela began to hum quietly, that frail voice resonating deep down inside her chest. The solemn sounds grew weaker with each breath, while the unspoken words from thirty years ago grew steadily louder inside Sean's head, tolling a familiar refrain.

Chapter Nineteen

Sean muttered, "Didn't notice that before," as he ran past the entrance to what appeared to be a paved macadam path intersecting Lake Road, and immediately realized it was the route of the old West Shore railroad that once ran along the top of the man-made ridge bordering the north side of the reservoir.

Discounting the fact that it was beginning to get dark, he slowed and circled back, hurdling the low-slung galvanized chain strung across the entrance to the leaf-covered path. With the trees almost bare and the air as crisp and clear as well water, he could see for miles on either side of the long, curving ridge as he slipped back into stride and checked his pulse: He had been running faster than he usually did, faster than he knew he should, pushing his heart above 165, the maximum rate for a man his age.

"Theoretical max," he countered as he glanced down and found himself running in a path kicked through the leaves, and not too long ago either. His curious gaze raced ahead of him, following the trail of what he guessed was another runner, until the late-afternoon shadows cast by the barren branches chopped up everything into jagged patches of black and gray and tarnished autumn gold.

Recalling the route he had walked more times than he could count—going from Blue Fields to Pearl River to see Judith, and the return trips after midnight—he shortened his stride to the metered pace he had once mastered; that of a hobo walking the line. He shuffled from one imaginary railroad tie to the next, while pumping his arms back and forth in perfect time like the pistons of an old steam engine. The pace quickly proved awkward and he broke into a sprint, slipping back into a smooth, running stride.

But that was the only thing that was smooth for Sean as he found himself running the gauntlet all over again, ducking and covering up from everything he had seen and heard earlier this morning at the hospital. *Stay out of this!* rang the loudest as he winced from the memory of Carmen's blow, struck in anger as if she were

Pamela's guardian and he some sort of dangerous predator.

You're all hypocrites, he thought as he recalled Carmen's comments after she had downed her third Cointreau in less than half an hour, having opted for alcohol instead of caffeine for her fix. "Face it, Sean, it's the only rational explanation. She must have overheard me talking with Bob Jeffrey about my going up to Blue Fields to look for my grandmother's grave. So when she heard our banter about the cemetery, her subconscious probably kicked in."

Carmen had been quick to tack on with a certain clinical aloofness, "It's a coincidence, nothing more. As for my reaction, that was simply the unresolved pain of a young girl who had once been abandoned by her grandmother. That can happen to anyone when they haven't reached closure with a traumatic event in their life."

Sean snarled, "Closure my ass." As far as he was concerned, the idea of closure was nothing more than feel-good, eighties psychobabble. You never reach closure, you just learn to live with whatever happened and bury the pain as deep as you can. And pray it doesn't climb back out; because if it does, it'll return with a vengeance and sink its teeth into you even deeper.

In the time it had taken them to walk from Pamela's hospital room to some sleazy, twenty-four-hour diner/bar around the corner from the hospital—which Carmen had claimed the doctors all frequented, though not one was to be found there—she had filled him in on how she had come to know Pamela. She had told her story using a colorful montage of snapshots from a summer in the Hamptons—afternoons sailing, nights chasing men and mornings that had been slept away until brunch. While sailing was one of the many pieces of the complex puzzle Sean knew Pamela to be, the others didn't fit the woman he knew. And he had never once heard her speak Spanish.

Confused, especially about when this had all taken place, he had tried to get Carmen to tell him more. But each time he asked, though admittedly in a roundabout way—certainly not the way Pamela would have asked—she had held up one glitzy snapshot after another, sidestepping his questions with the grace of a matador.

As she parried his moves, now and then sticking a word of Spanish into her evasive replies, he had found himself thinking that behind her pictorial cape she was hiding a *banderilla,* that deadly barbed spear the *banderillero* drives deep into the shoulders of the tormented bull, for no other reason than to fuel his rage.

Whatever suspicions Sean had begun to harbor, however, had been tempered by what Carmen had said to him after her fourth drink and another newsreel of sketchy, and at times bawdy recollections. Speaking in a secretive voice, her words slurred, which had once again teased up thoughts of that woman he had seen in the cemetery years ago, she had said, "I didn't tell any of my colleagues this . . . and if you repeat it, I'll deny it . . . but after I had repaired the damage to Pamela's artery and had begun to examine her heart, my fingers suddenly felt numb. And I couldn't let go, even though I tried. It was as if something—"

It was here that she had stopped in midsentence, shook her head and muttered, "I really shouldn't be telling you this." Then, without saying another word, she had gotten up and walked out.

Is that where you are now? Sean wondered, and started running even faster. *Why her and not me? What the hell are you waiting for?* Angered by the absence of answers, still struggling with the fact that he had accepted as true what couldn't possibly be true, Sean lowered his head and pushed himself still faster. Yet with each step taken he seemed to be moving slower, as if he was running in sand. His lungs began burning as his chest caught on fire, and his legs suddenly felt like they were filled with lead.

He finally gave up and wound down to a walk, gulping air as he gasped, "What the fuck do you want from me?"

But he had no answer, his mind, like his body, empty.

About to turn back, he spotted a shadowy figure not far up ahead, jogging at a leisurely pace. Wearing a hooded sweatshirt and baggy sweatpants, he couldn't tell in the thickening twilight whether the stranger was a man or a woman. Ever curious, recalling with an affectionate smile Pamela's concern over which of his feline lives he was on, Sean skipped into a lazy jog. As he drew closer, the stranger appeared to speed up, as if they were trying to keep their distance. His competitive nature quickly got the better of him and he sped up too, only to see that the stranger had kicked into a sprint. This drove him even harder, forcing him to call upon what little reserve he had left as he closed the gap.

It's a woman, he thought the moment he was able to make out the subtle but unmistakable movements beneath the loose-fitting sweatpants. No sooner had he realized this than he took the image he'd created in his mind to the next level and tried to sculpt a womanly figure to match the imaginary hips and ass.

Before he could complete his fantasy, he found himself wondering, *What the hell is a woman doing out here alone, and at this time of day?* Concerned, he quickened his pace, but abruptly eased up and turned back when he realized that

169

his pursuit of her was probably the cause of her running faster.

Wearing only running shorts and a sweatshirt, both of which were now soaking wet, Sean soon began shivering from the chilling bite of the rising October wind. Left with no other way to get warm, he started jogging again, running on empty.

A hundred yards later—the muscles in his legs screaming at him, the salty sweat rolling off his forehead and burning his eyes—he grumbled, "Fuck this shit," and slowed to a labored walk.

As he ambled down the shadowy path, lazily kicking his feet through the leaves, he began to rehash everything Carmen had said to him. He compared her every word, every glib description, with what Pamela had told him of her life before she had met him. Lost in his thoughts, he was unaware that the stranger had turned around and was now following him. While matching him step for step, she kept her distance. After a few minutes, she nodded and began to increase her pace, but cautiously, as if she was stalking him.

Each time he discredited one of Carmen's snapshots, he kicked at the leaves. The shuffling noise muffled the footsteps of the stranger as she drew steadily closer.

Wait a second. He pulled up. *How could she have known about the rosary beads?* "You blind son of a bitch! How could you—"

Startled by the sudden rustle of leaves behind him, Sean jumped aside, his heart racing, as the stranger kicked past him.

Annie? Without thinking, he started after her, only to feel the muscles in his legs cramp up. "Shit." He limped back down to a walk, trying to work out the knots as he watched her pull away. For a split second he thought he heard her laughing but decided what he heard was the echo of his own bruised ego. Before he could call her back, she slowed and made a U-turn. Yanking off the hood of her sweatshirt, she shook out her long red hair and stood with her hands on her hips, smiling, waiting for him to catch up to her.

He shook his head. "What the hell are you doing out here?"

Annie sounded somewhat defiant when she said, "I decided last night that I was fed up with being fat . . . and sick and tired of spending my nights alone." Spreading her arms wide, she turned full circle and asked cautiously, "So, do I look like a runner?"

With a playful brush of her hand across his chest—her copper green eyes as clear as stained glass for a fleeting moment, then dark and clouded—Annie smiled and started walking backwards, as if she were trying to tease him into following her.

Sensing something in his throat, a flutter in his chest, Sean glanced down to see that his pulse had risen above 120 and was still climbing. He quickly passed it off as his heart simply doing its job and trying to cool him down as he started after her.

"Listen . . . I'm sorry about last night. I fell asleep—"

"Forget it," Annie said with a sharp wave of her hand, cutting him off. "You don't owe me any explanations."

Sean smiled to himself at the familiar gesture as she spun away and skipped farther ahead, then turned and started walking backwards again. "Wanna try again tonight?" she asked, just as she tripped on something buried in the leaves and stumbled backwards.

Lunging forward, he snared a fistful of her sweatshirt and pulled her back. When she fell against him, he knew immediately that she was anything but fat. Using the womanly curves he now felt pressed against his body, aided by a photoplay of reawakened memories, he completed his unfinished sculpture from moments ago.

"Yuck!" Annie laughed as she pulled away and gingerly patted his chest with the tips of her fingers. "You're soaking wet; you're going to freeze to death out here," she said as she slipped her hand beneath her sweatshirt and retrieved a palm-sized cell phone.

Sean instantly felt a thump in his chest and was about to check his pulse again when the sight of Annie holding the phone and punching in a series of numbers on the dimly lit face called up thoughts of Pamela and brought a private smile to his lips.

"I'm calling us a cab," she announced officiously and waved, urging him to follow her. "Then I'm going to see that you get a nice hot shower and some dry clothes." She smiled again. "And a decent meal . . . not that horrid hospital food."

Concerned that his pulse had not yet begun to drop, Sean said with a nervous shake of his head, "I really think I should—"

"Betty? It's me, Annie. I need a cab at the new bike path on Lake Road, near the intersection of Old Western—"

She smiled and shook her head. "I'm okay . . . really, I just need a cab for a friend and me. We were jogging and—"

She glanced away, her gaze cast off in the distance, as she said without the slightest reservation in her voice, "My house."

Oh, no, we're not.

"Yes," she said softly but firmly. It was as if she'd read his thoughts. She then reached out, placing her hand on his shoulder, her gentle touch erasing his every conscious thought.

She laughed, "No such luck . . . we're just old friends."

Chapter Twenty

Pamela floated to the surface and opened her eyes to a burst of bright, fluorescent light. Wincing from the harsh, antiseptic glare, she shut her eyes and lay perfectly still, wondering if this was just another wishful dream. She took a slow, cautious breath: there was nothing, not even a prick. Always the doubter, she took another, as deep as she possibly could. *Yes!* she thought as the fireworks exploded in her chest like the Fourth of July.

But her skepticism refused to allow her the luxury of hope. She tested every muscle, every joint. She closed and opened her hands, making a fist and squeezing so tight that her fingernails dug into her skin. She relished the fires that had begun to burn throughout her body, fanned hotter by the winds of consciousness.

As if she was cheating at a game of hide and seek, she cracked open her eyelids just enough to see through the narrow slits. When she turned her head side to side, panning the brightly lit room, her blurred gaze fell upon a petite, dark-skinned woman.

Turned aside but not facing away, she was wearing a white hospital coat and unfashionable black-rimmed glasses, and quietly reading something on a clipboard. Her shiny black hair was cinched into a long, girlish ponytail that curled down her neck.

Pamela searched the many faceless names drifting through her mind for one that matched the look of this exotic woman. When she found it, she wondered if she could even speak, and if she could, if it would hurt. Anxious, but nonetheless determined, she finally asked in a guarded whisper, "Dr. Faraahd . . . is that you?"

Galeal spun around, her dark eyes wide open and filled with wonder. "Pamela! . . . I mean, Dr. Eagleston." Stepping forward, she took Pamela's outstretched hand in hers and laughed, but more with a note of relief in her voice than humor. "It's a miracle."

There were a hundred things Pamela wanted to say—to shout, if her throat wasn't so raw.

They all clamored to be said first, but the one thing that had plagued her every conscious moment, stealing her most intimate thoughts, suddenly took center stage. She tried to swallow away the soreness in her throat but met with little success. "I have to talk to Sean. Please get me a phone."

When she tried to sit up, she doubled over and fell onto her side, clutching her chest while squeezing Galeal's hand. She tried to speak but could only mouth her thoughts.

Clearly upset, Galeal said with obvious concern and an equal measure of compassion, "Let me increase your—"

"No!" Pamela rasped and refused to let go of Galeal's hand when she tried to pull away. "No more . . . *please* . . . I—"

She gasped, her breath stolen when the pain kicked in again without warning. After a moment, tears in her eyes, she said in a wavering voice, a frail smile on her face, "I like the pain."

Galeal frowned, her expression half-curious, half-bewildered as she tried to free herself from Pamela's grasp but couldn't.

Pamela sought to counter Galeal's obvious doubt with a broader but still weak smile. "It's okay, really. It's my friend, if that makes any sense. It tells me that I'm alive, and that she—"

Pamela caught herself, fearful that Judith might still have a hold on her—somehow, some-

where—however tenuous. She cleared her mind and renewed her request of Galeal, only this time she spoke in a calm and solicitous voice. "Would you *please* get me a phone?" Though polite, the taut thread stringing her words together left no doubt about her determination.

Weakened by her efforts, she closed her eyes to rest.

In that brief moment, Galeal succeeded in slipping free of her hold. "I have to get Doctor—"

"No!" Pamela protested, sounding still weaker. "I don't want that self-righteous son of a bitch anywhere near me . . . especially not after the way he treated you when you tried to tell him—"

"I knew it!" Galeal said excitedly. "You really were conscious, weren't you?"

Pamela could only smile meekly and nod in response.

Galeal suddenly became still, her face, her whole body calm, as she returned to the side of the bed. Cradling Pamela's hand in hers, she held it close to her as she asked in a secretive voice, "You were raped . . . weren't you?"

The mere sound of that word—*raped!*—instantly dug up the nightmare Pamela thought she had buried somewhere deep inside her psyche. Before she could catch it and entomb it again, and bury it much deeper this time, those frightening thoughts broke free to invade her mind and body, ripping and tearing at her flesh all over again. "You goddamn bitch!" she cried out and shut her eyes tight, as if that could somehow blind her to what was happening.

But the onslaught continued, clawing and scratching at her body and soul as she began to shiver uncontrollably.

Galeal darted around the bed and said reassuringly, "Everything will be all right . . . trust me."

Calling upon what little strength she had left, Pamela grabbed hold of Galeal's coat and pulled her down close to her. Steadying herself, she said through clenched teeth, her words scraping over her vocal chords like barbed wire, "I told you . . . *no more drugs.*"

Galeal shook her head. "I can't let you suffer like this."

Knowing that there was no way she could possibly tell Galeal what had really happened to her, not without her thinking that she'd lost her mind, Pamela said in a calm and rational voice, "She almost killed me . . . and if she—"

"*She?*" Galeal gasped. "Did you say *she?*"

Pamela could see the confusion clouding Galeal's eyes as she recoiled in disbelief. She wanted to tell her the truth, tell her who Judith was and what she had done. She now knew Judith as well as Judith knew herself. She knew her every thought, her every wish, her bitter taste for cruelty and her desire for revenge.

But the most frightening parcel of knowledge that she now possessed was that Judith also knew her. And in so doing, she now knew Sean better than she ever had: She knew him as Pamela knew him, as a man, knew his every manly desire and his every weakness.

"Please," Pamela whispered prayerfully in the desperate attempt to plead for Sean's safety, to somehow hold him harmless from what she now feared Judith might do if she succeeded in seducing him one last time. "I must speak to Sean; his life—"

The sound of that fateful click caused Pamela to shake her head in denial as she braced herself, though she knew all too well that she was too weak to fight what was about to happen.

Aware of the precious few seconds of consciousness left to her, she chose her words carefully. "Tell Sean not to—"

"You *must* rest," Galeal said and pressed the button again.

Dear God . . . please . . . no—

Chapter Twenty-one

Still in her sweats and sneakers, waiting for Sean to get out of the shower, Annie propped her hands on her hips and stepped back to admire the table she had set—complete with an antique lace tablecloth, her best china and crystal, sterling silver flatware, tapered candles and a bottle of red wine left uncorked to breathe.

With a satisfied smile, she shrugged off the yoke of guilt that had been trying for the last half hour to collar her for what she had done to Sean. *He didn't have a prayer,* passed through her mind, causing her to wonder if that thought was hers or not, as she recalled what Betty Hayes, her best friend and owner of the Blue Fields Taxi and Limousine Service, had said once she assured herself that Annie was safe. "You oughta have your head examined, Potter!" she said as only one friend could speak to another, "What were you thinking, girl, out running alone? And after dark! Don't you know that writer guy is still here, and *he's* always running somewhere? Everyone says that he looks like he's in a trance when he runs. You know those literary types; he's probably on drugs or something. And let me tell you another thing, sweetie, after reading that book of his you gave me, as far as I'm concerned that man is not all there. What if you had met *him* on the bike path and not your friend here . . . there's no telling what might have happened!"

Annie stood motionless, listening to the water running overhead. For a moment—as long as it took her to realize that she didn't have the courage—she toyed with the thought of sneaking upstairs and slipping into the shower with Sean. Laughing quietly to herself at what she thought might be his reaction, she whispered, as if Betty Hayes was standing beside her, "He was never *all there;* that's one of the things I loved most about him."

Annie smiled warmly. "That, and the way he—"

She caught herself; there was no way in hell she was going down that path again. *One sleepless night was enough!*

Shaking her head, she spun around and

slipped the two-handled silver platter off the kitchen counter and surveyed the store-bought appetizers that she'd artfully arranged on the platter: slices of pâté, thin wedges of overripe Brie, small pastry cups filled with red and black caviar, chopped egg, chopped onion, capers, dozens of cookie-cutter toast rounds and crumbled Stilton.

Setting the platter down, she poked at the wedges of cheese, nudging them into a perfect oval surrounding the slices of pâté that were fanned out in the center of the tray. As she licked the gooey Brie off her finger, she couldn't help wondering if she was wasting her time, knowing that there was no way she could possibly compete with Pamela. She thought about the night she'd met Pamela at the library, and recalled word for word what Pamela had said to Sean, how she had said it and especially how she looked at him.

Although she had liked her, and admittedly envied her, Pamela was not the kind of woman she would ever have pictured Sean with. But then, she had known the boy, not the man. She hadn't been jealous then, but she was now, which surprised her. A wry smile slipped onto her face as she muttered, "She's too butch for him," then evaporated just as quickly, as if she was unaware of it.

In the time it took her to circle the table—

squaring up the silverware, primping the napkins, straightening the candles and sliding open
the tiny box of wooden matches—Annie had
poured herself a glass of wine and drained it.
Without a second thought, she refilled the glass,
dimmed the lights and slipped out of the kitchen.
After turning down the living room lights, she
started toward the foyer. The only thought now
on her mind was getting out of her grungy sweats
and into a nice, hot tub.

She shook her head and sighed, "No can do,"
when she realized that she wouldn't have enough
hot water for a good soak, and that a quick
shower would have to do.

As she started up the stairs, there was a sharp
rap on the front door. *Don't answer it.* She kept
right on going, nursing her glass of wine. A few
steps later, the knock was repeated, this time
with an irritating determination. *If someone
broke into that library again . . . and that's the
police . . . I'm going to scream.*

She reluctantly backed down the steps and
peered through the peephole in the front door.
Damn. Slipping off the chain, she opened the
door and planted herself squarely in the doorway, hand on her hip. "This better be good," she
snarled playfully.

Grinning like a Cheshire cat, Peter Murphy
gave her the once-over, head to toe. When he
finally spoke, there was an obvious tone of

amusement in his voice. "I wouldn't have believed it if I hadn't seen it with my own eyes. You look like you *really* were running." He tried peering past her into the house. "Is Dr. MacDonald in there with you, by any chance?"

Betty, you have a big mouth. Annie half-closed the door behind her, letting Murphy know that she didn't appreciate his nosing around. "What makes you think Sean MacDonald is here?"

Appearing miffed by her gesture, Murphy caught a frown before it could get out of hand and replaced it with a sly smile. It was that I-know-what-you're-doing look. She let Peter know that she didn't appreciate his unspoken snide attitude when she snapped, "I'm in no mood for games, Peter. Spit it out; what do you want?"

Murphy stood a bit taller, his shoulders back. He nodded, as if to apologize, and said respectfully, "A Dr. Faraahd from the hospital is trying to reach Sean." He was quick to add, "It's not an emergency. She just wants to talk to him about something."

Murphy stuck his hand into his shirt pocket and pulled out a small, folded-over piece of paper. "She left these numbers with the desk sergeant when she called the station." He handed the paper to Annie. "The first one there is her beeper, the other one is her apartment. She said that she's on duty until eight tomorrow morning.

After that he can call her at home. She said it's okay."

Murphy started down the curving flagstone path toward the driveway. Just before getting into his car, he waved and said with a presumptuous air of authority, "See that Sean gets the message."

By the time Annie had reached the second-floor landing her glass was empty again. She thought of darting downstairs for another refill, but instead hurried down the hall toward her bedroom. She faltered to a stop beside the bathroom door and glanced at the note. She appeared to look right through it, her mind suddenly blank. Tossing it onto the drop-leaf table to the left of the door, she topped it with her glass. About to continue on her way, she paused, her head turned. Not hearing the water running, she imagined Sean drying himself off and immediately found herself wondering what he looked like after all these years.

Annie willingly held on to that thought as she walked toward her bedroom, struggling out of her grungy old sweatshirt and wriggling out of a soaking-wet, long-sleeved turtleneck. Reaching behind her, she deftly unhooked her bra.

"Oops!" She laughed and came to an abrupt halt when she caught sight of Sean standing beside the bed, naked, drying his hair.

Not bothering to cover herself up, which she

reconsidered, but only for a second, Annie smiled as she reacquainted herself with the boy she had once known. *You've grown into a man.* She was about to say just that, too, but thought better of it when she saw that Sean was blushing. His reaction drew an amused smile from her as she watched him wrap the towel around his waist, cinch it tight and look at her straight on, the hint of a blush still there.

"Did I hear Peter Murphy's voice?" he asked.

Annie began to answer him, to tell him about the message, but stopped. Her thoughts were swirling inside her head, a voice telling her it could wait, that it wasn't an emergency.

"Yes," she finally said, though apprehensively. "He—"

She slipped Sean's expectant gaze. "He was just checking up. Betty Hayes has an overactive imagination. I told him—"

She shook her head. "It was nothing," she said quietly.

Without looking at Sean, she walked over and snatched up one of the bath towels she'd set out on the bed and started back to the door. Halfway down the hall, she called out in a lyrical voice, "You'll find a man's bathrobe buried in my closet. It's on the left side. It's plaid. Never been worn. It should fit you."

* * *

Sean hovered over the kitchen table like a hawk circling its prey, drawn between the growl in his stomach and his conscience, which told him to wait for Annie. Looking for an excuse—just about anything would do, given his hunger—he noticed that one of the wineglasses was missing and recalled having seen one on the table in the hallway upstairs, empty and sitting on a make-shift coaster. He checked the bottle of wine and saw that it was only half full, which instantly erased any doubts he might have had.

Filling a glass, he topped one of the toast rounds with a healthy dollop of black caviar and proceeded to alternate, taking a small bite, then a sip of wine, until it was gone. After pouring himself another glass, he began to surf the platter. Although he had practically drowned himself under the shower in an attempt to quench his thirst from running, it resurfaced with a vengeance, and he unwittingly downed the wine as if it were water. It wasn't until he found himself holding an empty bottle upside down over an empty glass that he realized what he'd done.

Just don't pass out like some kid, he told himself as he stole another slice of pâté and skillfully covered up his theft.

Intent upon doing the same with the empty bottle of wine, Sean began to poke around the kitchen, quietly opening and closing the cupboard doors in search of a replacement bottle.

The walk-in pantry gave up its secret, along with a corkscrew. Finding a mate to the empty bottle, he rearranged the bottles in the rack. No sooner had he done this than he started laughing to himself, remembering the times he and Annie had done the same thing in her father's wine cellar to cover up what they'd stolen.

In that moment, trapped in the past, whatever defenses Sean had thrown up to keep Annie at a safe distance were torn down. Other memories quickly burst through the broken barricades as he tried in vain to rebuild the ramparts of his mind. He finally gave up when he was set upon by the unexpected thought that what he was really afraid of was his own feelings, which opened the door to the fear of what might happen if he let Annie get too close to him.

Although he rejected that thought out of hand, it refused to die. As if to test his resolve, Sean risked replaying the images of Annie walking into the bedroom, naked from the waist up and not appearing the least bit shy. He immediately realized that he'd been wrong and tried to get away from what he'd seen, to distance himself from what he had felt. His imaginary flight was slowed by the wine, leaving him easy prey to his resurrected feelings.

But he stood his ground. "No . . . I'm tired of running."

"Then stop," Annie said in a soft, but nonetheless serious tone of voice, which also had a slightly seductive ring to it.

As he turned around to explain what he had meant—knowing that he couldn't possibly tell her the truth—Annie switched off the kitchen lights. The soft amber glow from the living room carved out a womanly silhouette in the doorway that momentarily took his breath away. After what seemed like an eternity, she reached back and turned off the living room lights.

Cloaked in the dark, she walked up to the table. With the strike of a match, the satin caftan clinging to her body burst into a shimmer of midnight blue reflections as the sulfurous sparkle turned her long red hair to liquid bronze, her skin to ancient ivory. When she bent forward and lit the candles, the flickering flames exposed the swell of her breasts straining against the thin, shiny fabric. Although she had laced up the front, she had not drawn the laces snug, allowing the candle light to slip deep down between her sumptuous breasts, inviting the eye to follow.

The girl Sean had tried telling himself hadn't changed—a chrysalis of the mind he thought he'd safely wrapped in silken memories—had suddenly emerged from her cocoon and spread her wings. As he watched her pour a glass of wine and take a long, lingering sip—revealing a womanly hunger he hadn't noticed until now—he fought to extinguish the fire that started burning in his loins. Her every move, a sensuous swallow, her tongue moving over her moistened lips, fanned the flames even hotter.

She gestured with her now-empty glass toward the bottle of wine and said, as if she was talking to herself, "I wonder if Daddy knew what we were doing . . . and just never said anything to us?"

With a whimsical smile, she refilled her glass and gracefully moved beyond the reach of the faint but nonetheless revealing candlelight. She stood staring out the window into the moonless night, her every move, however slight—a smile, a frown, a nod, a shake of her head—creating the illusion she was talking to herself. Unsure of himself, Sean said quietly, "I'm sorry about what happened with John. I can't possibly understand why—"

"You mean pity, don't you?" Annie said bitterly and turned around, her face hard as stone. There was an unmistakable twist to her body, as if she were knotted with pain.

Uneasy with her sudden change of mood, unable to explain why or what it was that had suddenly taken hold of her, Sean said softly, "No . . . I don't pity you. I think what I felt was—"

"Guilt?" she asked, the razor-sharp edge of her question severing Sean's thoughts from his intended reply.

Annie moved toward him and asked in a somber tone of voice, "Why did you leave me, Sean?"

Grabbing his wrists, she held them tight.

He tried making sense of her question, but to no avail.

"What are you talking about?" he finally asked. He tried to step back but found himself tethered in her vicelike grip.

She growled, "You know what I'm talking about," and moved still closer, her eyes colorless holes sucking up every last photon of light, turning gray to black.

He dove into her icy gaze, searching the frozen depths for the girl he thought he knew. She instantly turned away, something she had never done with him before.

Perplexed by her reaction, he asked, "Are you all right?"

She abruptly released her hold on him and walked over to the table. She appeared to hesitate and stand motionless, as if she was waiting or listening for something. After a moment, she nodded and blew out one of the candles. When she turned and began to loosen the laces of her caftan, her movements appeared stilted, reluctant. With a suggestive shrug of her shoulders, her mood having suddenly changed, she began to squirm out of her satin skin.

For a moment, it clung to her breasts, caught on her nipples, before sliding down and gathering around her hips, creating the image of a

Greek goddess. A casual brush of her hands and a sensuous twist of her body sent the silky folds falling to the floor around her bare feet. Framed by a halo of candlelight, she was as much illusion as reality. But not even the veil of darkness could mask the woman she was. Her full breasts, the tuck of her waist, the womanly swell of her tummy—still youthful—and her broad but shapely hips spoke not a word of her thirty-year affair with time.

All too aware of the fire spreading throughout his body, engulfing his thoughts and melting his resolve, Sean said in a deliberately dipassionate voice, "Annie . . . listen . . . why don't we think about—"

"No!" she snapped, her eyes filled with a light of their own.

When she spoke again, her voice was decades older and surprisingly frail. "I've had a thousand lifetimes to think."

Confused, Sean stepped away, only to have his escape thwarted when she reached out. Before he could move, she slipped her hand inside his robe, her touch taking his breath away. When he tried to move her hand, she pulled his bathrobe open and stepped closer, her breasts, her nipples touching his chest, her body melting into his. Afraid of his own feelings, he placed his hands on her shoulders and tried to gently push her away. Evading his grasp once again, she stepped around him and slipped the bathrobe off his shoulders, throwing it to the floor. When he spun around, naked, she wrapped her arms around him and covered his mouth with hers. Her lips were warm and moist, her tongue hot and hard and searching for his as the honey-sweet fragrance of her desire filled the air.

Though he tried, he was unable to keep from responding to her unspoken invitation. He grew firmer with every heartbeat, his hard body pressing into the soft flesh of her thighs as he inhaled the past, hungry for the present and a taste of this mysterious woman.

As if she had read his thoughts, Annie stepped back and slowly kicked the bathrobe into a makeshift blanket. Kneeling down, she gracefully laid back, her legs spread, inviting him to follow.

Sean knelt down as thoughts of summer and dried hay and warm breezes swirled inside his head. When he pressed against her, she opened like a rose, the petals covered with drops of dew. About to slip inside, he pulled back and said quietly, "I can't—"

"*Can't* . . . or won't?" she replied in a deep-throated growl and locked her legs around his waist, pulling him down to her.

He stiffened, holding himself back, even though he was aching with desire to plunge deep inside her. "No," he said with a shake of his head and squirmed free. "This isn't right; I—"

"Damn you! Damn you both!" she cried out, her words dripping with venom as she violently kicked him away.

Struggling to her feet, Annie stumbled over to the table and, with a clench of her fist, snuffed out the last candle, casting the room into darkness as she gasped for air and asked in a voice on the verge of exploding into rage, "Aren't I good enough for you?"

Clutching his sides, Sean got to his feet and started toward her. "Annie . . . please . . . it's me, not—"

"Get out!" she screamed and spun around, her arms flailing, her nails raking across his chest, digging deep into his flesh.

Chapter Twenty-two

Pamela awoke with a start, her heart racing. She was warm and damp with perspiration, but not feverish. She lay perfectly still, her eyes shut— feigning that drug-induced stupor she knew only too well—as she struggled to see the images playing out in her head.

Shrouded in darkness, she could barely make out the faceless figure of a man standing over her, though she could see clearly that he was naked and aroused. As he knelt down before her, she realized that she was aflame with a passion equal to his.

Without any conscious effort to resist—to question who this man was or why she was doing this—she spread her legs, inviting him to quench the fire burning in her loins. She struggled to see his face as the engorged head of his rigid shaft seared her swollen flesh. When he hesitated, a woman's voice—faint, more thought than word—urged him on. About to slip inside her, he paused and turned away. In that moment of hesitation, the flickering light of a candle erased his anonymity, revealing that this was not another one of her hidden memories of Sean about to be stolen, or one of Judith's that she had left behind out of cruelty: It was happening now, with another woman, in a place she didn't recognize.

Pamela was startled when she heard Sean say in a quiet sigh, as if he was there in bed with her, "I can't—"

That distant voice whispered, "Yes you can," followed by a woman's deep-throated growl, demanding to know, *"Can't . . . or won't?"*

She felt her legs tightening around Sean's waist and trying to pull him back down to her, the two voices in her mind arguing—one desperately wanting him inside her, the other unsure—and her tentative resolve growing weaker with every unclear word spoken.

She tried to stop herself but couldn't. *Don't do this!* she pleaded as she tried to push Sean away.

As if he'd heard her, felt her touch, he held himself back and said, "No," with a determined shake of his head as he squirmed free of her reluctant grasp.

That faraway voice, now close to rage, began shouting bitter taunts and venomous threats, yet not a single word was spoken.

Sean whispered, "This isn't right, I—"

"You bastard!" could be heard erupting from afar.

"Damn you . . . damn you both!" echoed loudly in reply.

You fucking bitch! rang out in cacophonous refrain inside Pamela's head when Sean doubled over, clutching his side.

She reached out to pull him to her, to hold him, to comfort him, but something burned her hand. Then everything went black, the air filled with the acrid odor of soot and melted wax.

Both voices—one angry, the other hurt, one drawing close, the other pulling back—asked in unison, "Aren't I good enough for you?"

"Annie . . . please . . . it's me, not—"

Pamela bolted up in bed. *Annie? Annie! What the hell—*

Get out! startled Pamela into silence as she felt her nails raking across Sean's chest. Tears squeezed from her eyes as she fell back onto the bed, sickened by the nauseating sensation of something soft and wet and warm wedged under her fingernails.

Chapter Twenty-three

Annie's midnight-blue caftan was lying on the wood-planked floor, floating in the soft gray shadows of dawn. A few feet away was the plaid terry-cloth bathrobe Sean had been wearing. On the floor near the bay window was a mismatched pair of empty wine bottles, one standing upright, the other tipped over onto its side.

Annie was sitting motionless on the cushion in one corner of the window seat, naked, immune to the cold. Her head was bowed, her eyes shut, her long red hair hiding her face as it fell down over her gently sloping breasts. Her stomach, soft and relaxed, was smeared with streaks of blood. Her hands, balled up into fists, were lying in her lap. While the wine had silenced the angry voice raging inside her head, the forgiving nectar had failed to give her the sleep she so desperately wanted. But at least she was finally alone.

Uncurling her fists, she sat staring in disbelief at her bloodstained fingers. Using her thumbnail, she picked at the bits and pieces of skin and strands of hair caught under her nails.

"What got into you?" she asked and waited. But there was no answer to her question, only that sickening feeling in the pit of her stomach from the look on Sean's face when she'd scraped her nails across his chest. In that fleeting moment, the special light in his eyes that she had always thought was only for her had been snuffed out. It was a flame she desperately wanted to relight, while also rekindling the womanly emotions she thought had been extinguished a lifetime ago. She didn't regret for a single moment having wanted him, or having dressed and acted the part of a temptress, though it was an unfamiliar role for her.

Annie stood up, suddenly no longer tired, her thoughts once again her own. It was as if there were two of her, one for the night, another for the day, and they had just traded places.

She collected the bathrobe and her caftan and went upstairs.

As she walked past the table in the second-floor hallway, she was reminded of the note she hadn't given Sean. Slipping into the bathroom, she resolved to find him and tell him what she'd done, and ask him to forgive her. *That's if he'll even talk to you. You were a real bitch last night. You were just like her.*

No sooner had she said this than she found herself wondering what Sean had seen in Judith, and it wasn't a new question either. *You must have known, or was she that good of a lay you didn't care?*

"Maybe it's about time someone told you—"

A bitter cold suddenly knifed deep down into her chest. Frightened, she tried telling herself that it was just the shakes, something she knew all too well. She bent down and turned on the water, adjusting it to the hottest setting she could possibly stand. About to step into the shower, she was seized again by whatever it was that had grabbed hold of her, only this time the icy grip was stronger and colder, freezing her thoughts.

After a moment, her gaze locked onto something in the distant past, she said with a shake of her head, as if talking to someone she knew, "I told you, I will *not* do it," and stepped into the shower.

She gasped and jumped back at the sudden shock of the steaming-hot water. Yet at the same time it felt good, creating the odd sensation that it was melting the ice inside her chest, easing the pain. Curious, recalling what the wine had done to her, Annie braced herself and ducked beneath the water, the scalding hot spray pricking her skin like a thousand needles, freeing her thoughts.

Chapter Twenty-four

Sean drew back the shower curtain and snatched a towel off the row of wooden pegs stuck in the wall and started drying himself off. He had a definite routine, one which he never wavered from: standing in the tub, he first dried off his face, his hair, then his feet and legs, before stepping out.

After he and Pamela had been together for awhile, she had noticed him going through this same drill whenever they showered, and asked if there was a reason why he did it. He didn't have an explanation; he wasn't even aware he was doing it. "It's probably your obsessive-compulsive nature," she had told him. "But I guess that's to be expected . . . after all, you're a writer," she quipped, and playfully snapped him on his bare butt with a wet towel.

"Obsessive, maybe . . . but I'm *not* compulsive." Sean laughed, recalling that scene—Pamela giggling and darting naked and still wet out of the bathroom, he no more than two steps behind her, the two of them diving into her queen-sized bed and making love.

Sean was instantly drenched beneath a wave of remorse about what he'd done last night. Before the guilt could drown him, he tried shaking it off by telling himself, *You're damn lucky nothing really happened.* But it wasn't so easy this time, no more than he could easily rid himself of the pain in his belly, a dull, twisting knot that felt like something was alive inside him.

Adding to his discomfort were the baseball-sized bruises on his hips where Annie had kicked him, her heels digging deep into his sides. Each time he brushed the towel over them, though gently, the pain sparked another unwanted image. Strangely missing from those thoughts, however, was what Annie had said and done. It was as if his memory of her had been wiped clean when she'd raked her nails over his chest: erasing the sound of her speaking in a voice not her own, snuffing out the distant light in her eyes that faded to black the moment he knelt between her legs, the foul smell of her breath and the startling sensation of her flesh suddenly turning ice cold—her loins a glacial crevice, the chasm rapidly freezing over—just as he began to slip inside her.

After her violent outburst, she had spun away and begun talking to herself. When he couldn't get her to listen to him—she acted as if he wasn't even there—he had gone upstairs, slipped into his sweat-soaked clothes and left. An hour later, cold and damp and aching all over, he had collapsed into bed and fallen sound asleep. He might have slept all day had he not been woken by the tug of war in his gut, which he passed off as hunger pangs until he sat up and doubled over onto his side.

Though it was too late now, he knew that he should have listened to his instincts and said no the moment he'd heard Annie telling the dispatcher they were going back to her house. But something had stopped him. *What the hell were you thinking?*

When Sean wiped off the mirror over the sink and stepped back, he immediately shook his head at what he saw. With the scabbed-over furrows scratched across his chest, the blackened bruises on his hips and the road map of stitches crisscrossing his side from where he'd caught himself on Murphy's car door, he looked like he'd been in a fight. *And with a woman . . . and you lost!*

His laughter instantly reawakened the spasms in his gut and started him pawing through the travel case sitting on the vanity beside the sink. Uncertain if it was still there—it had been over a year since he last used the belladonna—he began to empty out the contents of the small leather case: a tube of toothpaste, a toothbrush, a comb he never used anymore now that he'd cut his hair short, a handful of Band-Aids, a bunch of Q-Tips, his shaving gear and a styptic pencil that he hadn't used in at least ten years.

Fishing out the brown prescription bottle, he twisted off the cap and took a sip, estimating a teaspoon. He took another for good measure. After checking the date—figuring the belladonna had lost some of its strength—he proceeded to drain the bottle.

Sean was numb as a rock from his chest to his butt. But the belladonna hadn't done a damn thing for the throbbing ache where Annie's heels had dug deep into his hips. When he broke into a lazy jog it got even worse, but he kept right on running.

After a half-mile or so, he noticed that his pulse was a little higher than normal but passed it off as a natural response to the pain, which he decided would only go away with a healthy dose of his own endorphins. So he sped up, wincing with every jarring strike of his heels. Though it hurt to run, he welcomed the sharp bite in his side. In a strange sort of way it felt good: It was a clean, clear pain, and there wasn't the slightest doubt in his mind what it was, or what was causing it.

It's your penance, he told himself, ignoring the fact that he had stricken that word from his vocabulary thirty years earlier, along with the litany of superstitious lies that had been nailed to his conscience before he had been old enough to know better.

With each yard of macadam swallowed up, every pinch of pain stoically absorbed, his thoughts grew steadily clearer, until there was only one person in his mind—Pamela—and only one thought, that he loved her and wanted to be with her.

About to turn back, he glanced down, intent upon tapping the button to see what time it was. *Shit!* His pulse was 175. He immediately slowed to a walk, telling himself *Don't stop . . . keep the blood pumping . . . don't starve the heart.* But the numbers kept climbing. He pressed his finger to his neck, his carotid artery, comparing the beat of his heart with the flashing dot on the tiny monitor. They were in synch, and his pulse had now risen to 190.

He frantically ran through the drill: He wasn't short of breath, there was no pressure in his throat, no pain in his jaw, no needle under his tongue, no spike shooting down his arm, not even a tingling sensation in his fingers. And there wasn't the slightest bit of pressure in his chest, no sign of that dreaded six-hundred-pound gorilla sitting on him, crushing his ribs.

What the hell is happening?

He pulled up to a wavering stop, his heart skipping and thumping wildly against his chest, the numbers on the display continuing their relentless, infuriating climb.

His thoughts were spinning just as fast, driven by fear: but not the fear that he would die, the fear that he might live forever, locked in Judith's—

"You're it!" Annie laughed and tapped his shoulder as she darted past and turned around, pulling to a stop facing him.

"My God!" She took his hands in hers. "Sean, what's wrong?"

His vision began to blur. *You stupid man! How could*—

"Sean!" Annie gasped as he collapsed to the ground.

Chapter Twenty-five

Pamela bolted up in bed, her arms open and out-stretched, accidentally striking the nurse drawing her blood and sending her stumbling backward. In spite of the impact, Eku Malawa-tumba, tall and thin, with huge hands—her face a work of art from African antiquity—managed to palm the small glass vial and keep from dropping it. With a relieved shake of her head, Eku said in a deep, lyrical voice, "You should have known better . . . she started talking in her sleep again." She set the blood-filled tube into a slot in the blue plastic tote sitting on the nightstand.

Pamela fell back and shut her eyes, waiting for the unsettling sight of Sean collapsing to the ground to return. But he wasn't to be found, his startled face lost amid a crowd of unfamiliar silhouettes and strange voices firing questions and answers back and forth at each other, their pitch and tenor rising with every anxious exchange. Refusing to give up, she continued her vigil as the nurse busied herself reattaching the line for the IV saline drip that had pulled free from her right arm. Eku then began checking to see if she was still tethered to the spider's web of multi-colored wires growing out of her body. With each tap of the electrodes tapped to her chest and ribs, the lines tracking her heartbeat across the amber-green monitor mounted to the wall overhead jumped and skittered and skipped across the face of the screen. After reaching beneath the sheet for a discreet check of the Folly catheter, Eku scurried around and gave a knowing tug on the morphine trap in Pamela's left forearm, then smiled to herself.

Frustrated and growing angrier by the moment, Pamela found herself once again wondering how she could get out of the hospital, *Out of this goddamned prison! Before that bitch*—

"Take it easy," Eku urged in a soothing voice and placed her large hand on Pamela's arm. "Your heart's doing handstands. Are you in any pain?"

The word *pain* had come to mean one thing to Pamela: a free fall into a sea of black—separating mind from body—drowning her thoughts as time passed her by. With a shake of her head, she said as calmly as she possibly could through a forced smile, "Must be aftershocks from the nightmare . . . I'll be okay in a minute."

Telling herself to try a different tack, Pamela turned to a blank page and asked sweetly, "Would you please help me sit up?"

Raising her head off the pillow, she peered at the shiny brass nameplate pinned to the nurse's uniform and asked apologetically, "Is it pronounced *Malawa* . . . tumba?"

A broad smile spread across Eku's face. "The emphasis is on the last two syllables. So it's *toom-bah,*" she said with a throaty, bass-drum cadence as she propped her hands on her hips and cocked her head to one side, looking about as doubtful as a wife holding a lipstick-smeared shirt. "As for the sitting up part, Ms. Eagleston, the doctor has left strict orders for you not to be moving about. It's been touch-and-go with you, young lady."

Before Pamela could try out her best pout, Eku laughed. "But I suppose since you already sat up, and you don't seem to be in any *real* pain . . . and you've got a nice normal sinus rhythm now . . . I don't suppose there's any harm in letting you sit up for awhile."

Eku was quick to wag her finger. "But if your heart starts to act up, I'm cranking you right back down . . . and I don't want any arguments out of you . . . understand?"

Pamela smiled and scratched an *X* in the air over her chest. "I promise . . . cross my heart and hope to—"

"We'll have no dying on my shift," Eku said with a made-up scowl that was followed by a grin as she pressed a button on the keypad built into the polished steel frame at the foot of the bed.

Pamela held her breath and smiled—masking every pinch and spike of pain—until she was sitting upright. *Step one*, she thought, and said with a curious frown, "I feel a little dizzy."

Eku responded with a knowing nod. "That's to be expected. It should go away in a minute or so. If it doesn't, you tell me."

Pamela glanced about the room as if she was testing her eyes. With a casual turn of her head, she discreetly scanned the contents of the tote tray on the nightstand to her right. Then she turned and gave the appearance she was looking at the nightstand to her left, but only for show. She made an effort to clear her throat and asked in a hoarse whisper, "Is the prisoner allowed ice water?"

Eku raised her hand, her finger in the air. *"That* you can have." Spinning around, she walked out of the room, moving with a certain grace and elegance that matched her regal appearance.

The moment she was out of earshot, Pamela reached into the tote tray and grabbed a handful

Donald Beman

of sealed paper packets from one compartment, then a few more from another. Reading the contents of each one—pleased with what she'd pilfered—she let two of the packets drop into her lap and returned the others. At the sound of footsteps approaching, she snatched up her bounty and stuffed it under the pillow behind her as Eku reappeared carrying a pitcher and a stack of plastic glasses wrapped in clear plastic film.

"Just fluffing up," Pamela said with a comfy sigh. "I feel so much better now. And I'm not dizzy anymore, either. It just goes to show you that doctors don't know everything, now do they?"

Eku grumbled, "You got that right," as she walked over and set everything down on the nightstand. Without comment, she unwrapped a glass and poured it half full. Handing it to Pamela, she said in a maternal sort of way, "Now, just take a few baby sips at first . . . wait for it to settle . . . then try a little more."

Pamela did exactly what she was told even though she wanted to chug it down, and the rest of the pitcher, too.

Eku nodded approvingly as she patted the drug meter standing beside her. "You're scheduled for meds in half an hour, although it seems silly, since I don't see any sign of you being in pain."

Pamela was quick to affirm Eku's observation

with a shake of her head in the hope that it might weigh in her favor when she made her feelings known about not wanting another drop of morphine.

Eku gave the drug dispenser a light tap. "Maybe you should ask the doctor to cut the dose back. This stuff can be addicting for some people . . . but you don't strike me as being the type."

Pamela chose her words carefully so as to make certain that her feelings about Dr. Jeffrey didn't accidentally show through.

"That's a good idea. Who do you suggest I speak with?"

Eku appeared to struggle with her thoughts before saying with a distinct note of reservation, "I know that Dr. Jeffrey is your attending physician. But if I were—"

She caught herself. "You didn't hear this from me, mind you, but the specialist on call . . . the one who cut you open and saved your life . . . is not only one of the best heart surgeons we have on staff here at Presby, but also a first-rate cardiologist."

A smile began to work its way onto Eku's face. "I think you'd like her, too. Dr. Evangelista is as smart as they come. Too smart, I'm afraid, for some of the men around here. Especially the older ones like—"

Eku shook her head and went silent.

Carmen? "Is Dr. Evangelista by any chance—"

Can't be, she thought, and muttered, "Thanks for the advice."

"Not *my* advice, mind you . . . I'm just a nurse."

Snatching up the tote, Eku was about to leave, but paused and said in a suddenly serious vein, "Just so you know . . . everyone here's pulling for you." She became quiet, her gaze steady, and said respectfully, "We know who you are, and what you and your foundation have done for the hospital. Especially the children's ward." She gave Pamela an affectionate pat and a rub on the thigh. "You want anything, *anything,* you just ask." She winked. "Okay?"

Pamela wanted to say, *How about my clothes and a cab?*

Instead, she said in a quiet and contrite, but nonetheless serious tone of voice, "Thank you . . . I'll keep that in mind."

As Eku slipped out into the hall, she turned back and winked again. "Why don't I call and have one of the volunteers stop up?"

She began toying with a smile. "They can do something with that hospital hair of yours, make you feel like a woman again."

Without waiting for a reply, Eku turned and disappeared down the hall, her throaty laugh trailing after her.

Pamela listened intently as her footsteps faded into the background of murmuring voices, squeaky carts, guarded whispers and the occasional twitter of nervous laughter. Once she was certain that she was alone, she reclaimed her booty. Without checking the contents, she hastily tore open one of the packets and immediately braced herself when a syringe fell into her lap. The moment she saw that the needle end was safely jacketed with a plastic sleeve, she gave up a sigh of relief and whispered, "Stupid is lucky."

Doing her best to rein in her excitement, she moved quickly. With her gaze fixed on her intended task, and listening for the slightest telltale sound of someone approaching, she peeled back one side of the tape holding down the trap for the morphine feed.

An unfamiliar sound startled her into slipping her arm beneath the sheets and holding her breath—listening and waiting. After an endless moment of silence, she told herself, "It's just your imagination," and bit the plastic sleeve protecting the needle end of the syringe. Pulling it off ever so carefully, she spit it as far away from the bed as she could. While holding the IV line between her teeth to keep it from pulling the trap out, she used the needle to prick holes in the thin plastic tubing for the length of an inch or so above the point where the trap pierced her skin.

Next, but with greater care, she lifted the feed line just short of pulling out the trap and did the same to the underneath side of the tubing. After setting the syringe down on the bed and making certain it wouldn't roll off, she ripped open the other packet and shook out a small, square, padded bandage. Peeling it apart, she pressed it to her arm just beneath the IV line where it was peppered with pinholes, which had begun to ooze a crystal clear liquid.

A creaking noise brought her efforts to a breathless halt again. Her immediate reaction was to slip her arm under the sheet and lie back, waiting and watching and praying. A candy-striper, blond and blue-eyed and barely eighteen, smiled innocently as she walked past the open door pushing a snack cart with squeaky wheels.

Alone again, Pamela resecured the trap and meticulously smoothed out the wrinkles in the tape so that it looked like nothing had been touched. With a scoop of her hand, she palmed the shreds of paper from the packets and pinched up the backing from the bandage. She ignored the dull throbbing in her chest as she fell back into the pillows and began wondering if what she had done would work. And if it did, how much morphine would leak out and how much would make its way into her veins. And whether or not what leaked out could be absorbed through her skin. She even tried to guess how much time she had before someone found out what she'd done and put it all back the way it was. Unlike most everything else in her life, however, now Pamela didn't have a single answer.

The sound of footsteps approaching, and not the distinctive strike of Eku's long, graceful stride, abruptly ended her inquiry.

"Damn," she whispered when she realized she was holding her own incriminating evidence.

About to stuff it under the pillow again, she surprised herself by hurling the syringe across the room. Striking the wall, it shattered and fell to the floor in hundreds of barely visible chards. She was about to pop the paper into her mouth and eat it, but instead slipped her hand beneath the sheets and tucked the evidence under her thigh. She shut her eyes in an effort to feign sleep just as the footsteps appeared at her door, followed by a woman saying playfully, "Welcome back from the dead, PJ."

PJ? Pamela looked up. *"Evi . . . is that you?"*

"In the flesh . . . or should I say bones." Carmen laughed. "A good forty pounds lighter and ten years older. But . . . and excuse my French . . . as happy as the proverbial pig in shit."

Carmen stepped up and gave Pamela an affectionate kiss on the cheek. "But I'm even happier to see that you're okay."

Pamela instantly felt safe for the first time since waking up and finding herself in the hospital. Her newly discovered sense of security was

Donald Beman

quickly replaced by curiosity as she watched Carmen slip the stethoscope from around her neck. There was something about her, something different, and not just the ten years that had separated them, or the weight she had lost. "What happened to being a lawyer?" Pamela asked as she tried but failed to catch Carmen's gaze. "Too easy for the girl genius from Barcelona?"

Carmen shook her head. "Nope . . . too sleazy. I went back to medical school. Never should have dropped out in the first place."

She seemed to force a laugh, yet there wasn't an ounce of humor in her voice when she said drolly, "Never should have gotten married, either. Found out too late . . . no, I finally faced the truth about myself . . . that marriage just wasn't meant to be, at least not for *this* girl. But then, you probably suspected that."

Confused by Carmen's reply, Pamela asked, "I don't understand; what are you trying to—"

"And you?" Carmen asked, cutting Pamela off. "Ever make it down the aisle, or haven't you found anyone who can keep up with you?" Appearing not to need an answer to her question, Carmen carefully opened Pamela's surgical gown, exposing a nest of wires and terminals and crisscrossing strips of tape securing the foot-long incision down her chest from her neck to her stomach.

"Okay . . . let's have a listen to that heart of yours."

"Think it's still there?" Pamela asked and smiled, but quickly frowned when she glanced down and saw for the first time what her chest looked like. "I guess I won't be needing my bikini anymore!"

Smiling, Carmen pressed her finger to her lips as she tenderly placed the business end of the stethoscope against Pamela's bare skin and turned her head. Seconds ticked off. "If you can," she said in a quiet voice, "take a deep breath and hold it."

Pamela obeyed enthusiastically, only to wince and shut her eyes. "Sorry." She sighed and took a moment to catch her breath.

"Take your time; I'm in no hurry. You're my last stop, then I'm out of here. And it's none too soon, either. It's been one crisis after another for fourteen hours." She smiled and said with a twist of irony, "And for once . . . *thank God* . . . it wasn't you."

Pamela took a deep breath, only this time more slowly.

Carmen whispered, "Good girl . . . now hold it." She closed her eyes. "Okay, breathe normally." She placed the stethoscope on Pamela's neck, over her carotid artery, then slowly moved it down the side and over her chest. She stopped just to the left of the taped-over incision marking

219

the spot where they had cracked Pamela open. "Can you roll over onto your right side?"

Pamela said a bit hesitantly, "I *think* so."

Carmen placed her hand on Pamela's shoulder, stopping her.

"Would you like me to give you a hit of morphine and wait a bit for it to take effect?"

Pamela shook her head as she rolled over onto her side and said with a throaty growl, "I want that goddamned machine out of here. Now. I don't need that shit anymore. I *hate* it! I'd rather have the pain than what that damned drug does to me."

Carmen mumbled to herself, "Still gotta be in control, I see."

Ignoring the comment, Pamela caught her breath and asked, "Can you arrange to have that thing disconnected?"

Carmen shook her head. "I'm not your attending—"

"You are now," Pamela said with unquestioned authority.

"Not so fast, PJ. We're friends. As a matter of ethics . . . and according to the policy here at Presbyterian . . . I'm not—"

"That didn't stop you from cutting me open, now did it?"

Carmen shot back, *"That's* different. I didn't know it was you until *after* the anesthesiologist told me that I better be careful, because I was operating on one of the hospital's biggest patrons."

She chuckled and said with a certain pompous, yet playful inflection, "Dr. Pamela J. Eagleston, Chairman of—"

"Okay, okay . . . I get the message. But I still want you as my attending physician . . . not that insensitive son of a—"

"I see that you two have met," Eku said in a bubbly voice as she walked in carrying a clipboard in her hand and made a beeline for the drug dispenser. "It says here that you get—"

"No!" Pamela snarled and reached out, blocking Eku's path.

"I don't want that goddamned—"

"Take it easy, PJ," Carmen ordered with a comforting rub of Pamela's bare back. "You're giving your heart fits, which is *exactly* why Dr. Jeffrey prescribed the morphine. You must—"

"I like the pain," Pamela insisted. "It reminds me how much I hate the bitch who did this to me."

Carmen exchanged perplexed glances with Eku, frowned and asked, *"Bitch?* What are you trying to—"

Pamela suddenly gasped and arched her back and shut her eyes as her fingers balled up into rock-hard fists. Shaking, she whispered through her clenched teeth, "Evi . . . you know me . . . and you know that I've never lied to you. Please don't do this. If you'll cancel the drug script, I'll be a good girl. I promise."

She forced herself to take a deep breath and let it out slowly as she asked with a heartfelt sigh, "Please?"

"PJ . . . this isn't fair. There's a protocol, and I—"

"Screw fair!" Pamela said with an awkward laugh and immediately winced again. "And to hell with your *goddamned* protocol. Since when did *you* ever follow the—"

A loud beeping startled Pamela into silence.

"That's me," Carmen announced and checked the pager clipped to the inside of her hip pocket. Easing Pamela onto her back, she withdrew a palm-sized cell phone from her other pocket.

"Excuse me," she said with an apologetic smile and stepped away from the bed.

Eku chimed in, "Dr. Evangelista . . . if you won't be needing me here, may I go now?" She casually let her hand come to rest on Pamela's arm and started tapping her finger, as if she was sending a secret message. "I don't see a need for the meds . . . do you?"

Carmen pursed her lips into a thoughtful but harmless scowl. She appeared to bite her lip, then nodded and waved Eku off.

Eku gave Pamela a discreet pat and left.

Pamela couldn't help staring at the cell phone and trying to figure out how she could talk Carmen into leaving it with her.

Fat chance!

Carmen turned away and tapped in a few numbers. When she spoke, her words were guarded, making it impossible for Pamela to hear what she was saying, though she tried. The exchange was brief and pointed. Carmen clapped the phone shut and turned back.

Seizing the opportunity, Pamela asked, "Mind if I borrow that cell phone to make a few calls?" She raised her hands in a posture of surrender and said with an innocent smile, "No business . . . just a few personal calls . . . I promise."

Carmen stood staring at Pamela, a look of suspicion in her eyes, which evaporated when she handed over the phone. "I'm going to tell Eku to give you ten minutes . . . or less, if Dr. Jeffrey shows up on the floor . . . then she's to come in and take the phone away from you. And don't give her a hard time . . . understand?"

Not wanting to risk saying anything that might possibly change Carmen's mind and jeopardize her use of the phone, Pamela held her tongue and tried her best to look compliant: not an easy task.

Carmen gestured to the other side of the bed. "I really shouldn't do this, but I'm going to put a hold on the morphine. But I'm leaving strict instructions for it to be resumed . . . and at full dosage . . . if you start acting up again. That should keep Bob Jeffrey out of here, at least until he speaks with me. At any rate, he's *not* going to be happy about this."

Carmen gave Pamela a womanly scowl and said with a clear warning, "And if he . . . or anyone else . . . comes in here in the next ten minutes, you better not get caught with that phone. Make believe you're out of it from the morphine. Play dead. You should be pretty good at that by now," she said with a nervous laugh.

Her face suddenly went blank. "I gotta go," Carmen said and darted out of the room before Pamela could even thank her.

With both hands shaking, unable to believe her good luck, Pamela sorted out her options. She considered how much time she had, what she had to do and in what order. With a determined nod, she entered a number and hit the SEND button. Pressing the phone to her ear as if it were a security blanket, she kept her other ear tuned to the sounds in the hall as she watched for silent shadows on the wall. Sitting up, she said excitedly, "John, it's me."

She smiled. "I'm fine, thank you."

Her jaw tightened. "Just listen and don't ask any questions. I want you to pack an overnighter for me, the usual stuff, then drive up to Blue Fields and find Dr. MacDonald. In case I haven't been able to reach him . . . he could be out running . . . tell him I called and told you to do this. Then come get me out of here."

Pamela's eyes flickered. She nodded. "Good

point. Then get hold of Charles Andrews and have him make a few calls to—"

She stopped and held her breath when she heard Eku talking to someone down the hall. She was speaking unusually loud, even for her. She smiled. *You're a sweetheart.*

"Gotta go," she whispered into the phone. "Ciao."

Scanning the keypad, frantically looking for a MUTE RING button but not finding one, she impatiently clapped the phone shut and with a smile tucked it under her butt. *Now play dead,* she told herself and shut her eyes, turning up her blind senses and tuning them to the familiar sound of Sean's strong, confident stride.

The first footstep into the room raised a doubt; the second confirmed it. *Damn.* The stranger took another few steps—seemed to hesitate— then slowly walked up to the foot of the bed and stopped. Pamela considered the possibility that it might be Dr. Jeffrey but rejected that thought when she remembered that he had never once been in her room without an entourage of groveling residents, or at the very least a pair of nurses. Galeal Faraahd's face slipped into her thoughts, then right back out when she recalled the heavier stride of the faceless visitor.

Her next thought was that the press had picked up on what had happened, which meant that this stranger could be any one of a hundred people who knew her. Faces began flashing through her mind—staffers from the foundation, trustees from the Met, even more from the dozen non-profit boards she sat on—not one of whom she could honestly call a friend, someone who would simply walk in without first having had a secretary call for them. That thought, not having a friend, had never crossed her mind before. Now that it had, it left her feeling alone, which only added to her growing sense of uneasiness with a nameless and faceless stranger at her bedside. She suddenly felt vulnerable, which instantly ignited a firestorm of memories that were just as quickly doused when she recalled Eku's parting words, "Why don't I call and have one of the volunteers stop up?"

Relieved, and feeling stupid, she was about to open her eyes when she was startled by a hand on her chest, followed by a frigid cold crystallizing throughout her body and freezing every muscle, dulling her thoughts, encasing her heart in a block of ice. *You!*

Though soft and plastic-sounding, the endless clicking was deafening. She braced herself, hoping that what she'd done would work as she forced herself to think, *He doesn't love me anymore,* repeating it in her mind in metered time with every infuriating tap of the button until everything went black.

Chapter Twenty-six

Thank God I'm alive was the first thought that passed through Sean's mind when he was startled awake by the bone-jarring sounds of metal striking metal, out-of-breath grunts and groans and a tornado of muted voices swirling around him. Hidden in the cacophony was a familiar voice, an oasis of calm amid the chaos. A microsecond later he heard a second voice. Though her words were faint, causing him to wonder if he'd heard them or thought them, the tenor of her angry reply—the sound of someone scratching their fingernails across a chalkboard—was crystal clear.

He raised his head off the pillow to find Carmen standing at the foot of the bed. Her face was blank, a sheet of black ice, her cold blue eyes floating just beneath the frozen surface. She folded her arms into a wiry knot and asked, "So, how do we feel?"

We? We! He was instantly obsessed with what she had said, in spite of the fact that he knew it was nothing more than a figure of speech. He waited for a sign from her—a reassuring word, a touch of her hand, a caring smile—anything that would tell him that he was all right. Nothing. He wanted to shout, *Say something for chrissake!* even though he knew that she couldn't tell him what he wanted to know; what he now feared. *Where the hell is she?* exploded in his mind as he replayed his last few seconds of consciousness, his heart racing out of control.

He knew she hadn't been herself ever since he saw her in the cemetery. She hadn't been the Annie Parker he had known and once loved, and perhaps still did in some way. Or was it the memory of her he loved? *You don't even know who she is!* And he didn't, after all; it had been years since they had seen each other. She would have changed. *She must have changed.* And she had; he just didn't want to believe it, he wanted her to be a touchstone—an island in his mind—a place where he could go and feel safe.

How could you have been so blind?

Fearing the worst, knowing all too well what could have happened last night if his instincts were right, he shut his eyes and imagined that he was inside himself—his body, not his mind. He'd done this hundreds of times before, but always while running, and for other reasons. He knew exactly what to listen for, knew every subtle sound and telltale symptom. He had taken the time to learn every part of his anatomy—the major arteries, the veins, the vital organs, even the neural pathways—so he would know precisely where to cut. He had convinced himself he could do it, and before he lost consciousness, to a point where he had taken to carrying a small pocket knife with him whenever he went running, the blade honed to a surgically sharp edge. It was a scene that he'd written and rewritten in his mind at least a thousand times—turning fantasy into reality as he so often did—cutting himself open and spreading his ribs and slipping his hand inside his chest, massaging his heart back to life before it could fail him.

Silence. *Shit!* Frantic, his thoughts caught in a time warp, the Universal Clock approaching the speed of light, the hands about to stop and turn back—leaving him stranded somewhere in time, lost and forgotten—he took a shallow breath and held on to it, listening. Still nothing. He took another sip of that heavenly nectar, which was nonetheless bitter with worry. He drew the air deep down into his lungs, savoring every delicious drop of the life-giving elixir. To his relief all he could feel was the slow, steady, rhythmic beating of his heart, sending a solitary message of hope. "I feel fine," he finally said with a tentative smile.

Carmen pursed her face into an unreadable frown as she stuffed her hands into the pockets of her white hospital coat. In so doing, she pulled the fabric into taut, parallel folds, creating the grotesque illusion that she was clutching fistfuls of steel cables hidden inside her coat and wound through her body, holding her together: a Borg posing as a human. "Problems?" Sean asked warily and fought to stifle a nervous laugh. "Did you find—"

He broke off his question, knowing he couldn't ask what he really wanted to know. "It was just a mild heart attack, right?"

"Just a mild heart attack! Do you have any idea—"

"Save the speech," Sean snapped, surprising himself with his impatient outburst. "Just tell me what you found."

Carmen stiffened for a moment, then appeared to relax. But outside, not inside. Her words were just as taut as the folds in her white coat when she said slowly, "Your cardiac enzymes were normal. But we'll keep drawing blood to make sure. So was your EKG . . . except for a slight ST elevation. At this point, I can't say for certain what caused your heart to race the way it did, or for you to pass out. Thankfully, the paramedics got to you right away and wired you up and transmitted everything to our emergency CCU.

"When I saw the heart rate and the nature of the arrhythmia . . . you've what I would guess are benign premature ventricular complexes . . . coupled with the fact that your pulse-ox was ninety-eight and you were responsive, even though you were unconscious . . . which didn't make any sense given the symptoms, and still doesn't . . . I told them to give you a shot of Atenolol to try and slow down your heart."

Grasping hold of what Carmen had said, ignoring his instincts, ignoring what he knew he'd felt, Sean thought, *See, it wasn't her!* It was as if he was arguing with himself, pitting science and reason against intuition. *If it was her, she wouldn't have let Annie call an ambulance; she had what she wanted.* A shiver rippled through his body, the sensation of someone stepping on his grave, followed by the question, *But what if that's not what she wants?*

Carmen smiled and said with a sense of pride, "The Atenolol worked like a charm."

Pulling her hand out of her pocket, she held up a folded-over piece of paper the size of a credit card. On one side was bone-white block lettering set against a magenta background spelling out the words STENT IMPLANT CARD. On the flip side was a thinly drawn sketch in black of a human heart crawling with arteries. One of the larger arteries had three xs struck over it, one near the top, another in the middle and a third close to the narrowed base of the heart. Waving the card at him, she asked in a condescending voice, "Would you mind telling me what the *hell* you were thinking of when you went running? Are you crazy . . . or do you have a death wish?"

Sean tried snatching it away from her, only to find that he couldn't move his hand. When he glanced down, he saw that his wrist was tied to the side of the bed and a flattened baseball-sized wad of gauze was tapped to the inside of his arm, just below his armpit. His expression must have said what he was thinking, because before he could ask what had happened, Carmen told him, "I did an emergency angiogram . . . that's the pressure bandage over the arterial incision. The restraint is to keep you from moving."

Sean wanted to shout, "What the fuck do you think you were doing?" Instead, he asked calmly, "Was that *really* necessary?"

But the pitch of his voice had sent a different message, one that if spoken would have been an octave above a primal scream.

Carmen fanned the card in his face again as if to taunt him. "I did the angio because the paramedics found *this* in the pocket of your running shorts. Since the stents were less than six months old . . . and there was a slight abnormality in your EKG . . . I was concerned that you might have experienced a failure in one of the stents. If you had, considering it was your right coronary artery, you could have been experiencing a reduction of blood flow to the sinoatrial node, which might have explained the tachycardia. On the other hand, you could have been facing a massive coronary. Either way, I wasn't about to take any chances with a wait-and-see approach. That's not my style. So I went in and took a look for myself. If the stents had gone bad . . . or had been blocked and couldn't be cleared . . . you'd now have a foot-long scar down the center of your chest from a bypass. Or you might be dead."

She reached her free hand into her pocket and pulled out a small pen knife. "The EMTs also found *this* along with the stent implant card. I figure it's got to be some sort guy thing, right?"

With an explanation out of the question, Sean simply nodded.

Carmen responded by tapping his nose with the card. "For the record, your stents are fine. And no, you did *not* have a heart attack, so you can relax. Unless the tox screen I ordered shows me something else, I'm afraid all I can do is classify the cause as idiopathic. One thing I can tell you, however, is that most men your age . . . and many much younger than you . . . would not have fared as well as you did. With a sustained heart rate of over two hundred, it's doubtful that their hearts could have kept up for very long, which is a testimony to the condition you're in."

Sean flashed a smug grin, then just as quickly frowned as he asked, "Tox screen . . . as in drugs? But I don't use—"

"Not just recreational drugs, but anything that might have sparked this unexplained tachycardia. If we can't find an organic cause, I strongly suggest that you consider further tests to see if there's a problem somewhere, and correct it so this doesn't happen again." She paused for a moment. "It could be something as simple as an electrolyte imbalance . . . or something far more serious. At any rate, if left unchecked, it could well be fatal. So for now, just take it easy . . . and no running . . . understand?"

Carmen affectionately patted Sean on his side, causing him to wince. Pulling the sheet back, she placed her open hand on his abdomen and slowly moved it around, while gently pressing down.

When he jumped again, she asked, "Where does it hurt?"

In an effort to cover himself in case she lifted the hospital gown and took a look for herself and saw the bruises on his sides, he told her, "I tripped and fell against one of those headstones."

"Does it hurt here too?" she asked, pressing down on the center of his belly.

"Not anymore. The belladonna I took must have—"

"You took *what?*"

"Belladonna elixir. I had some left over from—"

"I don't believe it! How much did you take?" she demanded.

Sean frowned, thought for a moment and gave a casual shrug. "Two, maybe three tea-spoonfuls . . . maybe more? . . . I'm not sure."

"Do you have any idea what a drug like that can do to the heart? You could have—"

Carmen paused and shook her head in obvious dismay. "Stupid is lucky," she muttered to herself, though she sounded more like she was talking to someone else. "What are you trying to prove by this running . . . that you're twenty instead of fortysomething?"

The last thing that Sean needed right now was a self-appointed bedside shrink. As far as he was concerned, running made him feel good . . . and it kept him alive . . . *period, end of discussion.*

Carmen laughed, but more to herself, and appeared to relax, revealing an unusual turn of mood Sean hadn't seen in her before.

"Trying to stay a few steps ahead of the Devil?" she asked.

Sean recoiled upon hearing her repeat almost word-for-word what he had said to Annie. He tried telling himself that Annie must have said something, no doubt amused by his comment. But it didn't help; his instincts told him that something wasn't right.

She stepped away from the bed. "I suppose I really shouldn't talk. After all, I used to run thirty . . . maybe forty miles a week. But there's precious little time for that now."

Her eyes suddenly lit up as an unusually feminine smile spread across her face, adding to Sean's uneasiness. "As a matter of fact, PJ and I used to run the beaches in Bridge Hampton, and it was the *rare* guy who could keep up with us."

Sean asked quizzically, *"PJ . . . as in Pamela?"*

Carmen's reply was a quick nod.

He suddenly felt like a jerk for having been so wrapped up in himself that he hadn't thought to ask how she was. He sat up, but at a tilt because his hand was tethered to the side rail of the bed. Before he could ask, Carmen said brightly, "Relax; she's doing great, thank God." She didn't stop there, however, and went on to tell Sean about Pamela, drifting back and forth between her medical condition and touchy-feely girl-talk things from their summers in Bridge Hampton. The more she talked, the more it became evident that she really did know Pamela—and far too well not to have been the friend she had claimed to be—forcing Sean to recast once again the image he had formed in his mind, though reluctantly.

"We first met in Spain . . . in Cadiz . . . when—"

She abruptly changed course, replaying the

Bridge Hampton scenes, but not before Sean had been reminded of those perplexing exchanges in Spanish between Pamela and Carmen. And the angry bite from Carmen's words when she'd shouted, "Stay out of this!" and shoved him aside with a surprisingly powerful sweep of her arm.

Suddenly uncomfortable, his feelings having erased his thoughts as they so often did, Sean asked, "Where are my clothes?"

Carmen raised her hands in protest. "Not so fast. I want to admit you for observation . . . at least forty-eight hours . . . just to make sure that—"

A beeper sounded, cutting her off. As she reached into her pocket, a nurse pushed her way through the curtains and said in a tense whisper, "You've got code on the seventh floor."

"It's Pamela . . . isn't it?" Sean blurted out and stood up, only to be jerked back by the gauze handcuffing him to the bed.

"Get this fucking—"

"No!" Carmen ordered. "You can't—"

"Like hell I can't," Sean growled as he ripped the IV feed out of his arm and reached into her pocket, retrieving his knife.

Flipping it open, he cut himself free with a single swipe and pushed his way through the curtains with an angry sweep of his arm.

Chapter Twenty-seven

Eku Malawatumba and a young male resident, as white as she was black, were standing at the foot of Pamela's bed. Bent over, her head cocked, stethoscope in hand, Carmen was listening intently to Pamela's heart. Sean was standing on the opposite side of the bed, barefoot and wearing nothing more than his hospital gown. His forearm was covered with dried blood from where he'd ripped out the IV trap. Beside him was Dr. Faraahd, her mysterious gaze tracking Carmen's every move, even the blink of her eyes. The only sound breaking the solemn silence was a slow . . . beep . . . beep . . . beep.

"It doesn't make any sense," Carmen whispered to herself.

Unable to bear it any longer—certain that he

would explode if he couldn't touch her—Sean
reached out and gently brushed the hair off Pamela's forehead, earning Galeal's instant disapproval.

Pretending not to have seen her, he began to
trace the lines of Pamela's face with the tips of
his fingers. It was something he had often done
after they'd made love and she was lying beside
him, her eyes closed, drifting in and out of sleep.
When he caressed her cheek with his open hand,
the monitor began beeping faster, causing everyone but him to glance up at the screen.

With a soft clucking of her tongue and a shake
of her head, Galeal reached out to pull Sean's
hand away, but Carmen blocked her well-
intentioned effort with a gentle sweep of her
hand.

"It's all right," she said reassuringly.

A faint smile softened her dark mahogany face
long enough for her to say, "Women are like that
with the men they love," before she turned to
confront her colleagues at the foot of the bed.

Based upon what he had witnessed only moments earlier, when she charged into the room,
strafing everyone with rapid-fire questions and
bull's-eye orders, then calling a unilateral truce
with a decisive wave of her hand, Sean fully expected Carmen to pick up where she'd left off.
Judging from the way everyone was standing,
shoulders back, eyes forward, lacking only the

blindfolds, it appeared to him that they too expected the worst. Galeal, however, was preoccupied with the morphine pump and the IV line.

To Sean's surprise, Carmen was soft spoken when, through a sigh, she said to the young resident, "I want an EKG and a complete blood workup right away, and make sure the lab knows *who* wants it."

Her next order was handed down to Eku. "See if you can find a robe for Dr. MacDonald, then take care of his arm."

"Wait," Galeal said in a guarded tone of voice, freezing everyone in place. She tapped a button on the pump, calling up a digital display filled with a row of red zeros. "It's empty!"

Carmen was at her side in an instant, hitting the very same button and getting the same result. She did it again. "Damn."

Spinning around, she pointed to Eku and said, "I want epi, fifty cc's . . . *stat!*" and dispatched her with a wave of her hand.

She glanced up at Sean, her eyes filled with fire and ice.

"You'll have to—"

"Forget it," he snapped and placed his hand on Pamela's shoulder. "I'm not going anywhere."

When the beeping suddenly began to slow, sounding an alarm, Carmen shoved Sean up against the wall and turned around.

Dead Love

"Eku!" she shouted. "Where the hell is that—"

Bursting into the room, Eku lunged forward and slipped a syringe into Carmen's outstretched hand with the practiced skill of an Olympic sprinter handing off a baton in a 4 × 100 relay race.

"It's twenty," she gasped. "It's all we had on the floor."

Chapter Twenty-eight

With an empty glass in one hand and a half-full bottle of burgundy in the other, Annie stumbled into the soft, flickering candlelight of the bathroom and fell up against the wall. After taking a moment to steady herself, she slowly slid down onto her knees and clumsily poured another glass of wine. Then she set the bottle on the floor, taking care to put it within reach of the tub.

Cradling the glass in both hands, she took a long, lustful sip. Wine dribbled down her chin, spotting her white satin peignoir and dripping onto the tiled ceramic floor. Denied the sanctuary of her own mind, she quickly snuffed out the thoughts that were sparked by the startling contrast of the blood-red wine on the bone-white tiles and sat gazing blindly at the flames dancing atop the candles circling the sink.

An hour earlier, armed with her first bottle of wine, she had ringed the sink with candles and lit each one. She then turned the heat in the house all the way up and went about shuttering the windows and drawing the curtains and switching off every light. With each planful step taken she was peppered with one anxious question after another, asking—demanding!—to know what she was doing, and why. Her calm, reassuring replies, followed by a casual but deliberate sip of wine, had succeeded in masking her motive.

The only window not battened down was the large bay window in the kitchen that faced the old barn behind the house, and the open fields that bordered the creek feeding the reservoir. Perched on the window seat and working on her second bottle of wine, Annie had watched the cold, antiseptic gaze of the full moon cleanse the nightly landscape of its infectious shadows, leaving untouched the shadow poisoning her, as if it were immune to that heavenly light.

"I hate you," she growled through her teeth and suddenly sat up, fearful that her unguarded feelings might have once again betrayed her.

Without waiting to find out if the wine had begun to work its mysterious magic, she wiped her fingers back and forth through the telltale drops spotting the tiled floor, erasing the colorful abstract images before they could paint a revealing picture in her mind and expose her. Then, with a disconsolate sigh—as if she were being forced against her will—she struggled to her feet and stood facing the full-length mirror. Her movements were stiff and mechanical as she untied the peignoir and slipped it off her shoulders, letting it fall to the floor. She stood motionless, examining her undraped body. As if she had been programmed, she paused to consider every aspect of her full, womanly figure, finding flaws where there were none. She hesitated and waited obediently to hear the criticism that had become a constant refrain, but to her surprise not a single cruel word was uttered.

Relieved, but nonetheless wary, she peered into the reflection of her own eyes, expecting to find that all-too-familiar emptiness: a bottomless pit filled with the private thoughts and intimate deeds stolen from the dozens of faceless and nameless women she had come to know, waiting to be toyed with for Judith's perverse pleasure. Was she finally alone? Was her plan working? Or was this just another game of hers? Annie forced herself to wait, even though time was not on her side. She knew all too well that if she risked a careless thought, allowed a feeling to slip out—or permitted even the slightest flicker of hope to flare up in her heart—she would be pounced upon, her silent screams of protest added to the deafening chorus of cries now trapped inside her head.

It had become a game of cat and mouse: she the prey, her thoughts and feelings the scent, the lure, the bait; the unseen silhouette lurking inside her the insatiable predator, stalking body and mind, as yet unable to capture her soul. But Annie now knew that it wasn't her she wanted. She was simply a means to an end, as were all the other women before her, necessary hosts providing nourishment and amusement: a single night from the weakest, a year at best from the strongest, but usually only a month or two as Judith waited impatiently for what she wanted most.

"Not if I can help it," Annie whispered as she refilled her glass and drained it. Although she was already numb all over, she didn't want to take any chances, so she quickly topped it up again. She knew that if she was wrong, that if she misjudged even by a second, the pain would cripple her before she could do what she had to do—what she had decided to do the moment she had left Pamela's room—but dared not let herself think about.

With a bumbling slap of her hand, she closed the drain in the tub and turned on the water. At first she alternated hot and cold, then steadily turned on only the hot water. She knew it would burn her but didn't care. "You killed her," she snarled under her breath and immediately felt an icy chill stirring in her chest.

Frightened, she quickly drained the glass and refilled it.

Dizzy, the room spinning, she stepped into the tub, easing herself down into the steaming hot water, which instantly took her breath away. As the heat seeped into her body, melting the icy grip, she winced and sat up and said in a breathless yet calm and reassuring voice, "It's all right . . . relax . . . you'll be fine."

She waited, measuring her every heartbeat. Then she nodded, as if she had been given permission, and slowly slid back down until the water was circling her neck. After draining the glass again, she reached over the side of the tub and patted the air for the bottle of wine, only to knock it over. Striking the hard ceramic tile with a sharp crack, the bottle shattered into dozens of jagged green shards, spilling its contents all over the floor.

No sooner done than Annie whispered, "No," as she fought to stifle the carefully hidden thoughts that had been released from the depths of her soul against her will by the unnerving sight of the razor-sharp glass and the stark-white floor splattered with wine. Desperate—certain that she would be found out if she didn't do something, and quickly—she tipped her head back and shut her eyes and took a quiet breath, having decided to give up the only thing she had been able hold back, though the demands upon her had been fierce.

After taking another breath, bolstering her courage, she slipped her hand between her thighs and parted her unwilling flesh. The stirring she had felt in her chest only seconds earlier suddenly grew still, expectant. With every gentle stroke of her finger, she sensed an unwanted hunger that left a bitter taste in her mouth.

Numb to everything but her own touch, Annie raised her other hand and began to caress her breast, her nipple, while giving up thoughts that until now she had refused to relinquish. With each new image turned over, tears squeezing through her shuttered eyelids, the cold slowly released its deadly grip on her heart and mind as it slithered down into her belly, coiling itself— tighter and tighter—around the innermost depths of her loins. Warmed by the nutrient-rich flow of blood engorging her flesh, it hungrily fed upon the waves of pleasure, satisfying itself again and again, leaving her bloodied—the water stained red—but finally free.

Chapter Twenty-nine

With an impatient flipping of her hands, Carmen ushered Eku out of the room and closed the door. Turning around, she fell back against it and stood eyeing Pamela, who was sitting up in bed with the help of pillows stuffed all around her. With a shake of her finger, Carmen snarled affectionately, "You are one *lucky* woman."

She laughed. "And . . . I must admit . . . one smart cookie."

Fighting the lingering effects of the morphine in her system yet to be metabolized—she was anything but tired—all Pamela could manage was a halfhearted smile on the cocky side of proud.

Carmen shook her head, as if to say *of course, how stupid of me.* "Okay." She sighed. "It's just us girls now . . . not even the two cops outside your door can hear us . . . *talk* to me, PJ."

She walked over and collapsed into the armchair at Pamela's bedside, where she'd spent the better part of the last eight hours.

"And you can start by telling me what the hell *really* happened that night you landed here in the emergency room. Maybe that'll help explain why someone would want to try and kill you. And damnit, girl, you must have known . . . or at least suspected something . . . or you wouldn't have done what you did to the IV line."

Folding her arms over her chest, Carmen said with an exasperated sigh, "And take all the time you need, 'cause I'm not about to go anywhere. I'll be lucky if I can keep my eyes open."

An amused smile slowly worked its way onto her face as she kicked off her running shoes and propped her feet up on the bed. "And if I do nod off, at least this time . . . and I don't need to be reminded that no one knows it better than you! . . . it sure as hell won't be from having had too much to drink, now will it?"

"Nope," was all Pamela said. After all, given what she had been through with Carmen during their lost summer together—what for Carmen had been a nonstop binge, as if she were trying to drown something inside her—nothing more needed to be said.

Carmen sank down into the chair until her

chin was resting on her chest and mumbled, "I'm all ears. Just remember, it's *me* you're talking to . . . and not one of those detectives who were here . . . so you're going to have to try the truth this time."

In that instant Jack Nicholson's classic line from *A Few Good Men,* which he'd shouted at Tom Cruise from the witness stand—*You can't handle the truth!*—was all Pamela could think of as she sat staring at Carmen and toying with the idea of letting the cards fall where they may. But what was the truth? What she had seen in the cemetery, or more accurately what she hadn't seen? What she had heard, which could all too easily be rejected as imagined? And what about what she had felt; at least there was proof of that . . . *Just look at me!* . . . even though none of it made any sense, medical or otherwise. What about those unwanted images of Judith and Sean, and now Annie too—not only from now, but years ago—woven into a tawdry tapestry with her own intimate thoughts, to be replayed and relived, but for someone else's pleasure. And what about the memories that had been ripped from the hearts of dozens of other women and scattered throughout her mind?

"Truth or dare?" Pamela finally asked, smiling.

Carmen shrugged her shoulders. "Whatever."

"Okay. Let's start with the IV line. No, I didn't expect anyone to walk into my room and try to kill me. I was simply trying to keep you drug pushers from pumping that crap into me and turning me into a vegetable. So this *smart cookie* as you called me, was simply very lucky . . . not smart."

Carmen shook her head in denial. "Do you really expect—"

"Stuff it!" Pamela snapped. Then she said with an edge to her words, "You asked for the truth, now shut up and listen. I know you'll probably think I'm crazy when I tell you this, but—"

A shadow suddenly passed through Pamela's mind, distracting her. After regaining her thoughts, about to go on, it reappeared: It was a woman—*Annie?*—naked and standing directly in front of her, looking deep into her eyes. It was as if they were peering into each other's soul, one a mirrored image of the other. The gaze of yet another could also be seen, but in the distance and out of focus. As quickly as Annie had appeared, she was gone, replaced by a room, white and shiny, flickering lights spinning and smearing everything—thoughts and images—into a blur of white on white.

"Not if I can help it," Pamela mumbled to herself and sat up, startled, when she realized that the words were not her own.

She laughed, "And not *hers,* either, thank God."

Carmen playfully jiggled the bed with her foot

and asked, "What in the world are you talking about?"

Pamela suddenly felt numb all over. She began to touch her face, her cheeks, her lips. Frowning, she squeezed her hands into fists, then opened them and sat staring down into her palms as she started to rub the tips of her fingers with her thumbs.

Carmen stood up, wide-eyed, her gaze darting back and forth between the monitor over the bed and Pamela's face. She took hold of Pamela's wrist and began to nod reassuringly in perfect metered time—faster and faster—with every silent blip on the screen.

She gave Pamela a gentle shake. "PJ . . . you feel okay?"

Turning the tables, Pamela took Carmen's hand in her own and fell back into her throne of pillows. "It's really strange. It's as if she left part of herself behind, but only in my head, thank God! I can see and feel everything—"

She paused when Carmen scowled, disbelief written all over her face. "You want the goddamned truth or not?"

Clearly startled by Pamela's outburst, Carmen simply nodded.

"Then wipe that frown off your face and listen to me."

Stone-faced, Carmen pulled herself free of Pamela's grasp and sat down, doubt still flickering in her eyes and punctuating her words when she said in a controlled voice, "Okay, I'm listening."

Pamela took a much-needed breath and said quietly, "I can *literally* see what she sees. And I can feel what she feels, just like now. She's confused, or dazed . . . or something's wrong. And I'm just not sure whether those feelings are hers, Annie's or if what I'm feeling is what *she's* thinking, and I'm—"

Carmen raised her hands, signaling for a time out, and said in a leaden monotone, devoid of emotion, "Just who is this *she?*"

Pamela struck back as if she'd been hit. "The *bitch* who did this to me . . . that's who. And she's going to do the same—"

She suddenly began to shiver and braced herself, waiting, fearful. But nothing happened. After a moment, relieved but still wary, she realized that she hadn't actually felt the cold, but had instead thought it, which had prompted the unexpected shiver: a conditioned response—like anticipating the prick of a needle—learned through pain and not easily forgotten.

Before the illusion could fade, a wave of liquid heat washed over her, melting the icy grip of the chilling thoughts, followed by a ripple of angry demands. Slurred and unintelligible and fragile, as if frightened, they echoed harmlessly inside her head.

"PJ?" Carmen asked, her voice strained, the numbers steadily climbing on the monitor over the bed. "What is it?"

"It's all right . . . don't worry . . . I'll be fine," Pamela whispered, her words thin, vaporous, but not frail, as she closed her eyes. Unafraid, and deaf to Carmen's anxious calls, she sank deeper and deeper as the delicious heat warmed her body and mind.

She gracefully sidestepped the jagged images scattered about in her mind, ignoring the startling but harmless splatter of red on white. With each synaptic step taken, she deftly skirted the dendritic mines laid in the neural web Judith had spun throughout Annie's mind. Moving unseen and unheard, she methodically stole back bit by bit what had been taken from her. In exchange, she left behind hundreds of razor-sharp fragments from the broken dreams and shattered lives that had been scattered throughout her mind. She discarded the bitter shards of Judith's jealousy, growing stronger with every poisonous barb she plucked from her psyche and threw back. Fear and hate soon turned to vengeance.

As she slipped in and out of Annie's mind—sparked by what she felt but couldn't see—her own jealousy was slowly dissolved by compassion. Unable to find even one of Annie's tortured thoughts, she quickly realized that she too had learned to hide them from Judith. Tempted to try and help, certain that she knew where to look and what to say, she also knew . . . and painfully so . . . that if she did find even one of those precious thoughts, she could risk exposing them to Judith: a cold-blooded serpent coiled up somewhere inside Annie—in a corner of her mind, in an open wound of her ravaged body—lying in wait, silent and ready to strike and sink her fangs into the first sign of hope.

Determined to find every last piece of her mind, Pamela forced herself to turn away, though reluctantly, and left Annie to fight the battle that she herself had fought and, she desperately hoped, had won. She wanted those special memories, those intimate moments with Sean, however fleeting. She wanted every feeling, whether good or bad, every tender touch, and she wanted every one of those hidden secrets that only she knew. They were all hers and she wanted every one of them back, convinced that they were the memories that had built the bridge, the neural network, the link between Judith's thoughts and hers; and now Annie's too.

When she paused to toy with the idea of leaving behind lies of the heart, a few drops of her own poison, she felt something, someone—somewhere—stirring. Uncomfortable, about to pull herself free and grab hold of her consciousness, she was caught in a firestorm that flashed through her mind and leapt into her body; a circle of flames wildly dancing about and licking at her loins.

Trapped, an unwilling voyeur, she had no choice but to submit to the strange sensation of her flesh being warmed by the fire burning in another woman's body. As the flames grew hotter, fanned by the rancid breath of that sleeping serpent—awakened by lurid images crackling in Annie's mind, its blood no longer cold—it slithered down and coiled itself around Annie's body. Slowly, then steadily faster, its forked tongue flicked in and out, ripping Annie's engorged flesh as it satisfied its craven hunger.

Held prisoner by shackles not yet cast off, an unwilling witness—blood staining her thoughts darker—Pamela was forced to wait until Judith was sated and fell into a gluttonous sleep.

"C'mon, girl . . . wake up," Carmen pleaded, apprehension and fear in her voice as she wiped the tears from Pamela's eyes and flushed cheeks. "I don't understand what the hell—"

She stepped back, her hand resting on Pamela's shoulder, as if it were attached to her, and said to Galeal Faraahd, "Go find Dr. Everette. I want a neuro consult. Then schedule a—"

"No," Pamela said quietly, as if talking in her sleep.

Carmen spun around, wide-eyed. "You scared

the shitoutof me!" She started laughing. "Do you have any idea how long you—"

"I'm okay . . . really." She patted Carmen's hand as she glanced past her and asked politely but firmly, "Dr. Faraahd, would you please excuse us?"

Carmen shook her head. "PJ, there's no time to—"

Pamela grabbed hold of Carmen's hand to keep her from pulling away. "Evi . . . please . . . trust me. There's nothing wrong with me. Give me a chance and I'll—"

"Dammit, PJ, don't you try telling me—"

"Wait," Dr. Faraahd pleaded and smiled sheepishly, as if she was embarrassed by what she'd said. "Why don't I step outside and let you two work this out? Page me if you need me." Without waiting for an answer, she walked out, pulling the door closed behind her.

Before Carmen could say anything, Pamela patted the side of the bed and scrunched over. "Remember that truth you wanted?"

Carmen nodded as she sat down, her hands folded in her lap, striking a childlike pose. "Yes, I do. But after what I heard you say over the last half hour . . . and watched your reactions . . . I'm not quite sure that I really want to hear what you have to say."

Sensing Carmen's discomfort, Pamela said as

casually as she possibly could, "You know that *she* I started telling you about?"

Carmen nodded.

"She was . . . or should I say *is*—"

Pamela hesitated, as if for effect, although that wasn't her intention; she was simply having second thoughts about telling Carmen this, afraid that she would think she'd lost her mind.

After a moment, no less concerned or any less determined, she finally said, "She was Sean's first love."

"That's it . . . end of story?" Carmen asked, as if relieved.

"Not quite. There are a few small problems, the first one being that she died thirty years ago. The second *little* problem, and this isn't going to be easy to swallow, is that she isn't dead. Not the way you think of as dead. She's actually very much alive."

Carmen's eyes widened but at the same time grew darker, sucking up everything in sight, casting her face in a shadow.

Taking what she saw to mean that Carmen believed her, or was at the very least finally ready to listen—to open her mind and heart and hear what she was saying—Pamela began with what had happened that first afternoon in Blue Fields. She spoke slowly, revealing her every thought, every secret feeling, as she told of the woman who'd appeared out of nowhere that night and disappeared beneath the surface of the water. The scenes of Sean she painted with a few quick strokes of memory, borrowing his cryptic descriptions. She left nothing to the imagination, however, when it came to what had happened to her that night in the cemetery.

With every vengeful threat repeated, every ruthless blow and cruel, vicious thrust described in intimate detail, reopening wounds that would forever be tender, Pamela watched Carmen's gaze narrow and grow cold, her very soul chilled—at least in her mind's eye—by a fear that only another woman could know and feel.

Chapter Thirty

Early morning light, still stained gray from the night, filled the room as Annie walked across the kitchen and stopped at the counter. There wasn't the slightest hesitation in her movements as she opened the drawer and withdrew a large chef's knife. She moved with equal determination to the bay window, where she sat down. With a twist of her body, she slipped off the thin shoulder straps of the peignoir, letting the satiny folds collect around her broad hips. Grasping the knife firmly with both hands, she placed the tip of the blade against her abdomen, just below her rib cage. She lowered her hands ever so slightly, angling the razor-sharp knife toward her heart and pressed, but gently, barely breaking the skin. A tiny trickle of warm blood worked its way down her stomach and melted into the peignoir as she waited, wanting Judith to know what she was doing, to feel her fear, to hear her screams.

At the first sign of the bitter cold crystallizing inside her, trying to regain her heart and steal back her mind, Annie tightened her grip and growled through her clenched teeth . . . *"Fuck you."*

Chapter Thirty-one

Carmen had fallen into a dead sleep in the un-inviting wood and vinyl armchair. With her head bowed, her clothes wrinkled and disheveled, her hair awry and her arms flopped at her sides, she looked like a rag doll that a child had dressed up in doctor's clothes and played with for hours before tossing it aside.

Pamela on the other hand was rested and finally free of the aftereffects of the near-fatal morphine overdose. Having just picked clean two trays of hospital food, Carmen's and her own, she was now sitting quietly and methodically organizing her thoughts, deciding what she wanted to do, in what order, when and who she needed to help her. Getting out of the hospital and getting to Sean before Annie did, though it wasn't

Annie she feared, were at the top of her list. Everything else, a hundred business tasks left hanging—even her precious foundation—were now unimportant.

The solitary exception to her singular state of mind was dealing with what Carmen had said just before nodding off. While she had finally stopped doubting what Pamela had been trying to tell her about Judith, but only after Pamela's vivid description of what had happened to her in the cemetery, it was her own story that had left Pamela filled with unexpected doubts, and even more questions.

Appearing to choose her words carefully, she had said in a weary voice, "It was the strangest sensation I ever—"

It was here that Carmen paused, her face, her eyes, her whole body creating the impression that she didn't believe what Pamela was saying. She finally went on to say, "Even though I've gone over it in my mind a hundred times, it still doesn't make any medical sense to me whatsoever. After I had sewn up your aorta and stabilized you, I proceeded to look for any other internal trauma. The moment I took your heart in my hands, I felt a cold that instantly numbed my fingers. Before I could let go, not that I could have even if I had wanted to . . . which scared the hell out of me! . . . something shot up my arm and knifed into by chest, taking my breath away."

Carmen had stopped abruptly and looked around, as if someone had called her name. She sat in silence, nervously glancing about the room, her lips moving, as if she was talking to herself. After a moment or two, she went on. "I couldn't move. I couldn't even think! Then—and I know this sounds bizarre—whatever it was seemed to let go. I would have passed off the whole episode as my imagination, but my hands and fingers were left numb to the touch, as if I had suffered some sort of nerve damage. And that's not my imagination, either, since my patients have been telling me that my hands are ice cold when I touch them."

Waving off Pamela's startled response, Carmen had scrunched her face into a frown and asked apprehensively, "You don't think it's possible that what I—"

She then went silent again, leaving the question unasked.

Before hearing this, before she had slipped into Judith's mind, turning the tables, and Annie's too, everything had seemed so simple, so straightforward: She had one person to fear and hate, Judith, and another to stop, Annie. While she couldn't bring herself to hate Annie, she knew that she was nonetheless just as dangerous, if not more so, as long as her thoughts and actions were not her own. Now there was Carmen. Or was there? Had Judith left some part of her behind in Carmen, as she had with her, or had she retreated? And if she had, why did she? What had she sensed, if anything? Or was this just another one of her cruel tricks, and she really was there, coiled up and hiding and refusing to allow anyone, even Carmen, to feel her presence until the time was right?

Or had she already struck when Carmen had operated on Sean?

What had been as simple as black and white to Pamela, which is how she looked at life, had been turned into a monochromatic kaleidoscope: a thousand broken pieces of glass stained every possible shade of gray by the fragmented memories she had stumbled upon in Judith's mind and brought back with the others. She had thought they were hers to take, simply because she had caught glimpses of Sean in them. But they were Judith's. And to her surprise they were filled with a love as tender as the night. Though faded, they were still rich with color and warm with passion. An unexpected discovery, those memories had served to cool the hate Pamela had nurtured and kept alive, but they had failed to snuff out the scorching heat of her vengeance.

One of those memories, however, was unlike all the others. Still unable to make sense of what she had seen, Pamela retrieved those images, though cautiously, in the hope of learning what had happened. Just as before, she was inside Judith, but in her heart, not her mind, where she had always been before. She felt safe and secure and filled with a sense of unbridled excitement, joy tinged with apprehension, yet not an ounce of fear; a woman's once-in-a-lifetime feeling she had once known herself long ago, before Sean.

Now, as before, an unseen wind picked up, wrapping her, wrapping them both in a blanket of silence as the warm night air turned cold and damp and thick with decay. Although what was now happening was only a thought—no longer a victim of Judith's will, she was free to come and go—Pamela found herself struggling to breathe as vaporous shadows, one, and then another, raced through her mind. The unearthly silence was broken by whispered voices, then shattered by a deafening scream so real it could have been her own cry.

Gray turned to black as one of the figures drew near, the one at a distance, not the one between Judith's legs. Unaffected by the bitter cold freezing Judith's heart and mind—praying that she would be released from her mortal form just as she had once prayed for her own death—Pamela reached into their shared nightmare and took hold of that second shadow, pulling it closer, trying to—

"Dear God!" she gasped and sat up, a familiar face—caught but lost to her subconscious—replaced by Annie's reflection.

A profile, seen as if she was looking out of the corner of her eye, Annie was sitting by a window, naked from the waist up, her head bowed, her jaw square, a knife held to her heart. Safe, no longer the prey—wishing to see them both dead—Pamela watched with a certain curiosity as Annie's reflection slowly drew into focus, and she saw a hate in her eyes she knew all too well herself.

Though aflame with vengeance and poisoned by jealousy, Pamela told herself, *No . . . I can't let it happen . . . not this way.*

Slipping her hand beneath the covers, she retrieved the cell phone she'd hidden. She flipped it open and squeezed her eyes shut, trying to recall the number she wanted. Precious seconds ticked away. With a confident nod, she hastily tapped out a number and waited. Biting down on her words, making no effort to speak softly, she said, "I want to report a murder in progress."

Carmen suddenly sat up. "What the hell—"

Pamela silenced her with an angry shake of her head and a wave of her hand as she growled into the phone, "Will you *please* shut up and listen to me. There isn't much time!"

Chapter Thirty-two

"Are you *sure* there wasn't someone else in here with you?" Peter Murphy asked as he stuck the flashlight in Sean's face again, then turned full circle, slicing up the shadows in the cemetery with the razor-sharp halogen beam. "Reverend Sparks said that she heard you talking to someone." Peter shook his head. "What she actually said was that it sounded like two drunks were arguing."

Sean replied impatiently, "Why the hell didn't she just come over and find out, for chrissake, instead of calling the police?"

"I can't blame the woman for not wanting to come here, not at this hour. And *especially* not after all that's happened here. And with you sitting on this tombstone like some—"

Murphy paused and chortled, "Well . . . you know what I mean."

Shining the light in Sean's face, Peter asked softly, sounding honestly concerned, "Everything okay with you?"

Sean slapped the light away. "I'm fine." *But you won't be if you stick that fucking light in my face one more time.* "And it's *not* a tombstone," he grumbled. "It's a *sarcophagus.*"

"Whatever," Murphy said with a shrug.

Sean jumped down beside him. "I just couldn't sleep . . . which isn't like me . . . so I went for a walk and ended up here. I used to come here a lot when I was a kid." He laughed, but to himself. "Strange as it may sound, and I don't know why I'm telling you this, but I somehow always felt safe here. But that was before—"

His voice tailed off, leaving Peter Murphy hanging.

The truth was that Sean had been writing— only with a pencil and paper, not his laptop—as he usually did at this hour. But his thoughts kept drifting back to yesterday, to what had happened to him, forcing him to once again face a fear he didn't understand and couldn't deal with, or had simply refused to, so he didn't. Then he began thinking of Pamela, of what had happened to her and what she was going through—and who had done this to her—and for the first time in his life he wanted revenge. But how? And against whom?

Frustrated, left with no way to exact a pound of flesh, his vengeance only served to pour salt on the wounds. As he had a hundred times in the past, he had refused to face the fact that those wounds had existed for years and he'd kept them from becoming infected by taking regular doses of denial. Unable to concentrate, oblivious to the time, he had given up and gone running in the hope of getting some relief from his second drug of choice.

But things turned from bad to worse as he tripped and stumbled in the dark. Since he was forced to walk at what for him was an infuriating pace, his agitated state of mind had been raised to the boiling point by the time he found himself in the cemetery, wondering why the hell he had come here. Only he hadn't thought it, he had demanded it out loud. Unable to come up with an answer that made any sense to him, he had begun to argue with himself, his voice growing steadily louder, his words harsher with each angry exchange. By the time Murphy had shown up—shining the long-handled flashlight in his face and asking what Sean thought was one stupid question after another—he was ready to explode.

"So," he asked, his irritable edge not the least bit dulled. If anything it had been honed even sharper by his contentious confrontation with Peter Murphy. "Is it a crime to be in a cemetery after dark? Am I trespassing on *sacred ground?*"

Murphy sighed, "No. A bit strange maybe, but it's no crime."

He turned and gestured with his flashlight toward the back of the cemetery, the light bouncing off the shiny yellow ribbon strung from fence to tree to headstone and back to the fence, forming a lopsided square. When he spoke, it was clear from the guarded tone of his voice that he was no longer kidding around. "I hope you weren't thinking about mucking around back there. 'Cause if you were, you can just *forget it*. We're expecting some people from the Forensic Investigation Center in Albany to have a look around and make sure that our ME's guys didn't miss anything."

He turned to face Sean, waving his flashlight at him as if it was a wagging finger. "Remember, *no research,* understand?"

Batting the light away, Sean said on a sarcastic note, "A bit late for that, aren't we?"

Murphy stepped back, frowned and asked wryly, "Who yanked your chain?" Then he shook his head and turned to leave.

You shit, MacDonald. "Listen, Peter, I'm sorry. I—"

"Forget it," he said without looking back and gave a friendly wave as he began to use the beam

271

of his flashlight like a blind man's cane, tapping and feeling his way through the dark toward his patrol car. Parked broadside on the lawn just beyond the gate, the driver's side door was swung open, the engine left running, the head lights on, the radio squawking instructions in pidgin English.

About to call out and ask for a ride, Sean was silenced by the sight of Peter Murphy, an elusive silhouette, slipping in and out of the headstones and monuments. His thoughts tumbled back in time, pursuing an all-too-familiar shadow he dared not follow before now. Drawing near, he was startled back into the present when Murphy suddenly gunned the engine and backed off the lawn. The harsh glare of the headlights carved out an eerie skyline of crosses and angels and saints, creating the City of Necropolis.

Propelled by a screech of tires, the car spun around and sped away, the sweep of light twisting the stone icons to life.

Shadows were sent chasing after shadows, only to be dissolved by the early morning light crawling over the horizon. All but two, which were unlike all the others, driven out of hiding after all these years. The urge to run suddenly swept over him, but he refused that visceral call, choosing instead to follow the amorphous shapes as they drifted toward the rear of the cemetery. With each deliberate step he took—determined to finally confront what he had banished from his consciousness a lifetime ago—the past began to mix with the present. Thoughts of Pamela flipped through his mind like pages in a book, each one illustrated by the ragged black-and-white images from that October night thirty years before. Scene matched scene, old words echoed in discordant concert with new: the anxious call of his name, the frail and frightened cry for help, a terrified scream and that same cruel laughter.

Snagged by the thin plastic barrier, he angrily tore it down and stepped into the clearing to stand squarely inside the chalked outline of a grave still waiting to be dug. He shut his eyes to the distracting daylight creeping into the cemetery. One of the shadows suddenly moved toward him, its arms held out, it's—

"You fucking bitch!" he cried out and dropped to his knees, clawing at the ground, frantically trying to dig up the marker.

Driven by a rage he couldn't calm and a fear he couldn't see, Sean dug deeper, his nails breaking and tearing off, his blood turning the soil from brown to black. Grabbing the thin block of stone, he struggled to his feet and raised it high over his head, only to be blinded by an explosion of red and white and orange stroboscopic lights as a police car flew past, turning him into a hideous monster of the night: a Frankenstein of his own fears.

Thrown back into darkness, he lunged forward, hurling the tablet at one of the massive stone sentinels surrounding the clearing, his cries answering the scream of the siren.

Chapter Thirty-three

With a fresh pot of coffee in one hand and an empty mug in the other, Annie did her best to act surprised when Peter Murphy appeared at the kitchen window, his revolver drawn, his ravenous gaze devouring everything in sight. With a blink of his eyes, he zeroed in on her, raking her body, stripping her, searching her. He peered into her eyes, as if he were trying to read her thoughts.

The part of Annie that wasn't her was titillated by the feel of his hungry gaze and eager for more. Yet she was sickened by it.

She smiled and waved, hoping that he would give up and go away now that he saw she was okay, that everything was all right. But he didn't budge. Taking a deep breath, she collected her

thoughts, trying to think of what she could say—
what she would be allowed to say—that would
set his mind at ease and send him away before
Judith's insatiable appetite was whetted. A soft
but insistent rap on the glass startled her into
gesturing toward the back door with a wave of
the mug, reluctantly inviting Peter into the
house.

The moment he burst into the kitchen, she said
calmly, a relaxed but forced smile behind her
words, "Peter Murphy . . . what in the world are
you doing sneaking around at this hour of—"

"What are those stains on your nightgown?"
he demanded, trying not to stare at the thin, satiny peignoir clinging to her body, revealing every
womanly curve, every hollow, even those faint,
prickly halos, the swollen saturnal rings of soft,
dark flesh circling her nipples.

Annie glanced down. "Oh . . . *that.* Most of
it's wine, and a few drops of blood." She paused
and said with a casual shrug, "I cut myself on
some broken glass in the bathroom upstairs."

Peter glanced over her head into the pantry.
Nodding to himself reassuringly, he lowered his
revolver and growled though his teeth in a
throaty whisper, "What the *hell* is going on
here?"

Annie proceeded to fill her mug. When she
leaned forward to put the coffeepot on the table,
her hastily tied peignoir fell open, recapturing

Peter's virtuous gaze. Upon seeing his secretive glance, she began to cover herself up but was stopped against her will. "I don't understand," she said with convincing innocence as a discreet smile appeared on her face: a look that said she knew what she'd done and was pleased with the reaction she'd gotten.

Peter's brow wrinkled into a frown as he stepped back, his fierce gaze—cautious, probing, searching—now fixed on hers.

When he finally spoke, his words were barely audible, as if he was afraid that someone might hear him. "Are you okay?"

Annie wanted to shout, *Get out of here!* but all she could do was nod and say with a tired smile, "I'm fine . . . really."

When his gaze narrowed and hardened, she did everything she could to open her mind, her heart, giving him free rein. But she quickly paid the price when the searing pain took her breath away and shut her eyes, a cruel reminder of what Judith could mete out: just enough to bring her to her knees if necessary, begging for mercy, but never enough to answer her pleas for death, ending her unbearable misery. More vigilant than before, she was now coiled tightly around every vital organ in Annie's body.

After a moment of awkward silence, Peter nodded, as if he understood. Lowering his voice still further, he said, "I'm going to have a quick look around. You stay here . . . and *don't* move."

With a covert flick of his eyes, he gestured toward the living room as he turned away and raised his pistol, placing his trust, and unwittingly his very life, in Annie's hands.

Now! rang loudly inside her mind. But she stood firm, using what little strength she had left to resist Judith's command as she watched Peter slip into the shadows of the living room. Though he was out of sight, she could hear his every step, sense his every move—the turn of his head, his shifting gaze, his refocused aim. But that sixth sense wasn't hers, it was Judith's: the ultimate predator, she was waiting patiently for her prey to return.

Annie now knew all too vividly that Peter would not be kept alive as the women had, should Judith decide that she wanted him. Unwilling hosts, they had fed her and sustained her, vessels of nourishment and pleasure, giving to her again and again and again, and always against their will. And eventually giving her their lives, a few their very souls, their bodies and minds drained, no longer able to satisfy her voracious appetite.

When she whispered, "No, I won't do it," the sound of cold steel striking stone suddenly rang like a bell as twilight filled her mind. She saw an old man. He was bent over and trying to pry a small granite marker out of the ground with a long-handled shovel. She watched as he was thrown into the air, his clothes torn to shreds and stripped from his body, unseen fingers scratching and tearing his flesh, disemboweling and emasculating him. She shut her eyes and covered her ears, but she couldn't block out the screams, or the sight of his ravaged body impaled on the branches of a towering tree, its broad limbs, like his bones, broken and splintered by the raging wind howling inside her head.

In spite of her deceit and cunning, and her terrifying cruelty, Judith had failed to possess the one woman who could have easily given her what she wanted, for a purpose that no errant thought had yet revealed. That failure was now Annie's only consolation as she thought of her own failure—a knife held to her breast, ready to plunge it deep into her heart and take her life in order to end Judith's—only to pause and savor her vengeance; that tiny spark of hate resurrecting Judith from her sated sleep.

"Why are you doing this?" she asked, tears falling from her cheeks, adding yet another stain to her soiled satin peignoir as she slowly walked over and switched off the kitchen light.

She obediently disrobed to stand naked, waiting: She was now the unwilling but deadly predator, needing only her scent, her womanly form, her bare hands and Judith's surreal strength. As she tracked Peter through the house, she could feel her body tingling with anticipation: Her breasts were suddenly sensitive, her nipples alive, her loins warm and moist, her mind filled with unwanted thoughts of seduction. Slow and unhurried, she imagined herself melting Peter's resistance. She saw his clothes falling from his body by his own hand, his manly desire rising to match her womanly hunger. She was forced to picture herself taking him deep inside her, his heart beating harder and harder until she had drained every last drop of—

The creak of footsteps ended the repugnant fantasy.

Annie spun around, embarrassed by what she had thought and felt. Startled by her reflection in the window, she thought of what she'd been able to do the night Sean had been here, ending Judith's deadly quest. Seizing that glimmer of hope, she started for the back door, intent upon slipping outside and hiding in the dark. But she was stopped and thrown back into the center of the kitchen and forced to wait. Her only hope now, however dim, was that Peter would some-how be able to resist Judith's seductive lure.

Chapter Thirty-four

Pamela was kneeling on the bed and slumped back on her heels, dripping with sweat. At the feel of her teeth sinking into flesh again—blood filling her mouth, the warm liquid running down her throat—she gagged and lunged forward, grabbing fistfuls of sheet.

Hunching over, she retched and heaved like a sick dog, but there was nothing left in her stomach except for the acid regurgitated with every twist of her gut, the fiery fluid burning her throat and mingling with the bitter taste of blood nowhere to be seen in the patches of undigested food spotting the sheets.

"That's it . . . just spit it out," Galeal said in a soothing voice as she gently cradled Pamela's forehead in her small hand and wrapped her arm around her shoulders, trying to hold her steady.

Glancing across the bed, she told Eku, who was struggling to reattach the IV trap for the saline drip on Pamela's right arm, "When you finish with that, go get some hand towels and a pan of cold water . . . and a bucket of ice . . . I want to sponge—"

"No," Pamela rasped and slowly sat up, dizzy, unable to focus, her thoughts spinning into a sickening blur. "Nothing cold."

Though she was teetering and fighting to keep her balance, she managed to pull off her sweat-soaked hospital gown and throw it onto the floor. With a clumsy swipe of her arm, she wiped her mouth, which was smeared with crud. "Make it as hot as you think I can safely stand it. And get me a glass of hot water . . . nothing in it . . . I want to rinse out this disgusting taste in my mouth."

She settled back onto her heels and sighed, "Then go find Dr. Evangelista. I have to—"

"It's four in morning!" Galeal interrupted. "Besides, she's not on call tonight."

Pamela snarled, "I don't give a shit . . . you can drag her ass out of bed for all I care . . . I have to—

"Dear God . . . no!" she cried out, and dug her fingernails into the hollowed-out cavern of her belly. Clawing at her own flesh, she scratched it open, sending a jolt throughout her body that short-circuited the images being fed into her brain.

Afraid to let go lest they return, she tightened her grip, shivering from the pain as she bit down on her words. "I'm going to stop you . . . even if it means I have to kill *her* to do it."

Clearly startled by what she had said, Galeal and Eku exchanged worried glances. Before either one of them could say or do anything, Pamela turned to Galeal and demanded, "I want something to knock me out. I can't stand this anymore. Tell whoever you have to that I'm having nightmares, that I'm hallucinating . . . hysterical! . . . and you have to sedate me.

"*Lie* if you have to!"

Bathed and wrapped in a clean hospital gown, smelling of rubbing alcohol, Pamela slid down under the sheets and whispered into the cell phone buried in the pillow beneath her ear, "I don't care what Dr. Evangelista said, John . . . *I* know how I feel."

She shook her head, about to argue with him, when she felt the Demerol drip kick in, slowing her wits. "I don't care, wake him up! That's why I pay the man five-hundred dollars an hour."

Sensing that she was slipping fast, desperate, Pamela shouted, "Have him get a goddamn court order . . . just get me out of here!"

Chapter Thirty-five

After carefully nudging the broken glass from the wine bottle into one corner of the bathroom with her bare foot, Annie gingerly wriggled out of the bloodstained sweatpants and kicked them aside. Refusing to look at them, she grabbed fistfuls of her sweatshirt, about to pull it off over her head, but stopped.

What! She hesitated, her eyes flitting about. *You make a goddamn whore out of me, force me to kill a man for no reason, and you're bitching about not getting off! Who the hell do you—*

Annie caught herself when she suddenly realized this was the only part of her body she had any real control over when it came to Judith. Aware of the risks if she was found out—aware of what she would become if she did what she

284

was thinking—she quietly slipped into a corner of her mind Judith hadn't found yet. Hiding behind a mask of angry thoughts, she began to explore ways of manipulating Judith with what she had, what she could do and Judith couldn't and what Judith appeared to need, desperately so, as if it was what kept her spirit alive. She quickly devised ways of trading favor for favor, reminding herself to always take before giving: a moment of freedom to do what she wanted to do in exchange for a microsecond of pleasure—the rush, the high—that she now knew Judith would do anything for, and already had.

That's it! That's your ticket—

"What the hell do you want now?" she demanded, her defiant outburst a deliberate attempt to cover up her thoughts, fearful that she might have been overheard. "Go to hell," she snarled, ripping off her sweatshirt and throwing it at the wall. "There's no way I'm taking a bath . . . I know what you *really* want."

With a sharp twist of her hand, she turned on the water and flipped up the lever for the shower. Letting it run hot, she turned and reached for her hairbrush, only to be startled by her reflection in the full-length mirror. Naked—her ivory-white Irish skin mottled and stained red—she stood staring in disbelief at the stranger before her. Matted to the sides of her head and half-covering her bloodied face, her hair was knotted with clumps of flesh and covered with crust. Scratches crisscrossed her hands and forearms from the splintered bones she'd brushed up against.

With a disgusted shake of her head, Annie stepped into the shower. Shutting her eyes, she tipped her head back as beads of hot water pelted her face, her body, wrapping her in a veil of steam at it slowly dissolved the evidence of her sins. Before the heat could work its magic, a spike of cold was driven into her chest and hammered deeper with every beat of her heart. She flinched as one angry threat after another was hurled at her, every one a vivid reminder of something Judith had done in her cruel and ruthless effort to force her to bring Sean to her.

Catching her breath, she sighed. "All right, I'll do it."

Released from Judith's vengeful grasp, angry with herself for giving in, Annie reached down to shut the drain and draw a tub, only to be sickened by the sight of a mound of shredded flesh balled up with strands of blond hair, clogging the drain.

A mutilated body suddenly filled her thoughts, Peter's face replaced with Sean's, his expression the same one she'd seen after raking her nails across his chest. "No!" She stumbled out of the tub. "And I won't let you hurt him, either. You might as well kill me now." A smile found her lips. "But then you won't—"

Dead Love

Silenced by a baleful cry, Annie grew quiet as she leaned up against the wall, the crud from her hair streaking the white ceramic tiles and dripping onto the floor, staining her feet. She repeated in her mind every word Judith had to say, while trying her best to decode the subtle nuances in the pitch of her suddenly beguiling voice.

Why should I believe you? she asked, pushing herself off the wall and walking over to the tub. With a scoop of her hand, she cleared the drain and tossed the fistful of hairy scum into the toilet, flushing it away; out of sight, but not out of her mind.

After turning up the hot water, she grabbed the shampoo and stepped back under the steamy spray. There was a curious frown on her face as she lathered her hair and listened to Judith's plea.

Chapter Thirty-six

The walls of the bleached-white bathroom were decorated with an array of stainless-steel bars installed to accommodate every conceivable infirmity and handicap. Thankful for the one in the tiled shower stall, Pamela held on to it firmly as she reached out, tugging at the towel she'd tossed over yet another bar just outside the shower. Recalling as best she could Sean's routine, she dried off her face, her hair, then her feet and legs, before stepping out onto the stiff institutional terry-cloth floor mat. The memories that followed—beginning with the thought of her snapping Sean on his hairy butt, and his high-pitched squeal of surprise—lit up her face as she walked out of the bathroom and shut the door and stopped to look at herself in the full-length mirror, still wet.

Her red hair was longer than she usually wore it, almost covering her ears. What little fat she once had was gone, devoured by her own body, leaving behind a sinewy network of muscles and protruding veins snaking over arms and legs just beneath the skin.

She gingerly tapped a silver-dollar-sized welt, one of nine welts spotting her chest and rib cage from where the electrodes had been glued to her skin. Smiling, she cupped her breast in her hand. "You need to put on some weight!" She laughed and was about to continue drying herself off when she was startled by Carmen's reflection in the mirror just before she stepped away. In that instant, having seen the look on her face—not that of a doctor pleased with her patient's recovery—Pamela recalled Carmen's comment that she had finally faced the truth about myself, and now knew what she'd meant by it.

Unsure of what to say, she waited, expecting some sort of feeling—discomfort, disgust, repulsion?—to rise up inside her. But there was nothing there, not even curiosity: She didn't care. She wasn't even bothered by the thought that they'd shared a bed that whole summer in the Hamptons, showered naked together and had spent countless moonlit nights skinny-dipping in the ocean.

Cinching the towel around her, she was about to face Carmen when it struck her: *Maybe that's why she retreated? Maybe she could tell, and knew that you wouldn't be of any use to her?*

Before she could say anything, Carmen asked, "So, I understand that you had one hell of a night. Think it was something you ate?"

Shivering at Carmen's choice of words, Pamela replied, "Nope," and walked over to the bed. Grabbing a pair of panties, she hesitated, her gaze locked with Carmen's until she turned away. Dropping the towel, she stepped into the panties. A long-sleeved blue cashmere sweater was next, followed by a pair of designer jeans, which she slipped on with ease and looked two sizes too big on her.

"Was the sedative strong enough?" Carmen asked, turning back.

Pamela snatched a watch off the bed and slipped it on. "Worked like a charm." She tapped the face of the watch. "Knocked me out for nearly twelve hours. I could have been dead for all I knew."

"Feel better with a good night's sleep under your belt?"

"I feel *great* . . . especially now that I've taken a shower. I'd feel even better if I could get through to Sean. But every time I call, I get bounced back to the service. Other than that, the only thing this emaciated woman you see before you needs is a decent meal . . . and lots of chocolate milk shakes . . . which—"

"This stuff here," Carmen said, gesturing toward the clothes and small carry-on bag and two cell phones, one of them hers, the other Pamela's. "Did that gray-haired man standing outside the door . . . who looks vaguely familiar, though I can't place him . . . bring all of this here?"

Pamela dropped a shiny pair of loafers onto the floor and stuffed her bare feet into them. "The reason you recognize that *gray-haired man* is because you've met him. He's John Sutherland. He was my father's chauffeur, and now he's mine. And," she said with a sharp bite to her words, having suddenly grown impatient fencing with Carmen, "as you've no doubt guessed . . . I'm leaving."

Carmen said indignantly, "I haven't discharged you yet . . . you can't just up and—"

"Save it, Evi." Pamela pointed to a folded-up sheaf of papers on the bed. "That's the court order . . . my get-out-of-jail card. Read it if you like, but it won't make any—"

"She wasn't murdered!" Carmen snapped.

Confused, Pamela frowned and asked, "What are you—"

"The Parker woman. I had my cell phone service trace that call right after I left here. When I called the number myself . . . I told the police I was the one who called the first time . . . they told me that Officer Murphy had reported that she was fine, that it was just a small accident, and he'd already left her house."

Pamela sighed. "That was yesterday . . . he's dead now."

Not appearing the least bit phased by what Pamela had said, Carmen told her, "PJ . . . you've got to get some help before these fantasies of yours get you into—"

"Fantasies!" Pamela picked up Carmen's cell phone. "Here; call the station and ask if they've found Peter's body yet." She shoved the phone in Carmen's face. "Go ahead," she taunted.

Carmen pushed Pamela's hand away. "PJ, listen, I only—"

"*That's* why I was sick," Pamela said with disgust as she threw the phone onto the bed and began stuffing everything into the flight bag. She said in a dead calm whisper, "I could see—"

She paused, afraid that if she let those thoughts loose she would be sick all over again. After a moment, she said with a throaty sigh, "I could see *everything*. I could even taste—"

"I don't buy it," Carmen sneered. "The mind can trick us into thinking we're tasting blood; any first-year resident knows that!"

What? Pamela tossed her cell phone into the

flight bag, zipped it shut and stepped in front of Carmen. "I didn't say anything about blood, how did you know—"

"Eku, or maybe it was Galeal . . . one of them! . . . told—"

"No," Pamela said with a solemn shake of her head and placed her hands on Carmen's shoulders to keep her from pulling away. "I didn't tell a single soul what I saw, or what was making me sick. So they couldn't have—"

Startled by the sudden change in Carmen's appearance—her face was like carved stone, her eyes black as midnight and just as cold—Pamela stepped back. *I knew it! She's there, watching and listening, only I bet you don't know it, do you? You can see and hear for her, while I can see and hear what she sees . . . at least what she wants me to see. Yet I can't stop her anymore than you can, even though I know she's doing it. But she can't hear me, hear my thoughts, or see what I see . . . at least I don't think so.*

Pamela shook her head. *We're no more than goddamn puppets for that bitch, and she's pulling the strings!*

"I'm outta here," she said as she snatched up the flight bag and started for the door. "Thanks for saving my life, Evi. Let's hope it wasn't a waste of—"

"Wait! I'm coming with you," Carmen said with absolute authority and was at Pamela's side before she could say anything, slipping out into the hall with her. "You may need me."

Pamela's every instinct told her, *No! Don't trust her.* She turned to tell Carmen that she didn't want her to come with her. But that logical side of her didn't agree and held her tongue, forcing her to listen. *It doesn't make any sense. If she was going to do something . . . and no one would have been the wiser . . . why didn't she do it when she had the chance? A dozen chances!*

She finally nodded and started down the hall, her chauffeur on one side of her, Carmen on the other, not a word spoken by anyone. With every determined step she took, shadowy vignettes began to slip in and out of her mind. Annie appeared to be darting about her house in the dark. The fear of what she was doing, what she was thinking . . . *What is she so excited about?* . . . quickened Pamela's pace to the point where she was well ahead of the others.

Chapter Thirty-seven

The moment the deep, cathartic sleep that claimed him after he had stumbled his way back from the cemetery released its anesthetic hold—even before he could open his eyes—Sean knew there was no longer any doubt in his mind that Judith was alive.

But even now, in the light of day, he still couldn't help thinking that what he'd finally remembered was nothing more than a trick his mind had played on him, a waking dream that had turned into a never-ending nightmare. *What about what she did to those women? And what she did to Pamela. Those weren't goddamn dreams! And now she's in Annie, at least some part of her is. But how?*

That unconscious thought, a purely intuitive

response without any evidence to support it, prompted Sean to wonder, *If that's true, if only part of her is in Annie, then where's the rest of her spirit? Is it possible that she could have hidden some part of her in someone else's body? Pamela, Carmen, me?* raced through his mind. *What the hell do you want?* sent his thoughts spinning.

Sean opened his eyes and lay staring up at the cracked ceiling above his bed, waiting for the accusations to be hurled at him like falling pieces of old plaster—those rational, logical, left-brained arguments he had fabricated in a desperate attempt to explain everything away, second-guessing what he felt and what he thought, rejecting his intuition and attacking the very essence of who and what he was—hoping they would convince him that he was wrong.

But not a single dissenting voice was heard, not even a whisper of doubt. The only thing he felt was that subtle tension he had come to know and dread, his thoughts, his whole body slowly growing tighter and tighter: the uneasy sensation of a steel spring being wound up inside him, his running the only way he could unwind it, afraid that if he didn't run something might snap.

"Maybe *you're* the part that's missing!" He laughed as he rolled over onto his side and saw that the travel clock on the nightstand read 4:02. *That can't be right . . . I couldn't have slept that long.* He sat up and looked outside. *I'll be damned!*

Upset with himself that he'd nearly slept through the day, Sean felt around under the pillow for the cell phone he'd stashed there in the hope that someone might call—the hospital, Peter Murphy, even Pamela!—only to come up empty-handed. Tossing off the sheets, he saw the phone down by his feet and reached for it, determined to call the hospital and see how Pamela was doing.

When he hit the POWER ON button nothing happened: no friendly musical greeting, no start-up messages on the display. *Shit.*

Hopping out of bed, he began to rummage through Pamela's things, certain that she had to have another phone hidden somewhere in her clothes. *Nope.* About to give up, he spotted the flight bag she had shoved under the bed the night she'd driven up from the city. Scooping it out, he sat down and dropped the canvas bag in his lap. The moment he unzipped it, Pamela's smell filled the air, causing him to pause and think about how much he missed her.

But that thought lasted only until another was pulled out of his head: *I don't know how, but I'll stop her, even if I have—*

Surprised by the hatred boiling up inside him, Sean forced himself to calm down by carefully taking out one article after another and neatly arranging everything on the bed beside him.

He smiled at the feel of something hard inside the bag, only to frown just as quickly, when—instead of coming up with another cell phone—he withdrew a revolver, which instantly sparked the realization that if Pamela had thought to bring her pistol, she had to have known something, while he was still unable to face it.

Questions began exploding in his head. *Maybe it was that woman we saw at the reservoir? No, it couldn't have been her; she never touched her. Wait. It had to be the afternoon I showed her the marker, because we started arguing with each other after that. It was that wind, the same thing I felt. That's got to be it!*

Angry with himself, knowing that he had unwittingly exposed Pamela to Judith, to her venomous hatred—that what had happened to her was his fault—Sean suddenly threw the bag onto the floor and stood up, every conscious, analytical thought erased from his mind. Driven by pure instinct, he grabbed his shorts and slipped them on, wincing at the fact that they were still damp. His socks and running shoes were next. Kneeling down, he laced the shoes tight, the way he did for cross-country, and didn't question why.

Then, without a second's hesitation, he donned the shoulder holster—fumbled with the buckle in order to fit the strap around his larger chest—and popped his sweatshirt over his head.

*   *   *

"PJ! You're shaking like a leaf and you're white as a—"

"Shhh!"

Pamela covered her ears with her hands and sat as still as a stone sculpture in the backseat, trying to focus on the distant voices drifting in and out of her mind as the Rolls-Royce flew past the other cars on the parkway in majestic silence—the digital speedometer frozen at 100— a wraith outrunning the wind.

"What is it?" Carmen asked and slid over beside her, pressing her fingers to Pamela's carotid artery and checking her pulse.

Pamela brushed her hand away and fell back into the plush leather seat, tears filling her eyes as she said, "She's in Sean now . . . by a thread, but she's there . . . and he doesn't know it."

"What? Why?"

There was the bitter taste of irony in Pamela's voice when she said quietly, "She wants me to see what he sees . . . feel everything that he feels . . . and know that I can't do anything to stop—"

She grew quiet again and shut her eyes.

"What is it . . . what's the matter?" Carmen asked.

It was too late; Pamela had already blocked out everything around her and was now following Sean—memorizing every scene, creating a road map in her mind so that she could find him—her every thought, even the beat of her heart, in synch with his.

Without questioning where he was going, Sean threaded his way through the cemetery and came to a rigid stop in front of the small stone marker bearing the name ISABELLE EVANGELISTA. In the time it took him to insert Carmen for Isabelle and repeat the name to himself aloud—giving it a sharp, Spanish flair—the pieces of the puzzle that was Carmen Evangelista fell into place for him.

He wasn't going to try and analyze how he knew, playing back everything he had seen: the way she moved; her age, a deliberate deception; her many faces, those she showed him and the others she wore when she thought he wasn't looking; her unsettling yet at the same time soothing touch; her startling blue eyes, her gaze alive one second, cold and empty the next; or compare her with that old woman he had seen three decades ago, only to watch her reappear inside Pamela as fragments of another life stolen and discarded.

I should have known the moment I saw her; I just wasn't—

Before he could complete his thought, Sean was called to account by his own conscience. *You knew. You've known for years, you were just afraid to face it . . . afraid of what she does to you, how she makes you feel. That's why you didn't want to come back; you knew that you wanted her, wanted what she could give you . . . what no other woman can. You're running from your own feelings.*

Sean was confused by the sound of an unfamiliar voice, as if someone else was speaking to him, not his alter ego. While he knew there was some truth to what had been said—that he had known it was Judith, though not consciously, and that he had been unable to face it, but because he was frightened by what was happening to him—*Who wouldn't be!*—he was nonetheless angered by the accusation that he desired her, desired the bizarre sexual fantasies aroused in him against his will by the women she had sent to seduce him.

He turned and started for the gate. *Do whatever it takes, just get her the hell out of that hospital,* he told himself as he skirted the clearing where Judith's headstone had been, giving it a wide berth only to circle back when something caught his eye.

Set into the crater left behind when he'd ripped up the thin slab of granite and shattered it against a nearby funereal urn, were chunks of stone that appeared to have been fused together, restoring Judith's headstone to its rightful place. Imbedded in the ground beside it was another

marker, identical in size and shape, the epitaph—
ANNIE . . . LIE HERE WITH US IN LOVING MEM-
ORY—etched into the stone with the same grace-
ful hand as its mate.

What? Startled, Sean turned full circle, peering into the late-afternoon shadows.

"Annie . . . is that you?" he called out apprehensively and held his breath, listening to a distant reply rising above the whisper of the wind.
Confused, he wondered, *What the hell is happening?*

He stepped back, as if pushed, his head
cocked. *Where?*

Pamela buried her face in her hands and said
barely above a whisper, "Don't go . . . please . . .
she's just playing with you."

Spinning around, Sean darted out of the cemetery and started running, that invisible spring inside him rachetting down with every powerful
kick as he pushed himself to the limit and beyond, blinded to what might happen if the spring
wound too tight.

"PJ . . . can you hear me?"

Chapter Thirty-eight

Sean broke stride and hurdled the hedge bordering Western Highway, then sprinted across the lawn, ignoring the front door and circling around the house to find the back door ajar.

I knew it! he thought without questioning how he'd known, and shoved the door open, sending it slamming against the wall as he burst into the kitchen and stopped dead, something he knew he should never do. He stood with his hands on his hips, gasping for air, his heart—a machine gun—firing wildly inside his chest.

He glanced at his wrist out of habit. *Shit!*

Frantic, not knowing what his runaway pulse was, Sean fought to catch his breath and calm himself down as he looked around the kitchen—into the pantry, out into the darkened living room and back into the kitchen—searching for any sign of—

A barely visible trail of spots snaking its way through the kitchen over the wood-planked floor caught his eye. He hoped it was nothing more than spilled wine as he reached down and swiped his finger through one of the splotches. Breaking through the dried crust, he came up with a smudge on his fingertip that smeared into a flaky red paste when he rubbed it with his thumb. *Damn!*

He stood up, dripping wet; the sweat had finally caught up with him, cooling him down and slowing his heart. He brushed his face with his sleeve as he walked through the living room.

With his blurred gaze riveted to the second-floor landing, alert for the slightest shadow, he slowly climbed the stairs, wincing at the noisy protest from the wooden steps squeaking under his weight. Halfway up, he paused to listen for the sound of running water, footsteps or the rustle of fabric. Nothing.

The moment he stepped onto the landing, he saw that the bathroom door was closed but not shut tight, allowing light to leak out all around the edges. He tried convincing himself that Annie was taking a bath, that the voice he'd heard in the cemetery was his imagination and everything was all right. But that spring inside him—

winding tighter by the minute—told him that he was wrong.

He strode down the hall and stopped at the door, his head turned, listening. "What did you say?" he asked and leaned closer, before it struck him that the voice he'd heard telling him *No!* had been Pamela's, and he had unwittingly drowned out the rest of her anxious plea with his own hasty reply.

Confused and angry with himself, he threw open the door.

The bathroom was empty, the tiled floor and walls and tub sparkling white in the bright incandescent light. The air was filled with the damp, antiseptic smell of bleach so thick it burned the back of his throat, forcing him to try and swallow it away.

The bedroom was next, but gave up nothing.

"It's not there . . . he must have taken it," Pamela said as she closed the car door behind her and sat back, quietly staring out the window at the front of Mike Gordon's bed-and-breakfast.

After a moment, she slid to the edge of her seat, reached across the divider and said in a businesslike manner, "Give me the one in the glove compartment." She took the short-barreled .357 from her chauffeur. After checking the safety, she slipped the revolver under her sweater and into the waistband of her jeans.

"PJ . . . what the *hell* are you doing?"

Pamela shut her eyes, losing herself in her thoughts.

Carmen frowned and shook her head. "I don't like what's happening here. I think we should go to the—"

"You can hear me!" Pamela whispered.

"What did you say?"

Sitting up, Pamela asked, "John, do you know where Miss Parker lives?"

John simply nodded and pulled around the circular drive.

With a guarded sigh, Pamela fell back and shut her eyes.

The blood . . . follow the trail before it's too dark!

Sean bounded down the stairs and raced through the living room into the kitchen. He glanced outside. The sun was just above the horizon. *Flashlight,* he told himself and began rifling through the kitchen drawers like a madman. Finding one, he tested it. *Women!*

He whacked it and got a faint beam of light in response.

"Save it 'til you need it," he told himself and slipped the rubber-handled flashlight into the waistband of his running shorts.

About to leave, he hesitated and glanced around the kitchen as if he'd heard something.

He waited. Nothing. Lowering his head, he followed the trail of blood out through the open door and across the back lawn, heading for the field of overgrown corn grass beyond the barn.

"What did you say?" Carmen asked.

Bent over, her face buried in her hands, Pamela didn't answer.

Carmen reached out, but pulled back when Pamela raised her hand, blocking her gesture. Her voice was strained when she said, "As your doctor, I'm asking you to stop. Your heart can't keep up, especially not at this rate." She said it as if she somehow knew that Pamela's pulse had begun to climb, matching Sean's beat for beat.

Pamela shook her head and muttered something under her breath.

Carmen slid closer and asked softly, "What do you see?"

Go to hell . . . do you really think I'm that stupid?

Chapter Thirty-nine

The dense waist-high grass—dry as tinder—crackled like a creeping brushfire as Sean waded across the field toward the towering wall of leafless trees climbing a steep hillside. He knew right where he was: The reservoir was just on the other side of the hill, and the bike path—hidden among the trees—was snaking its way along the top of the ridge.

But that comforting thought didn't help his growing anxiety, which was being cranked up, his lumbering pace increased, by the sight of more and more blood spotting the blades of dried grass.

Pamela emerged from the shadows of Annie's living room and leaned up against the doorway, her shoulders slumped, her arms hanging limply at her sides. Even with her size, the shiny .357 Magnum made her hand look small.

She glanced down at Carmen, who was kneeling on the kitchen floor and bending over, and asked, "What are you doing?"

"It's blood," she replied and stood up, holding out a swatch of paper towel with a dark burgundy smudge. "But it's at least a day old, so it's not Sean's. Must be from the Parker woman."

Pamela sighed. "No." She slipped the pistol back into her jeans. Ignoring Carmen's doubtful frown, she stepped around her and walked to the bay window. "It's Peter Murphy's blood," she said quietly and flopped down into the corner of the window seat.

Discouraged and tired, forced to accept the fact that her body wasn't as strong as she'd convinced herself it was, Pamela tipped her head back and closed her eyes, sifting through her thoughts.

Sean stopped and covered his ears with his hands, blocking out the howl of the wind and straining to hear the plaintive call.

After a moment, he started back across the field, retracing the path he'd trampled through the grass, which was now little more than a serpentine shadow. His mind was clear except for thoughts of Pamela: He found himself wondering if she was all right, if she was strong enough to come home, and *Where the hell is Carmen?*

Pamela suddenly sat up and looked outside. "I'm all right! I'm here!" she said excitedly, and squinted into the thickening dusk, trying to see. She shook her head. "Don't worry about her."

Sean frowned, nodded, then spun around and started running. He slowed to climb the weed-infested fieldstone wall bordering the woods. Leaping down, he focused his gaze on the faint slivers of rapidly fading twilight falling between the barren trees, offering him safe passage as he climbed the rocky hillside, following as best he could the broken line of overturned leaves.

"No!" Pamela cried and lowered her head, her arms spread out, her fingers desperately scratching at the glass.

Carmen was at her side. "PJ . . . what is it . . . are you—"

"You stupid woman." Pamela sighed. "What have you done?"

As Sean neared the top of the ridge, fighting for every finger-and toe-hold, the ground began to crumble and slip out from underfoot. He crawled the last ten yards and stood up, his hands and knees scraped and bleeding from the razor-sharp cinders once used as a bed for the train tracks and bulldozed aside when the bike path was built. The only light was from the smoldering fire along the horizon, a remnant of the setting sun, filling the sky with smoke. He paused to catch his breath and pick the specks of ash out of his skin as he glanced down, searching for the trail of blood. But the ground had swallowed up every morsel of light.

Reaching back, he grabbed the flashlight out of his shorts and thumbed the switch. *Shit.* He gave it a smack. It glowed to life, giving off a faint yellow beam just bright enough to melt the dark.

"Jesus Christ!" He stumbled backward, choking on the vomit caught in his throat and spitting it out as he tried but couldn't look away from Peter Murphy's naked body—his belly and loins were clawed to shreds, stripping him of his manhood, his chest was ripped open, his ribs broken and splintered. But his face was untouched, except for the horror burned into his wide-open eyes.

A voice whispered, "Don't be frightened; I won't hurt you."

Sean dropped the flashlight and whirled around, peering down the path—a tunnel with no light at the end except for a shadowy figure standing in the center of the vortex. Without thinking, without asking himself why or who it was, he started running. His only guide was the tip of a tree branch that stung his arm, another that scratched his leg, and one that poked him in the face—turning his head—whenever he drifted too close to the edge of the path.

Pamela stopped a few steps into the deep grass. Her face and neck and hands started glistening from perspiration. She didn't pull away this time when Carmen reached out and placed a finger over her carotid artery after tapping a button on the side of her watch, lighting the face.

"My God . . . your pulse is one forty and climbing!"

She took hold of Pamela's arm. "You've got to lie down, PJ. The way you're perspiring . . . and with your heart racing like this . . . you're exhibiting the classic signs for a heart attack."

Pamela casually slipped free of Carmen's grasp. "Don't—"

She gasped, suddenly short of breath. She began to breathe faster and deeper. Jagged images began to fly past on either side of her as she found herself running in the dark. She tried to blink away the sweat in her eyes but gave up when she was startled by a sudden slap on her arm, as real as if she'd been whipped. She was hit again and again on her arms and legs and face until she was numb, her only salve her free will.

Dead Love

But instead of pulling back, knowing that her link with Sean reached beyond just thought, she allowed herself to be drawn deeper and deeper into the maelstrom.

Chapter Forty

As Sean raced headlong down the leaf-covered path, he felt something in his chest. It wasn't warm or cold, and to his surprise he wasn't frightened by it the way he had been that night in the library, which confused him. Although he knew it was virtually impossible to feel his pulse over the pounding of his feet, he had to check; he had to know for certain if what he thought he'd felt—a subtle double beat of his heart—was real.

Grabbing his neck, he placed his thumb over his left carotid artery, his middle fingers over the right artery. *Shit.*

He slowed to a brisk walk, telling himself that it must have been the delayed pulse in his thumb. But he wasn't convinced.

Using only his finger this time, he held his breath and checked again and immediately pulled to a dead stop when he felt another heartbeat a microsecond out of synch with the beat of his own heart. *What the hell—*

Pamela clenched her fists as she looked up into the night sky and whispered, "Thank you."

Then she shut her eyes. *It's all right . . . it's me, not her.*

Confused and feeling uneasy, and unwilling to take any chances, Sean slipped his hand beneath his sweatshirt and withdrew the Luger. He released the safety, cocked the slide and spun around, his aim jumping from one imagined shadow to the next.

"No! There's no one there! She only wants you to—"

A shot rang out, startling Pamela into opening her eyes.

"Sean, don't waste—"

Two more followed in rapid-fire succession, their sharp report ricochetting across the field and disappearing into the night.

Pamela concentrated all of her energy, blocking out Carmen's frantic pleas for her to stop this insanity and repeated to herself, "You only have six rounds left . . . *save them!*"

*   *   *

Though he felt stupid for having fired at nothing more than his own fears, Sean now knew that if he had to, if it meant stopping Judith, he was capable of killing someone. He holstered the pistol and turned around to the sweep of headlights off in the distance, lighting a figure standing on the side of the road at the start of the path. He couldn't explain why—perhaps it was the insinuating twist of her body, the disdainful turn of her head or the way her hands were propped on her hips—but his immediate reaction was that she was amused, laughing at what he'd done.

He started running, but instead of gauging himself, holding back out of fear for what might happen if he pushed the envelope, he let go and turned himself over to the rage inside him boiling over into revenge for the years of being toyed with and taunted, like now. He was determined to stop her, knowing full well that he might have to take Annie's life to do it. *She's dead anyway.*

Pamela cried out, "Damn you!" the moment she realized that the figure in her mind growing steadily closer was Sean, which meant that she was now in Annie's head, watching him. Yet she had begun to perspire again, which told her that she was somehow still connected to him and could still feel what he felt. But had she been cut off from his thoughts, and from those feelings of the mind that both precede and follow the body's pain and pleasure? Could she still feel his hate burning inside her when it flared up in him, taste his bitter desire for revenge, know his fear of death or feel the terror in his heart when he saw Peter's mutilated body? She had no way of knowing, except to wait and watch. And hope.

You bitch! That's exactly what you want, isn't it? You're not content with me just knowing what he's going through, feeling his pain, his fear; you also want me to see it on his face, in his eyes. But how the hell do you know what I see, what I'm feeling—

Of course! She turned to face Carmen, who was standing a few steps behind her. *You told her. Only you didn't actually tell her; she could see everything I was doing, hear everything I said.*

So much for logic and reason and your dominant male side!

"I should have known," she muttered and shook her head.

"Known what?" Carmen asked and stepped closer. "Talk to me."

Pamela sighed, "Nothing . . . just talking to myself."

Lighting the dial of her watch, Carmen pressed her finger to Pamela's neck. "Let's see what that heart of yours is doing."

Grabbing Carmen's hand, Pamela grumbled,

"It doesn't matter anymore," and took her in tow as she started back across the lawn toward the Rolls. Parked behind the house, the overhead interior lights in the car were switched on and John was sitting behind the wheel, his arm braced in the open window, quietly reading a book.

Carmen gave Pamela a playful tug. "Where are we going?"

"Back to New York," Pamela replied and quickened her pace.

"That's it . . . it's over . . . you're giving up?"

Pamela simply smiled as she opened the rear door and hit the button to raise the divider. "After you, Evi."

"You're not making any sense, PJ. I don't believe that—"

"Get in, goddammit!" Pamela shouted as she jerked Carmen's arm and shoved her into the backseat. Slamming the door, she leaned up against it and ordered, "John, override the rear windows and door locks." At the muffled sound of a chorus of switches clicking in unison, she stepped away from the car and said without looking back, "Take Dr. Evangelista home . . . by way of Hartford."

Chapter Forty-one

Sean's desire for revenge was like a drug, a powerful opiate he inhaled with every breath—allowing him to run without fear—as he drew steadily closer to the figure running ahead of him on Lake Road. But as with so many potent drugs, there was a dangerous side effect to this one too: his instincts had been dulled, and the voices in his head, pulling and tugging at his conscience—forcing him to question what he was doing, and why—had been silenced.

He now had only one thought in his mind: to free himself of Judith. *Any fucking way I can,* he told himself, and started running faster, having grown impatient with the game she was playing.

* * *

Pamela didn't need a light to guide her as she slowly threaded her way up the hill: every invisible tree, every loose stone, every blind step had been etched deep into her subconscious, and not just once but twice. Nearing the top, short of breath, she was forced to stop and rest. But only until she was reminded that Judith was the reason for her infirmity. Angry, she willed herself the last ten yards over the spilled cinders. She remembered just in time to step aside and avoid tripping over Peter Murphy's body as she reached the top of the ridge and stumbled onto the leafy path.

Something—perhaps it was the desperate hope that what she'd seen had been nothing more than a cruel trick—made her turn back.

"Dear God!" she gasped when she saw Peter's mutilated and disemboweled body sprawled out amid a splash of colorless leaves, a black, amorphous shape except for the whites of his eyes, which seemed to glow like dying embers beneath the starry sky.

Shaking, Pamela stepped closer and knelt down and brushed her fingers over Peter's face, closing his eyelids. Sickened by the sour stench of decay, she jumped up and stepped back. Dizzy from rising too fast, she momentarily lost her bearings until she found the shadowy fragments in her mind, layer upon layer of black on gray, then felt the sharp sting on her arms and legs and face.

Spinning around, she started running, blindly following the path that Sean had taken, only to pull back to a slow, labored walk, straining for every breath. Before her frustration could reignite her anger, tears filled her eyes when she felt the heat of Sean's rage flare up inside her like a wildfire and realized that she had her wish. Not only were they one in body—her heart his to claim, its strength his to take in pursuit of Judith—but they were now also one in spirit. She could taste his desire for revenge, knew that he would do anything to have it, and that his vengeance had blinded him to the fire of Judith's hellish desires, while rendering him deaf to her own desperate pleas. At the same time, she could also feel Judith's growing excitement, feel her passion electrifying Annie's mind and body. She could even taste what Judith wanted, feel the warm, moist flesh, a raw, carnal lust, burning inside her, the flames growing hotter as Sean drew near.

Pamela stopped abruptly. *That's what you get off on. But the fear is just foreplay for you. It's the anger . . . the rage . . . that really cranks you over, isn't it? That's why you played with me so long. You don't want them to give in, or give up, do you?*

That's just what you're doing with him, isn't it!
"What a fool I've—"

Pamela caught herself and cleared her mind, hiding her thoughts and her feelings—*just in case*—and started running. She was risking both their lives as she pushed herself in the desperate attempt to steal back her heart, and her strength.

Chapter Forty-two

She had played with him for the last mile or so, sprinting ahead every time he drew close and called to her. Not once had she replied, although she'd turned and glanced back over her shoulder at him a few times, as if she was about to say something, before snapping her head back around. That wasn't Annie, and Sean knew it.

Once, he got close enough to reach out and grab a pinch of her sweatshirt, only to watch her twist free of his tenuous hold, his fingers slipping through her long red hair as she effortlessly pulled away, laughing at him instead of looking back. That laugh, a mean, condescending sneer, would have been the final fix for Sean's addictive desire had it not been for what he thought he saw in Annie's eyes when she looked back at him.

In those fleeting seconds, he had seen a stone-cold fear that served as a sobering reminder of what he'd seen in Pamela's eyes, of what Judith's playthings had looked like, teasing and taunting him, and what might happen to him if he was wrong and he couldn't stop her.

Instead of heeding Annie's silent warning, he started running with abandon, as if he were trying to catch the wind. He was hooked: The synthetic adrenaline extracted from his fear and concentrated by his hate was too intoxicating for him to resist.

Pamela burst out of the claustrophobic tunnel of trees and bushes and wiry branches and stumbled to a stop in the middle of Lake Road. She stood with her hands on her hips, her head thrown back, gulping down the cool night air. Unwilling to risk losing what she had been able to wrestle back from Sean—steadily gaining strength, reclaiming what she had unwittingly turned over to him—she started running without concern for where she was or where she was going; she just knew, her head filled with hundreds of small, pieced-together fragments from shattered images, leading the way.

Soaking wet, she began to pluck at her cashmere sweater in an effort to cool down. But it stuck to her skin, refusing to give her any relief. Angry, she grabbed a fistful of the soft woolen fabric and yanked it away from her chest, only to feel it clump in her fist like dirty wet hair.

Damn!

She didn't need to reach under her sweater and feel it to be sure, or place her finger on the tip of her tongue and taste it; she knew that the sweat had loosened the surgical tape, and the flexing of her chest from breathing so hard had finally pulled open the incision. *Just like you said it would,* she thought, recalling Carmen's warning to her of what would happen if she didn't settle down. She also knew that if she kept running, her heart would pump the blood out of her body, aided by the blood thinner she was taking.

She tried convincing herself it couldn't be that bad. But the thought of collapsing and lying on the side of the road and bleeding to death after all she'd gone through—especially the thought of Judith winning—forced her to slip her clean hand under her sweater and run her fingers down the foot-long scar between her breasts. There were no steady trickles! No pulsating spurts! Just droplets of blood weeping from the ridge of knotted flesh.

Relieved, she wiped her hands on the sleeves of her sweater and pushed herself even harder. But something held her to a slow, steady pace—her breathing unconsciously metered out—when the questions she'd failed to ask and answer filled her mind with doubt. How much blood had she already lost? Would the scar tissue continue to tear open? Would the bleeding get worse? Would she find Sean before she'd lost so much blood that she wouldn't have the strength to do anything, to help him? To stop her! And one question she didn't want to hear: Was she already too late?

No!

Sean suddenly hit the wall—that invisible but impenetrable barrier separating mind from body. He'd been here before and always managed to slip through that wormhole connecting the real to the surreal. Refusing to give in to his earthly limitations, he pushed himself—searching for the opening—only to be thrown back into reality. Exhausted, he gave up and sank to his knees as he watched Annie veer off Lake Road onto Western Highway and slip out of sight, followed by a sweep of headlights. Too weak to stop himself, he pitched forward, falling onto his side and rolling over into the tall dried grass growing along the side of the road. He lay on his back, numb, his eyes shut, as if he were dead. He waited for the oxygen to bubble back into his legs, his arms, his gut, his brain. His nerves started firing and misfiring. His legs began twitching and he started shivering uncontrollably, telling him that he was cooling down too fast, and if he didn't get up and start walking, his muscles would cramp into useless knots.

Taking a deep breath, Sean sat up and struggled to his feet. Dizzy, he teetered sideways and nearly tripped back into the culvert, but caught himself and started walking. His movements were stilted, forced—sketching the shadow of an old man—as he worked the stiffness out of his joints, his thighs, his calves. He slipped into a shuffling run, feeling stronger with every step.

Be patient. "Besides, you know where she's going anyway," he muttered and suddenly eased up, surprised by what he'd said. But he shouldn't have been. He should have known that when he pushed himself to the wall, draining his body of every drop of energy, he had also emptied his veins of that powerful drug. He was clean, no longer under the influence. But the edge was still there; he could feel it, cold as case-hardened steel and honed razor sharp.

He followed his instincts and walked into the woods. Guided by long-forgotten memories of a shortcut, he started running, but slowly, carefully working his way toward the rear of the cemetery. He knew where she would be, could see her in his mind, waiting for him. It had all started there, and it was only fitting it end there.

Chapter Forty-three

Pamela felt herself running through eddies of hot and cold air as a figure appeared in her mind no more than an arm's length away. She heard Sean calling Annie's name and saw herself reaching out. Yet she felt a hand graze her shoulder and heard herself laugh. She was running and breathless but not out of breath, all at the same time. She watched Annie disappear around a sharp bend in the road up ahead. She felt herself hitting the ground and rolling over—numb and cold and spent—yet she was still running, and through the woods now. Confused by these conflicting ripples of telepathic energy, she stopped and tried to sort out which were deliberate illusions created by Judith, and which were real images seen by Sean. Frustrated, unable to think clearly, she reacted purely on instinct and pursued the silhouette of Annie left in her mind. She pushed herself even harder to make up for lost time.

Sean's hunch was right; the abandoned service road led straight to the back of the cemetery, cutting the distance to the cemetery by at least a mile and saving him a good ten minutes. *No, more, the way you're running!* He tried climbing the eight-foot-high fence but quickly found he didn't have the strength to pull himself up. Forced to walk the perimeter, he kept glancing nervously through the bars for a sign of Annie. She wasn't anywhere to be seen. The gate was closed, confirming that he'd gotten here before her. *Don't be so sure,* he told himself as he wound his way toward the clearing in the back of the cemetery.

The moment Pamela spotted the Rolls-Royce pulled onto the shoulder, the lights off, she grabbed the .357 from the waistband of her jeans. Wiping the blood and sweat off the walnut grip, she approached the car behind a stiff-armed, two-handed point of the gun. She stopped at the rear bumper when she saw that the glass divider separating the passengers from the driver had been smashed.

Shit!

She rushed forward. The rear compartment was empty.

Dammit!

Pulling open the passenger-side front door, Pamela found her chauffeur lying face-up on the seat. His eyes were wide open, his head twisted and floppy in a way that told her that his neck was broken. Fighting back a primal scream—a vivid replay of the sights and smells from Peter Murphy's disemboweled body gagging her—she slammed the car door and jammed the pistol back into her jeans.

As she started running toward the outline of the church steeple etched into the night sky off in the distance, she heard footsteps behind her and glanced over her shoulder to see Carmen gaining on her. A second later, she was struck in the back and sent stumbling to the ground, the wind knocked out of her. Before she could roll away, Carmen was on her, straddling her and pinning her down. Pamela braced herself for the hands on her back to reach inside and try to rob her strength and steal her thoughts. But they were just there—holding her at bay—a chilling reminder. More angry at herself than frightened—fear was no longer death's handmaiden for her—she waited for Judith to reveal herself. She knew that she would, either through Annie's eyes or Sean's, whichever would give her the most pleasure, and Pamela the most pain.

Although it felt like an eternity—the runaway beat of her heart racing ahead of time—Pamela's wait was brief as a shattered image began to materialize in her mind. It was like watching a stained-glass window being assembled and disassembled, only these translucent shards were fragments of faces and figures, not colored glass. She saw her own dark amber eyes, Annie's ivory-white skin, Carmen's wry, bewitching smile, the moonlit breasts of the woman lost to the depths of the reservoir, the rain-soaked hair of the lady in the library, the striking blue of the eyes of a young woman she'd never seen and glimpses of other women, both young and old.

With each successive metamorphosis of face and figure, Pamela sensed a subtle weakening of the pressure on her back, yet at the same time she felt herself growing stronger. It was then that she knew for certain that some part of Judith was inside Carmen, and another part still inside her too. Once again held prisoner in her own body, Pamela could only watch and wait in silence for the slightest slip of a hand on her back. Only this time, she was the predator.

Suddenly, behind the ever-changing portrait, she saw yet another figure begin to drift in and out of focus—a ghostly apparition—as if it were trapped inside the window. *Sean?*

Chapter Forty-four

The moment she started toward Sean, she blurred into a grotesque silhouette, like ink smeared across a slate blackboard.

Yes! Rolling over, Pamela knocked Carmen off balance with a backhanded sweep of her arm. When she reached for her gun, she was struck with a crushing, two-fisted blow to her chest that sent a shockwave through her body. Stunned, unable to move, Pamela could only watch as Carmen tore open her sweater and dug her fingernails deep into the tender flesh surrounding the ropelike scar on her chest and growled, "Move and I'll rip out your heart."

* * *

Dead Love

Sean demanded, "Who are you? Where's Annie? What did you do to her, goddammit!" He stepped back beyond her reach, only to have his hasty retreat blocked when he bumped into the fence and found himself a prisoner of the rusted iron bars.

She came to a wavering stop in front of him, her distorted image slowly resolving itself into a young woman wrapped in a diaphanous gown of shadows. She was little more than a thin film, a murky emulsion, like an old black-and-white negative. Except for her eyes, which shone like cerulean stars in a moonless, midnight sky. As if blown by a cosmic wind, her long silvery hair swirled around her head, covering and uncovering her face. "Judith?"

Taking his hand, she asked softly, "Do you still love me?"

"What!"

He twisted free of her vaporous grip. But he could still feel the imprint of her cold hand—her long fingers curled around his wrist—and the bizarre sensation of a pulse far too fast for the beat of any human heart. The thought that she was now in him, a part of him—her unearthly genes forever bound to the double helix of his DNA—wound the spring inside Sean another notch tighter.

333

Donald Beman

Masking fear with contempt, he asked, "What is there to love?"

She appeared confused and hurt when she said, "Me."

Sean laughed incredulously, "But you're not real!"

Her bright blue eyes abruptly turned to cold, carbonaceous cinders as she sneered, "Ask your precious Pamela if I'm real."

Angered by her cruel words, his own guilt salt on the wound, Sean stepped closer, forcing her to look at him. He wanted what she had denied him, manipulating Annie, Carmen, even Pamela into refusing him access to the shadows of her mind in search of who—or what!—she really was. With an adoring smile, the look of innocence on her face, she gave herself up to him. He saw what he thought was his reflection in her eyes, only his face was too smooth, his hair still sandy brown and not yet brushed with gray. He was quickly surrounded by other images, those shadowy figures from his never-ending nightmare, their faces still hidden behind a veil of darkness. Only this time he saw them through her eyes, just like the thirty-year-old memory of himself. Confused, every logical thought in his mind telling him this wasn't happening, that he was imagining it, Sean found himself stumbling over his words.

"Judith . . . listen to me . . . please! I'm not

what you think . . . I'm not who I was . . . I've changed . . . *you've* changed!"

Close to tears, she asked, "You don't love me anymore?"

That invisible spring inside him wound another notch tighter.

"How can I love you . . . you're dead, for chrissake!"

Though soft-spoken, there was a razor-sharp edge to her words—the bone-chilling hush of an executioner's ax falling toward his neck—when she whispered, "You said you would always love me."

The spring coiled into a clenched fist of tempered steel.

Before he could slip away, he felt a hand graze his cheek, yet she hadn't moved. That unseen touch was followed by the sensation of lips brushing over his, warm and moist, leaving a taste in his mouth laced with all-too-familiar memories of Judith.

This is fucking insane!

Frightened by what he felt stirring inside him— a raw, sexual desire he couldn't control—he shoved her away, only to see his hands disappear into the dark and watch her break up into ripples of light. It looked as if he'd reached into a pond and disturbed her watery reflection. Seizing the opportunity, he lunged forward, scattering her watery image into thousands of angry screams.

* * *

Pamela suddenly broke free and punched Carmen in the face. She kept hitting her until she pitched over onto her side and her head slammed into the road with a dull, sickening crack. Grabbing the pistol out of her jeans, she jammed the barrel under Carmen's jaw and squeezed the trigger. The bullet exploded inside Carmen's head with a blinding flash of light, blowing away the top of her skull. Pamela rolled over and started retching and heaving.

Intent upon destroying everything associated with Judith, Sean hurled her pieced-together headstone against the huge marble sarcophagus and laughed when the small block of granite shattered. Then he fell to his knees and clawed at the earth until he loosened the marker bearing the epitaph ANNIE . . . LIE HERE WITH US IN LOVING MEMORY. Struggling to his feet, he raised the thin slab of stone above his head but stopped—wide-eyed—awestruck by the millions of microscopic particles connecting and reconnecting into a dense cloud of charged particles, wildly arcing into tiny blue flames.

Pamela struggled to her feet, her blood-soaked sweater hanging from her body in shreds. A steady stream of blood was now leaking from her open incision. Terrified at the thought that she could be bleeding to death—afraid that she might not make it—she panicked and froze. *Damn!* Her mind went blank.

After a moment, she growled through her teeth, "Fuck it!" and kicked her way through the fragments of bone and hair and blasted tissue littering the road. Once clear, she started running, but with a slow, shuffling gait this time, and weaving side to side.

Sean reached under his sweatshirt and withdrew the gun. The electrified cloud instantly engulfed him, igniting his clothes. Shielding his face, he backed away but tripped on the chunks of granite and fell, dropping the gun when his head struck the ground. Before he could get up, she was on him, numbing his body with her fiery sting. Desperate, Sean asked, "What the hell do you want?"

Judith solidified, straddling him.

"Look at me!" she demanded and bent over. Her face began to change—the pages of a book being turned—until she was his mirrored image, but years younger. "You said you would always love me." She leaned closer. "I want you back. I want you in me again." With her lips touching his, she sighed. "Can you feel me?"

The cold began to seep into his loins. He could feel himself responding to her against his will. The spring suddenly snapped. Bundles of nerves began uncoiling and whipping about inside his mind like barbed wire, shredding his thoughts. His heart started beating wildly, erratically, no longer controlled by the circadian clock ticking somewhere in the base of his reptilian brain, marking the rhythm of life. Sean cried out, "Why are you doing this?"

Leaning closer, Judith whispered in his ear, *"You promised."*

"And *you* promised me you wouldn't hurt him," Annie said as she walked out of the shadows and knelt down. Picking up the Luger, she pointed it at Judith. "You've had your fun; leave him alone."

Judith's laughter was laced with ridicule. "You always were the stupid one, weren't you? You can't shoot me. You *are* me. And I am you."

"We'll see," Annie said quietly as she pulled the trigger and instantly arched her back, as if she'd been shot. Breathless, she calmly squeezed off one round after another. Each incendiary burst of flame that erupted from the barrel of the pistol ignited another cluster of particles inside the collapsing cloud of light.

At the first sharp metallic strike of the firing pin, Annie rose to her feet, stepped out of her sweatpants and panties and eased herself down onto Sean, assuming Judith's amorphous shape.

Chapter Forty-five

Pamela smiled and breathed a quiet sigh of relief when Sean opened his eyes, his gaze locked onto the ceiling. She watched, amused and curious, as he slowly began to touch himself, his face, then his arms, before slipping his hand under the sheet.

Embarrassed, she laughed. "Don't worry . . . you're all there. And except for the nasty burns on your chest and stomach, and on your . . . well, you know . . . the doctor says you're fine. All you need is lots of—"

"Where is she?" Sean demanded and bolted upright, startling Pamela into doing the same thing in the chair beside his bed.

His wide-eyed gaze raked the hospital room

before zeroing in on the monitor over his bed. He clutched his chest.

Standing up, Pamela eased Sean back down and tucked the sheet in around him. "Your heart's fine too, sweetheart. Just relax."

He lay perfectly still, staring at her, touching every part of her with his gaze just as he'd done to himself with his hands.

After a moment, he frowned, as if something was hurting him.

Pamela waved him off and asked, "Are you okay?"

Sean simply nodded.

Taking his hand, Pamela sat down and said solemnly, "I owe your lady friend, Annie Parker, an apology. Not only did she save your life, but if it wasn't for her, I don't think I would—"

"Time for meds!" Eku Malawatumba announced cheerfully as she glided into the room, a warm smile spreading across her face.

Chapter Forty-six

Naked, Annie stood quietly in the center of the darkened bathroom holding a wooden match in one hand, a box of matches in the other. She was surrounded by a collection of small frosted glass jars, scented candles, scattered about the floor, around the sink, and one set in each corner of the shelf circling the tub. When she struck the match, the sulfurous orange flame burst into life, throwing her shadow onto the wall to dance with the steam rising up from the tub. She went from jar to jar—quickly, to keep from burning her fingers—filling the air with a fragrant spring bouquet.

With a shake of her hand, she snuffed out the match—tossed it into the sink—and started for the tub. She froze, caught, trapped by her nemesis; the full-length mirror on the back of the bathroom door. She blushed and turned away. *I can't do it!*

She stood motionless, trying to screw up her courage.

After a moment, she told herself, *Might as well get used to it, girl,* and hurried over to the tub, where she snatched up the nearly full glass of wine off the floor and grabbed the bottle standing beside it. With her hand shaking, she hungrily drained the glass and refilled it. She took another sip, as if for good measure, and stepped into the tub. Easing down into the steaming mountain of bubbles, she set the bottle quietly on the floor within easy reach, as if she was trying not to make any noise.

Annie settled back and sat nursing her wine and refilling the glass until the bottle was empty. She was now right where she wanted to be—where she needed to be—alone, her mind blank but still well shy of not knowing what she was doing. And still able to feel everything. She gingerly set the empty glass on the floor and slid down into the tub until the bubbles ringed her neck. Closing her eyes, she waited for the warm moist heat to dissolve away every last knot of inhibition left untouched by the wine.

Finally, with a relaxed sigh, she closed her eyes and began to slowly caress her breasts, reawakening memories she'd denied herself far too long.

She lazily circled her nipples with the tips of her fingers, drawing smaller and smaller circles. Now and then she brushed her thumbs back and forth and squeezed, but ever-so-gently. Those tender pinches sent a forgotten shower of sparks cascading through her body. This time, however, the fire they ignited in her loins was unlike anything she'd ever felt. Curious, but still cautious, she slipped her hand between her legs and began to toy with the strange yet delicious sensation of playing a game of tag with the breaking surf in the warm, wet sand, a hot, sultry wind blowing through her hair. As the waves grew stronger, she became even bolder, teasing the rising tide, yet holding herself safely beyond its watery reach. Her heart began to beat faster. Her breathing became shallow. She pulled back. It was too late; she was swept away. She tried fighting it, but the undertow was too strong, drowning her beneath wave upon wave as the pounding swell erupted inside her, filling her with its hot, salty brine.

Annie raised her leg and tapped the handle of the faucet with her toes until she had a slow, steady trickle of hot water.

You were asleep . . . I didn't want to wake you.

She smiled sheepishly, as if she was embarrassed.

Donald Beman

Because I always wanted to know what it was like for you.

Different . . . very different.

Her green eyes sparkled. *I loved it!*

But it all happened so fast. I'm not used to that.

Her face abruptly wrinkled into a curious frown.

I hadn't thought about it.

She laughed.

I guess 'til death do us part!

She gave a matter-of-fact shrug.

It just popped into my head . . . it's only a figure of speech.

Why are you so upset?

Annie sat quietly, her eyes darting back and forth.

She gave another casual shrug.

Whatever. Anyway, I think it's all sort of poetic. Judith has what she wanted . . . you . . . Pamela's happy . . . and so am I!

She grinned like the cat in Alice's Wonderland.

The doctor said you have the heart of a twenty-year-old!

Her grin spread into a smile.

Don't worry, I'm sure Judith will take very good care of that precious body of yours . . . not that you'll be needing it anymore.

Her grin bubbled up into laughter.

Because you have me!
Would you rather be dead?

She frowned again, but more of a disapproving scowl this time.

The only way that could happen would be for me to sleep with you . . . with your body, that is . . . which means I would have to sleep with Judith too. And I'm not into that, thank you!

Annie suddenly sat up—her eyes wide open—dead serious.

What?
How do you know?
It's not possible.

Because she was drawn into the neural void when I took you.

No! She's there, in your body; I felt her pass through me.

She shook her head in denial.

I would know if she were . . . I would be able to feel—

Annie took a sudden breath, startled by the sensation of a mouth on her breast. A tongue, warm and moist, began circling and licking her nipple. She tried to quench the fire smoldering in her belly, but a hand on her still-swollen flesh—touching her in a way only another woman would know—fanned the flames even hotter.

With a shake of her head, Annie shut her eyes and turned away. But she couldn't hide from the sensation of his tumescent flesh throbbing, growing firmer, harder, with every beat of her heart. She could feel the tide rising again. But slowly this time, a gentle ebb and flow stirred by a warm breeze, like the calm after a storm. *No!* he cried when Annie felt herself slipping inside another woman's body and heard Judith's words, *Welcome home, Sean,* echoing in her mind.

DONALD
BEMAN
AVATAR

When Sean MacDonald first meets sculptor Monique Gerard, he is fascinated. Her work is famous—some would say notorious—for its power, sensuality . . . and unbridled horror. But Sean didn't expect the reclusive genius to be as compellingly grotesque as her creations. Something about her and her work draws Sean in like a moth to a flame . . . or like a lamb to the slaughter.

___4376-9 $5.50 US/$6.50 CAN

VOICE
OF THE
BLOOD

JEMIAH JEFFERSON

Ariane is desperate for some change, some excitement to shake things up. She has no idea she is only one step away from a whole new world–a world of darkness and decay, of eternal life and eternal death. But once she falls prey to Ricari she will learn more about this world than she ever dreamt possible. More than anyone should dare to know . . . if they value their soul. For Ricari's is the world of the undead, the vampire, a world far beyond the myths and legends that the living think they know. From the clubs of San Francisco to a deserted Hollywood hotel known as Rotting Hxall, the denizens of this land of darkness hold sway over the night. Bur a seductive and erotic as these predators may be, Ariane will soon discover that a little knowledge can be a very dangerous thing indeed.

____4830-2 $5.99 US/$6.99 CAN

IN THE DARK

RICHARD LAYMON

Nothing much happens to Jane Kerry, a young librarian. Then one day Jane finds an envelope containing a fifty-dollar bill and a note instructing her to "Look homeward, angel." Jane pulls a copy of the Thomas Wolfe novel of that title off the shelf and finds a second envelope. This one contains a hundred-dollar bill and another clue. Both are signed, "MOG (Master of Games)." But this is no ordinary game. As it goes on, it requires more and more of Jane's ingenuity, and pushes her into actions that she knows are crazy, immoral or criminal—and it becomes continually more dangerous. More than once, Jane must fight for her life, and she soon learns that MOG won't let her quit this game. She'll have to play to the bitter end.

___4916-3 $5.99 US/$6.99 CAN

THE TRAVELING VAMPIRE SHOW
RICHARD LAYMON

It's a hot August morning in 1963. All over the rural town of Grandville, tacked to the power poles and trees, taped to store windows, flyers have appeared announcing the one-night-only performance of The Traveling Vampire Show. The promised highlight of the show is the gorgeous Valeria, the only living vampire in captivity.

For three local teenagers, two boys and a girl, this is a show they can't miss. Even though the flyers say no one under eighteen will be admitted, they're determined to find a way. What follows is a story of friendship and courage, temptation and terror, when three friends go where they shouldn't go, and find much more than they ever expected.

__4850-7 $5.99 US/$6.99 CAN

THE DECEASED
TOM
PICCIRILLI

Something is calling Jacob Maelstrom back to the isolated home of his childhood—to the scene of a living nightmare that almost cost him his life. Ten years ago his sister slaughtered their brother and parents, locked Jacob in a closet . . . then committed a hideous suicide. Now, as the anniversary of that dark night approaches, Jacob is drawn back to a house where the line between the living and the dead is constantly shifting.

But there's more than awful memories waiting for Jacob at the Maelstrom mansion. There are depraved secrets, evil legacies, and family ghosts that are all too real. There's the long-dead writer, whose mad fantasies continue to shape reality. And in the woods there are nameless creatures who patiently await the return of their creator.

___4752-7 $5.50 US/$6.50 CAN

Dorchester Publishing Co., Inc.
P.O. Box 6640
Wayne, PA 19087-8640

Please add $1.75 for shipping and handling for the first book and $.50 for each book thereafter. NY, NYC, and PA residents, please add appropriate sales tax. No cash, stamps, or C.O.D.s. All orders shipped within 6 weeks via postal service book rate. Canadian orders require $2.00 extra postage and must be paid in U.S. dollars through a U.S. banking facility.

Name_____
Address_____
City_____ State_____ Zip_____
I have enclosed $ _____ in payment for the checked book(s).
Payment <u>must</u> accompany all orders. ❏ Please send a free catalog.
CHECK OUT OUR WEBSITE! www.dorchesterpub.com